Molly Nichols has led a pretty much stable life — decent job at the local police department, a home she inherited from her uncle and one of her oldest friends Carrie, as her roommate. At least until recently — Carrie has time traveled back in time to be with the man she loves and her job is less than satisfying due to her boss who she refers to as the Red Queen. In her search for answers she ventures into Carrie's favorite shop, the Treasures Antique Store and its proprietor, Mr. Arthur Merle. There she meets Mr. Merle's nephew, a hunky, absolutely gorgeous blond named Gareth. But there is something a tad bit off about the handsome man and it's not just his way of speaking. When he starts to talk about where he is from and that he has woken because it is our time of greatest need, Molly is pretty sure there's something not quite right about him starting with what modern woman needs a knight in shining armor to rescue her?

With All Dispatch
Copyright © 2020 Regan Taylor
ISBN: 978-1-4874-2994-2
Cover art by Martine Jardin

Published by eXtasy Books Inc or
Devine Destinies, an imprint of eXtasy Books Inc

Look for us online at:
www.eXtasybooks.com or www.devinedestinies.com

WITH ALL DISPATCH
TREASURES ANTIQUE STORE
BOOK 2

BY

REGAN TAYLOR

DEDICATION

To Missy. Mommy misses you every day.

CHAPTER ONE

H ead spinning, Molly Nichols sat down on her roommate, Carrie Taylor's bed unable to breathe let alone move. Something that just couldn't happen, happened.

It just wasn't possible. No how. No way

"This has to be a joke, a really bad joke." She muttered, a photograph, an old photograph showing her roommate with a tall, handsome Indian, gripped tightly in her hand.

She looked around the room and weakly called, "You can come out now. The both of you. Really. Actually make that all three of you. Come on Taister, no playing silly cat games this morning."

Shaking ever so slightly Molly scooched off the bed and slid on to the floor. Not that she was worried about Carrie finding her in her room. After all, the twosome had been friends since they were kids. Growing up with her dark-haired friend had been an adventure with Carrie always finding something new and different for them to get in to. Then one day, not so long ago, Carrie brought home a photograph.

A very old photograph.

The very photograph Molly now held.

And damn if Carrie and her cat Taister weren't sitting in that very photograph this very minute looking like they'd both caught the canary.

Molly flipped it over and studied the paper. "Nope, this isn't the photo-shopped version of you and Black Eagle. Nope, nope, not at all. This is the real deal. Carrie, you really did it this time. Or not."

Lifting her hips off the floor Molly turned and peered under the white-eyelet comforter that covered Carrie's bed and spied nothing but a few of Taister's silky black cat hairs.

She sniffed. Nothing except the sulfur-like smell that greeted her when she first walked into Carrie's room minutes ago permeated the air. She brought the photograph up to eye level and shook her head, "At least you could have left a note."

She snickered to herself, "A note? That said what? Hi! I'm back in time with the man I love?"

She shook her head and then snapped her fingers. "Mr. Merle! I'll talk to Mr. Merle and he'll know what happened. Right? I mean, he's the one who gave you this darn photograph in the first place. He'll know where you've gone and if you're coming back."

She stood and walked over the Carrie's closet. Peering inside it was as neat and orderly as ever. It didn't appear that even a scarf was missing. Clearly Carrie hadn't packed before taking off to where ever she went.

"Not that anyone has time to pack before time traveling," Molly laughed, just short of hysterical. "Right. Like I have so much experience with time travel. Let's see what or who I know whose done it? There's Black Eagle coming here. And then there's Black Eagle going back to his home and yup, that's a lot of experience you have there, Molly. You're a virtual expert."

Molly turned to study her reflection in Carrie's mirror. "I suppose that's true though. I mean, how many people time travel or know people who do? Me and maybe Mr. Merle, if he'd admit to it. It's not the kind of thing you can bring up in every day conversation, 'say, Janice, did you happen to travel to Queen Elizabeth's coronation? Liz the first I mean. What did you think?' Nope can't exactly do that. If people didn't think you were crazy before they'd know it after a crack like that."

She padded back to Carrie's bed as if she carried the weight of the world in her hands rather than the yellowed photograph and sat. There they were, Carrie, Black Eagle and Taister, in the photograph . . . together, in time, forever. Carrie had made it back to her man.

"So now what do I do? Do I try to bring you home? Or let you live the rest of your life in the past sans latte's, microwaves and Jacuzzi's? Should I be happy for you or sad that I'll never see you again?"

With a sigh she rose and wearily plodded out of the room. Arthur Merle better have the answers she sought. There was the one definite option on the horizon. "At least I'm working swings these days . . ."

If nothing else, Molly Nichols was practical. She saw life in black and white with each event in its own box. If something didn't fit in a box, you shelved it till it did. This deserved a shelf of its own. Shelf? Hell, an entire closet. A massive walk in one at that.

In a daze she hit the shower and waited for her head to clear. "Oh shit! Work! Holy crap. There's no way Carrie called her office to say she'd be traveling back in time today." Molly scrambled out of the shower and dripping wet, headed for the phone and quickly dialed Carrie's office.

Fingers drumming on the table she contemplated the various stories she could and should tell her roommate's boss. After all, in the event Carrie came back to the present she'd probably want her job back. Then again, she might not. Telling the truth was out of the question. They'd not only not believe the story about Carrie and Black Eagle and the photograph, but they'd think Molly was certifiable.

All too soon one of Carrie's co-workers answered. After sputtering for a few seconds Molly managed to clear her throat and explain that she worked nights and with all the hubbub from the night before she forgot to set an alarm to call the office to let them know about Carrie. When asked what happened, the words that Carrie had a family emergency and had to leave town late the night before and they weren't sure when she'd be back, just flowed.

Relieved that that chore had been taken care of she finished her shower before setting about making a pot of coffee, all the while watching the clock and thinking she should have had the coffee before calling her friend's work. At least the message had been conveyed to them. Coffee set to brewing, she popped some bread in the toaster before getting dressed. A bit later, dressed and munching the toast a few minutes later she couldn't help but feel overwhelmed by the sheer stillness of the house. Even though Carrie left for work a couple of hours after Molly got in from her shift, her cat Taister, was always ambling about making his needs and desires known. The women would joke about how the long-haired black cat was putting in orders for shrimp, steak and a serving of filet of mouse, rare. Generally he was content with a can of his fishy-smelling cat food. Now, even he was gone and the silence made her unbelievably lonely.

Her dishes in the sink, she brushed her teeth, put on a little make-up, combed her hair and took off for Treasures and its elderly owner, muttering, "I knew Carrie always going in there was going to be trouble. Who'd a thunk it would be this kind of trouble?"

She grabbed a few apples to snack on during breaks at work and headed off for her shift as a dispatcher at the police department the next county over. On the way out, just in case she missed something earlier, Molly poked her head in Carrie's room one more time. Of course her roommate hadn't returned. If Carrie'd returned she would have called out to Molly and Taister would have hit the kitchen looking for food.

Fortunately no one was inside Treasures when she entered and spied Mr. Merle dusting off the glass enclosed box that held what seemed to be an ancient sword. "Mr. Merle?"

The elderly white-haired gentleman turned and looked down from the step-stool he stood on. "Why hello, Molly. What brings you here today? Is Carrie all right?"

"I think you might know the answer to that."

"Me?" He dropped the dust cloth on a counter and rubbed his hands along his hips. "Has something happened?"

"I don't know." She thrust the photograph at him and he studied it a minute.

"Is this the photo-shopped picture you two put together when Black Eagle disappeared and you tried to get him back?"

"No, Mr. Merle, it's the one you gave to Carrie. The magical one."

"Magical?"

"What else would you call it? It brought Black Eagle to our time and when he got rid of Dickless Dean, it sent Black Eagle back in time."

"What else indeed?" The jet-haired woman Molly remembered Mr. Merle introduced as his sister, Vivienne, stepped out of the kitchen. Vivienne's appearance made her wonder if her son or nephew, Gareth, might be with her. Neither Mr. Merle nor Vivienne ever quite explained who he was, not that it mattered. It was their family and nothing to do with Molly. Gareth, however, was a major piece of eye candy and then some. Well except for him parading around in a suit of armor, he seemed like someone she'd like to get to know. Mr. Merle said it was for some kind of re-enactment or play or something and there was some sort of relationship between the three but now was not the time to be thinking about that.

"Oh no. I'm sorry, I thought you were alone." Molly groaned.

"Pay me no mind, Merl . . .Arthur and I are as close as any brother and sister can be. There is little he does, or meddles in I am not eventually made privy to."

Molly cocked her head. The woman spoke with what sounded like a slight British accent. Thing was, it sounded almost as if she were still learning the language. Although the word "meddle" sure sounded about right for Mr. Merle. Carrie adored the man, thought he could do no wrong. Unfortunately, right now because of the elderly gent's stupid photograph, her roommate was stuck back in time. "Yeah, but this is crazy making talk. This is the kind of stuff that lands you in the psych ward. Trust me, I've taken enough calls on 5150's to know what I'm thinking is crazy."

"5150?" Vivienne asked.

Mr. Merle peered down at her. "It is their word for demon-possessed."

"Uh, not really. Everyone knows you can't be possessed by demons. That's just an old superstition and the stuff of fiction. Insanity is a break from reality either because of drugs or chemical imbalance or a medical condition."

"So your people have eliminated demons? Beware wizard, your race might be next." Vivienne practically purred.

If they were brother and sister, why did she call him "wizard"?

And speak of the devil, there was Gareth, once again dressed in some sort of odd costume. Talk about someone who needed to go 5150. This time instead of a costume of shiny armor he was wearing a red velvet looking tunic top on top of what black knicker-style pants. A silver buckle with a massive belt, along with a sword that didn't appear to be optional, completed the ensemble. She knew it probably wasn't the smartest thing to do. The police psychologist who offered training at the police department where Molly worked in the records department had told the staff you shouldn't challenge a suspect's belief system. Let them think what they want, don't address it and cut to the chase about what you need to know. Besides, he was so cute.

Still, she couldn't help herself, "So, lose your armor or was it too heavy to keep walking around in?"

"Lady Molly. Tis good to see you again." The blond Adonis grinned broadly at her. And dang he smelled good, like clean salt air. "Truly the armor is of no matter. I couldst easily defend you unarmed if need be."

The bow he gave her was nothing less than Hollywood courtly, even if he was a bit wacky. And aside from the fact he remembered her name, his smile. Carrie would have told her it was right out of one of her romance novels.

Molly looked from Mr. Merle to each of his guests. If she thought her day started out crazy, they weren't making it any better. "I'm dreaming this, aren't I? I'm going to wake up and find out the Carrie didn't end up in a photograph. Even better, I'm going to wake up and find out that she never bought it in the first place and an Indian named Black Eagle didn't end up in the future here with us for a couple of months. If it's not a dream, I'm having a killer hallucination and I need to find the antidote real quick."

She spun on her heel and made for the door. Between Gareth and his flowing red-blond hair calling Mr. Merle, Merlin, and the woman talking about Mr. Merle meddling and Mr. Merle talking about demon-possession Molly knew she had to make her escape and make it now with or without her answers.

"Gareth, dear boy, kindly stop Miss Molly, would you?" Mr. Merle spoke softly yet with authority from behind her.

For a guy as big as the blond was, he was surprisingly light on his feet and in a second had her by the arm, leading her back into the shop. " . . .and pray, sit and speak with us. Mayhap Merlin can set your world aright again."

"Merlin? Like in King Arthur's Merlin? I don't think so. Look, I can totally understand being part of the whole re-enactment and roll playing thing. Really. But you're carrying it a bit far now. I've got a problem and it started with Mr. Merle." She whispered looking over Gareth's shoulder toward the back of the shop.

"Gareth, come," Vivienne beckoned him to the kitchen. "Let my brother speak with the young woman."

Gareth looked from Molly to Vivienne and finally, with a shrug, followed the older woman into the kitchen.

"Please, Molly, accept my apologizes for not only my sister and nephew, but for all the mix up since you arrived. I can understand why you may be upset and they may have added to it. Will you have a seat and talk?"

"Um, not in here, okay. Your sister and nephew? I don't feel comfortable saying this in front of them. Could we maybe go out for a coffee and talk there? "

"Of course. Let me ask Vivienne to watch the shop and you and I will have a nice chat."

Molly nodded and waited by the door. "Man, I sure hope I wake up soon."

CHAPTER TWO

Settled at a table far from the other late-morning patrons Molly waited for Mr. Merle to return with their coffees. A swallow of the dark brew helped her to relax.

"Are you feeling a little better, dear?"

"I am, sort of. Thank you. Mr. Merle, none of this makes sense and I have to tell you, no offense, your relatives kind of freaked me out."

"None taken. Vivienne does tend a bit towards the dramatic and Gareth does like to play the knight in shining armor."

"Don't you think parading around in those costumes, first the armor and now that medieval get up, is taking it a bit far?" She put up her hand, "I'm sorry. That was rude. I shouldn't be commenting on your family. It's a defense mechanism to avoid dealing with the real issue."

"Actually, you are right where Gareth is concerned. I do need to speak to him about his dress. He'd only just popped in again when you arrived today. Now, tell me what happened with Carrie?"

She blew out a breath. "Where to begin?"

"The beginning?" The kindly old gent prodded.

"Right. Please, don't deny that you know about time travel, or at least that Black Eagle and Carrie went back in time."

"Go ahead." He told her without confirming or denying his knowledge.

"You knew when Black Eagle went back in time we tried to see if we could send Carrie back to him by putting her in

9

the photograph."

"I do, and that didn't work."

"No. But, well last night she was still feeling kind of down and turned in kind of early. At one point, later on, I thought maybe we were having an earthquake on account of how the house shook."

"Did you now?"

"Yes. You know how quakes are. You rock and roll and then everything settles back down. As long as the clock shows the time and there were no really loud crashes you figure it's a small one. This morning I got up and thought it was kind of odd with how quiet the house was. Not even Taister was looking for food and that's his major priority in life, you know. So I went to check on Carrie. Mr. Merle, her room looked like a tornado hit. Stuff was blown all over and there was this smell, kind of like what it smells like in the firing range at work. I picked up the photograph and there she was. *In* it. With Black Eagle."

Molly fumbled in her purse and pulled the picture out to him once again. "See, just like I showed you before. There she is and look who Black Eagle is holding. It's Taister. Mr. Merle, do you think they are back in time?"

"Maybe. If I know Carrie, she'd try to let you know where she went and that she was all right."

"That's true. If she could she would. But what if she can't? What if something else happened? If she's back there and happy that's cool. I can live with that. If something else happened though . . ."

"I'm thinking she'd try to send a message."

"But how? It's not like you can call from 1860 to today. Even with GPS a cell phone can only call the present."

"That's true. There are other ways though. Back then people wrote letters, you know?"

She would have been offended except when she saw the

twinkle in his eye Molly knew Mr. Merle was only trying to help her feel better. "You think she'll write me? I don't see how . . ."

"If I were you, I'd check in some of the antique furniture she told me one time you have in your house and see if maybe she didn't leave you a note."

Molly snapped her fingers, "That would be so like Carrie! Right out of one of her romance novels. She's read so many time travels she'll know exactly what to do, won't she?"

"I would think so. Molly, I know this is hard on you, so unexpected. Like Black Eagle's arrival in this time. Once you have a minute to catch your breath and relax you'll see, everything will turn out just fine. Do you have time to run home and check now?"

Molly glanced at her watch, "No. I need to get to work, the Red Queen, you know, Julie Prince, is on one of her rampages, looking for anything she can find to make my life miserable and it's my first week back on swings so she'll be foaming till I get there. As usual, I'm at the top of her hit list. If anyone belongs in a photograph, it's Julie Price. A nasty one too."

"Molly, why do you call her the Red Queen?"

"Come on Mr. Merle, from Alice in Wonderland. You know, the one always shouting 'off with their heads'. Well that's her."

"I see."

Fumbling in her purse for her keys she missed the glint in Mr. Merle's eye when she mumbled, "Man, I'm normally Ms. Practical, but what I wouldn't give some days for one of those knights in shining armor to walk off the cover of one of Carrie's books and right into my life. I bet one of those chivalry practicing guys would take care of Jules in one quick slash. I'd better get going. Thank you for the coffee."

"Let me know if you find a note or anything, will you?"

"I will. And Mr. Merle, if you think of anything, you'll let me know, right?"

"Certainly. We'll talk in a few days if not sooner, I'm sure of it."

Driving to work Molly replayed the morning's events over and over, searching for an answer to the puzzle. Despite believing Black Eagle had come forward in time, the idea of time travel simply wasn't possible. How could a man travel one hundred and something years into the future let alone go back? "Maybe I need to stop having my picture taken so I don't end up being sent somewhere. And what's with Mr. Merle's relatives? Okay, sure, with his white hair and that glint he gets in his eyes he could play Merlin in the movies, but to call him that?"

She tapped an aimless tattoo on her steering wheel, absent mindedly looking over the rolling Napa vineyards. "And right now I am spending way too much time on something that means nothing to me."

CHAPTER THREE

"Problems, old friend? Or should I say brother?" With the narrowing of her deep azure colored eyes and doubt-filled tone it was clear Vivienne knew there was some sort of trouble.

"No. No. And let's stick with brother in this time and place, please?"

"Hmm, you bring a man from the past to the present. Then, when what he came to do is done, he goes back in time without you knowing how or why. Then you send the woman he helped back to him."

With a slash of his hand he cut her off, "They are in love, Vivienne."

"Ah, and that makes it all right for you to interfere in their lives. Didn't you learn anything the first time?"

"Yes. I did. You realize, of course, if I hadn't of helped Uther achieve his heart's desire, Arthur would never have been born."

"You don't know that."

"Well what's done is done. What I need to do now is find a way for Carrie to let Molly know she is safe, sound and happy back in time."

"And how are you going to do that?"

"That? Oh. Well." He considered the question, almost absentmindedly looking over some runes nestled in one of the displays. "I believe I will go back to Black Eagle's village and suggest to Carrie she leave a note for Molly."

"And how is a woman living in an Indian village going to

do that?"

"Carrie knows. Well sort of knows, what I can do.

"Merlin! She suspects somehow you manipulated time, not how you did it. She still thinks you are the kindly old gentleman who owns this shop and it was your ancestor who took the photograph. From what you've said she believes you have family from around the world that send you an array of antiques and memorabilia. Neither Carrie nor Black Eagle have any idea who you truly are."

"I don't see as there is a reason for them to know."

"Most assuredly I agree with you. That issue aside, have you considered if you just pop up back then Carrie and Black Eagle will know you can move through time and that at any point you could have either brought him back to her or helped her to go to him?"

"That's not true. And I did help her get back to him. She's there now, isn't she? Vivienne, don't you think if that were possible I would have stopped so many things? Don't you think I would have gone back and done things differently, starting with keeping Morgause from Arthur's bed? Or kept Gwen and Lance apart?"

The dark-haired woman raised her hand as if to ward her old friend off, "Bah. It was Arthur and his son's destiny. The prophecy of his return at the time of the human race's greatest need would not have been fulfilled had you meddled with that. And as to Lance and Gwen? They too were destined to be together. There is another for Arthur."

"You have seen her?"

"Maybe. I cannot be sure. That is but a red herring. How will you explain your presence in Carrie's new time?"

"Well, I don't necessarily have to talk to Carrie. I could just have my ancestor talk to Black Eagle and have him suggest that Black Eagle have Carrie write a note."

Vivienne shook her head, the cobalt color of her eyes

turning to a dark sapphire, "You don't think he still believes your ancestor took his picture, do you?"

Merlin sat with a heavy groan, "At this point I don't know what they believe. All I know is that I need to make sure Molly knows they are okay. If not, well, she works for the police in this time. If I cannot prove Carrie is safe, well and happy, she will file what they call a missing person's report. That will start the police investigating and then I will have to move on before I planned to." He shook his head, the sadness of such an ending to his time in Napa heavy in the air.

"Have you need of a messenger?" Gareth appeared before the pair.

"I wish you wouldn't do that Gareth." Vivienne snapped.

"What?" The younger man looked truly bewildered.

"Sneaking into rooms and startling people." Mr. Merle softly told him.

"I did not sneak. I walked in and you, Vivienne, are not normal people."

"Well, make some sort of noise when you walk into a room, will you? People in this time don't like being surprised anymore than they did in our time. One would think a man of your size would make some sort of noise."

"And just where *is* here, Merlin?" The big blond asked.

"Oh. Well, this is Napa, California."

"I wake here a few weeks past and meet the Lady Molly. Suddenly I am again at rest only to wake again this day. Best you explain wizard."

Merlin waved a hand, "I will. I will. There is something I need to attend to first though. Vivienne, could you, that is . . ."

"You'd like me to bring Gareth up to date on life these days?"

"If you would. I'll be back in the blink of an eye."

In a barely there puff of smoke, the older man disappeared.

Gareth turned to Vivienne, "Do not think to go with your

old friend."

Vivienne waved her hand before Gareth. "I have no intention of leaving. I am determined to see just what mess he makes of this. Besides, we needs make certain you fit into this time."

"I would eat and then learn just what Merlin is about." Without a glance the blond strode back toward the kitchen.

With a flash of her hand the front door to Treasures locked and the closed sign prominently displayed. While Merlin might think he'd be right back, Vivienne had no doubt he'd bumble around the Indian village and forget when to come back to. Leave it to Merlin to dump explaining things to Gareth on her. Well she'd leave that one to Treasure's proprietor. He created the mess, he'd better fix it. With a glance at the old sword on the wall another thought caught her attention. If Gareth was here, awake in 2021, how long before his brothers and the rest of the knights appeared? And would the greatest one of them all also wake to join them?

CHAPTER FOUR

In the twinkle of an eye, Mr. Merle found himself on the outskirts of Black Eagle's *Sihásapa* village. In the distance he saw a few children running about, playing, while their mothers washed clothing in the nearby river. Deciding the best course was to assume the persona of his ancestor and convince Black Eagle to have Carrie write the note to Molly, with a flick of his hand he was dressed in the garb of 1860 in the American West and went in search of the Lakota warrior. It would really be so simple. Tell Black Eagle he'd heard he brought a woman back in time with him.

Well, no actually, that wouldn't work. After all, what if he misjudged the time jump and he arrived before Black Eagle went forward in time? Then the warrior'd be alerted to the fact it was happening or could happen or might happen and then when he arrived, if he arrived, in the future, he'd tell Carrie. Carrie would tell Molly and Molly would report him to the police unless Molly thought he was crazy and then she'd . . .

"*You!*" Black Eagle's deep voice made him jump.

Well, Merlin thought, no time like the present. The decision was made. Or partly made. Or . . .

"Have you come to steal my *wanagi* again? Or rip me from my *mitawin* and the woman I love?"

Wife? Woman he loves? Were they one and the same? Of course they were. Black Eagle wasn't the type of man to keep a mistress. Granted, his tribe permitted more than one wife, but would Carrie tolerate . . .

"Well, Mr. Arthur Merle? Are you here to steal another *wanagi*?"

"Black Eagle! How are you? I was in the neighborhood and I thought I'd stop by and . . ."

"Neighborhood? This is my village, not Napa, California. There is only one reason you would drop by and it cannot be for good."

For a man who spent life times in control, guiding kings and queens, for some reason the warrior concerned him. Not that Black Eagle could thwart his magic. Just the same—at least it seemed he arrived in the right time period.

"Well?"

"Well, ah, you see."

"The truth, Mr. Arthur Merle."

"I only need to get a message to Carrie."

The tall warrior considered the older man's statement. Tapping his chin, "What?"

"Well, you see. She needs to. Ah, Mo—"

"Mr. Arthur Merle, in both this time and in Carrie's, you hide behind word tricks. You are an *iktomi*, what your people call a trickster. Tell me the truth or I will not pass your message on to Carrie."

"I will. I will. I'm wondering though, is there somewhere we can sit down and talk for a few minutes?"

Black Eagle studied him, clearly looking for a trick before he grumbled, "This way."

He led Mr. Merle down the path leading to the river, stopping in a secluded spot away from prying eyes and ears. "Sit."

With a nod, the older man went to sit and then bent to the river, cupping the clear water in his hands and drinking deeply. "No water in the world like fresh river water, that's for certain. Now, what can I tell you so you don't doubt my intentions?"

"If you are my Mr. Arthur Merle, the one with the camera,

how do you know about Carrie?"

"I was afraid you'd ask me about that."

Unreadable, the warrior studied him. Even the combined efforts of Morgan and Morgause did not unsettle him quite the way Black Eagle's intent stare did.

"Well here's the story."

"Truth old man. No more stories."

"I'm getting to that. Okay, okay. I am the same man. In fact, I've been around for more years than you and I could both count."

"And no doubt have interfered more lives than we could both count."

"Some might say that. Yes indeed. They just might." Mr. Merle caught Black Eagle's deepening frown. "So, anyway, when I took your photograph, in this time, I took it only because you were an interesting man. There was something, I don't know, noble I suppose. You reminded me of the warriors of old. Men from a time of knights and chivalry and I wanted to remember that feeling. It certainly wasn't for any nefarious reason."

"So you did not intend to bring me to Carrie's time?"

"No. Not when I took the photograph. I lived through the years and . . ."

"You look no different in 2021 than you do, did, in my time."

"Yes, well one thing about my race, we don't age quite like yours does."

For a change Black Eagle's expression changed, the warrior clearly did not believe him.

"Well it's true. We don't. When I met Carrie, I felt bad for her. There she was, this warm, wonderful and caring woman and all she ever met were men that hurt her, made her feel bad. They just took and took from her and she needed a modern day knight in shining armor to come to her rescue."

"I am a warrior, not this knight in shining armor."

"No, no you're not. And heaven knows those knights could be more trouble than help. You have their qualities though. You wouldn't hurt someone just because you can, you are never cruel and you honor women. You'd never cheat on the woman you love. You were exactly the man Carrie needed in her life. The problem was you lived one hundred and sixty years apart."

"So you *did* send me to her time!"

Mr. Merle looked about the area, alert for anyone listening. "Shhhh, yes. But you can't tell anyone, especially Carrie."

"Why?"

"Because if she knows she might write it down and someone would know and then, well, questions would be asked. Questions we don't want to answer."

"Questions *you* do not want to answer. Tell me old man, why did I end up back in my time, without her?"

"I'm not so sure how that happened. I truly thought when you came forward you would stay. No one was sorrier than I when you returned to the past. I'll tell you, Carrie was beside herself. Molly was pretty worried. Do you know what they did?"

"I know Carrie was unhappy. She told me all when she arrived. Wait. What they did?"

"Yes. Do you know what they did?"

"Do you mean making the other photograph that had both Carrie and Taister in it with me? Yes. Why did it take so long for it to work?"

"I don't know about that either. Maybe after all these years I'm losing my touch. That or because I hadn't used my mag — skills in so many years it took a bit for the travel back in time to work. But let me ask you, Carrie arrived here — safe? She's well?"

Black Eagle smiled, pride illuminating his dark eyes, "She

and the babe she carries do very well."

"A baby! Well now that is good news. Very good news. How far along is she?"

Black Eagle narrowed his eyes, "You do not know how long she has been here, do you?"

"If you mean I don't know when in your life I landed, no. Does that matter?"

"No. It is just pleasant to know something you do not. We think maybe two moons."

"So Carrie's been here about two to three months. Good. Good."

Black Eagle put his hand on Mr. Merle's arm, "You do not think bad magic will pull her away?"

"No. Not that. Not at all." He crossed his fingers behind his back, "She is here to stay and because of that I need your help."

"My help?"

"Yes. Molly is worried about her. She needs to be reassured that Carrie is well and happy."

Black Eagle swept up a scoop of the sandy river dirt and watched it sift through his fingers. Only the occasional chirp of a bird disturbed the peaceful silence. "What is it you wish, old man?"

"It's very simple actually. Just have Carrie write a note that says she's happy and life is good and then leave it in a piece of furniture that will show up in her house in 2021."

"A note? Did you not just say we do not want her to write such things? Furniture? Mr. Arthur Merle, we are in an Indian Village. Where do you think to find this paper and that furniture?"

"Oh that." In the blink of an eye a sheet of parchment appeared in Mr. Merle's hand followed by a Bic pen. He studied the pen a moment before flicking his wrist and changing to a feathered quill."

"Ink?"

"It will write. And . . ." He glanced behind Black Eagle, blinked his eyes and with another flip of his wrist a desk appeared before the warrior. "There you go. A desk. The same one that now sits in Molly's house in Napa or will in the future."

"How will you explain this same desk being here in my village and later in Carrie and Molly's house in your time?"

"I'll just remind Molly that Carrie bought it in my shop a couple of years ago. Simple."

"Nothing is simple with you old man. And what would my people do with this desk?"

"Ah, well, they know Carrie's a white girl, right?"

"They are not fools."

"So you tell them she missed having one and you traded for it."

Black Eagle nodded.

Mr. Merle stood, eager to be on his way, "Well, give Carrie my best."

"You do not wish to see her?"

"I'm not sure that would be a good idea. If she sees me she might ask questions that are best left unanswered."

"Yes. That is so. I will bring her the desk and ask her to write the note. Do not be offended Mr. Arthur Merle. It is my wish you remain in your time and we will remain in mine."

"I certainly hope so, Black Eagle. With what I think is happening in my time having you there would only complicate things."

"Happening in your time? Is Molly safe?"

"Molly? Of course. In fact, if I'm not mistaken the man of her dreams may have recently arrived in town."

CHAPTER FIVE

"So, will she write the note?" Vivienne studied her friend.

"Already done. The note sits in a desk in Molly's house as we speak."

"How do you know for certain?"

"Moving from place to place in one time period is much easier than moving through time. When Molly returns home in the morning she will remember Carrie's antique desk, look in there and see Carrie's note."

"I ask you again, how can you know for certain?"

"I've just come from the house. The note is secure and explains she is safe and happy back in time. She even mentioned that she does not miss her lattes."

"What is this latte?" Gareth asked upon entering the room.

"Gareth, pay it no mind. Forget you heard of such." Mr. Merle grumbled at the interruption. He studied the younger man a moment and with a shake of his head raised his hands. He muttered a few words, flicked his fingers and closed his eyes. When he opened them he was surprised to find Gareth still standing before him and repeated the movements once more and once more again before Vivienne put her hand on his arm.

"You cannot send him back, my friend. I doubt you can even send him to Britain. He has woken and through no choice, has woken to live here and now."

"It cannot be."

"It is as it seems."

"Of all times, I do not need this now. Not with Carrie's

journey back in time and Molly asking questions."

"I have questions as well, wizard." Gareth deep voice rumbled in the stillness of the shop.

"I'm not sure I have the answers. It really would be much better if you went back to your rest."

"I would have answers, wizard, starting with this latte you and Vivienne have spoken of."

Mr. Merle sighed and looked upward as if the ceiling held the answers he sought. "I really do not need this right now."

"Then I will explain lattes to Gareth. Tis quite marvelous, dear boy." Vivienne cooed. "They take this brew called coffee. It's color a bit darker and flavor perhaps a tad more bitter than tea. Then they take milk and make it as frothy as freshly poured ale and pour it on top."

"Truly? I would have one of these lattes."

"Even better than its taste is the energy one has after they have drunk the brew. Quite tasty and I for one can remain awake for hours after imbibing one."

"Merlin! Can you procure one for me? Now?"

"No, Gareth. I cannot."

"Cannot or will not?" Vivienne smiled and with the flick of her wrist produced two large lattes for Gareth and herself. "And Merlin, shall I whip you up one of your peppermint mochas?"

The white haired man glanced at the door, "Hsst, Vivienne. Please restrain your use of magic! The people of this time do not believe."

"Not believe?" Gareth' brows rose in disbelief. "How is this so?"

"Ah, dear boy, much has changed since you walked the paths of Britain. Twas a time, not long past wise women were killed, murdered for their magical skills."

Suddenly aware of the beverage in his hand Gareth studied it before taking a tentative sip. With a smack of his lips he declared, "You speak aright Vivienne, tis quite tasty. I would return home now."

"I'm not sure that is possible," Mr. Merle shook his head.

"What mean you, Wizard?"

"What I mean is you are here because you have woken, not because you have traveled through time. What worries me even more is if you have woken, how long before the others do as well."

"Of course I have woken. I am standing here, once again, in this strange room. Again, I say I would return."

The older man shook his head, "This could not have happened at a worse time."

CHAPTER SIX

Pulling on to Miwok's main street Molly glanced at the car's clock and muttered to herself, "Hmmm, I've got just enough time to pick up a coffee before going into work."

She pulled into the police department's parking lot, slid her badge into the gate and waited for the fence to roll out and allow her to pull in. Off to the side she caught a slight movement in one of the patrol cars.

At first startled when the officer behind the wheel thrust his head back against the seat she fumbled for her phone to call for help. She'd just entered the nine when a blonde head popped up causing Molly to snicker, "Ole peanut butter legs is starting early this shift."

Molly shook her head in disgust at Kris, the department's resident badge bunny, otherwise known as BB for her sexual antics. Almost all the dispatchers slept rather indiscriminately with the officers. Kris was the worst. The woman was a disgrace to the department, but no one would do anything about it because her step-mother, Leslie, was one of the supervisors. Molly's direct supervisor to be exact, just below the Red Queen. Perhaps more important were Chief Crane's own words, "Kris is an asset to the department if for no other reason than how she single handedly boosts morale for us."

"Yeah," Molly muttered, "single hand and mouth and let us not forget her incredible, spreadable legs. It ain't morale she's boosting there, Chief." Man, she wanted to say the words out loud, but since rumor had it Kris had done the Chief a time or two it wouldn't go over too well. Ignoring the couple in the patrol car she head to Java, Java. Already she needed a quadruple shot extra mega latte. She needed a double when she got up this morning and found Carrie gone, a triple when she ran into Gareth and after witnessing ole BB's, morning snack, that fourth shot was a necessity.

Funny, she mused, it was almost four in the afternoon, but being on swings and graves for so many years it was morning to her, her and everyone else who'd been on swings for that long.

Walking into Java Java she spied Shannon, one of the newer employees. "Hey, Shannon! How's is going?"

"Okay. I never thought I'd think a three day weekend was too short, but it sure flew by."

"They do. Wait till you do a shift change and end up working six days straight."

"Does that happen?"

"Yeah, if you go from Sunday, Monday, Tuesday to Wednesday, Thursday, Friday, it does. I've done it a few times, but the past few years Karla and I bid the shift the other one wants and then we trade. What's worse is if you are going from graves to days because the Red Queen expects you to work the shifts as assigned. You could be up and running for twenty-four hours straight."

"Got it. Say, isn't having someone work twenty-four hours straight against the law?"

"According to Julie Prince, emergency personnel are exempt. She couches it in terms of public safety to have us do that. Some how she doesn't get it that working over fifteen hours straight, without a nap, could be a public safety issue. Besides, you don't want to challenge her. The few who have tried, including myself, have lived to regret it."

"Trust me, I learned that early on and it worries me because I'm still on probation."

"What happened?"

"I want to be a dispatcher. I paid for the classes, went to school for it and that's the job I applied for. At first, I believed her that I needed to know about records to have a foundation for dispatching, but after four months I asked her about it. She said something about us being at full staff and then two days later Katy Kimly comes in and is rushed through a background and gets a dispatch job. So I went back in to Julie and asked her how that happened."

"Let me guess. The list you were on expired and since you were doing so well in Records it never occurred to them that you would want the dispatch job. After all, why would you want to make almost a thousand dollars more a month and sit on your ass all day picking your nose?"

Shannon laughed, "Almost. Definitely on the money issue and being able to sit more would be better for my back. That's why I went after a dispatch job in the first place. I was in a car accident a few years ago and can't stand for long or lift much. Sitting at a computer terminal is really about all I can do. Now the picking my nose part, I hadn't considered that but it sounds like fun."

"Did you tell Julie that? About your back?"

"Yeah. I told her I was even willing to take on dispatch at my current salary as a reasonable accommodation. I can tell from the look on your face you know what happened."

"If I know Julie, things were great until then and as soon as you told her there was a remote issue of a disability she started to treat you like a leper."

"Pretty much. She started to make comments like she isn't sure she can accommodate my needs or modify my job duties so I don't get hurt. I haven't specifically asked for an accommodation. In fact, the only reason I mentioned it was I hoped it would land me in dispatch. If she notices Sally or Kaitlin going up to the front counter she calls me into her office and *reminds* me that doing the job means doing all the aspects, not just the ones I like and if I'm not physically capable of doing them I should think about quitting."

"She's done that before. We've lost some really great people by her doing that. Has she ever said anything to you about how you look?"

Shannon looked at her oddly for a moment and then shook her head, as if to herself. "Not directly. In fact, I was the one who said something."

"Which was?"

"Would I get a job in dispatch if I was a twenty-something blonde?"

"You didn't!"

"I did."

"What did she do?"

"Sat there and stared at me for about a minute and then told me that she cannot discriminate based on age or weight, and I never said a word about weight, but she pointed out dispatch does require the fast moving skills of a younger person."

"Sounds like Julie. She couches things in such a way that it's you that's the problem and that she is doing everything she can to obey the law."

"That's for sure. It looks like I'll never make it into dispatch at Miwok PD."

"Not likely, and you'll notice whenever you ask about training things will slow way down for you."

"Have you tried for it?"

"Every time a position opens up. Sometimes they make me retest from the git go, taking the P.O.S.T. battery and sometimes they just let me do an oral board. It's never going to happen here which is why — " Molly looked around the coffee bistro and when it was clear no one would hear, continued, "I'm applying elsewhere."

"Where?"

"Anywhere and everywhere there is an opening."

"I tried at the county, but they said I needed to pass probation here first. With Julie calling me in every time I turn around for just crap, I start to wonder if that will happen."

"It will. She needs a punching bag on the end of the week I don't work."

"Gees. You aren't joking, are you?"

"Nope. Before I came, Kaitlyn was her target. Before her Sally. Maria says that she was a target as well. However, since she's the only bilingual speaker and queen of the kiss asses in the department, Julie pretty much leaves her alone. Well, we should get going, shift starts in ten minutes and you know how Julie is about you having your headset on and ready to go the moment your shift starts."

"Yup, been written up for being thirty seconds late on that one twice."

"Violated public safety, did you?"

"Uh huh. Even though Sally, Kaitlyn *and* Maria were plugged in."

"Yes, well, even Miwok can have a mass casualty emergency."

"Have we ever?"

"Nope, but you never know."

Together they walked to the station. Molly came to a stop just inside the front door and pointed to several posters arranged on stands in the lobby. "What the heck is this?"

"Oh that," Shannon shook her head. "Remember that email a week or so ago about the community policing program? How we're supposed to get the community more involved in looking after themselves with budget cuts and all?"

"Right." Molly stepped toward one of the displayed posters.

"So this is part of the program."

Molly took a quick look at two of the posters, "Shannon,

these are serial killers."

"Yeah, I know. Julie said we need to be very careful because serial killers could appear in any community at any time."

"Right. Miwok with a serial killer."

"Uh huh, and all but one of them has been caught."

"Here in Miwok?"

"No, silly. All of them have been caught, tried and convicted but one."

"And which one hasn't been and do we think he's here?"

"Jack the Ripper. Jules said he was a favorite of hers."

"Why am I not surprised?"

The women were no sooner in the station and Julie came to the entrance to her office, "Molly, can I see you before you plug in please?"

Kaitlyn shook her head.

Her lips barely moving, Sally muttered, "That'll teach you to go on days off."

Matching Sally's ventriloquist technique and reaching into her locker for her headset, Molly asked, "Know what this is about?"

"Something didn't get done Tuesday morning at seven."

"I wasn't even here."

"Uh huh. Let me know if you need a union rep."

She was no sooner in the door and Julie directed her to close the door and have a seat. Clearly this was going to take some time. Not that that was a problem. Less paper for her to push at the start of her shift.

No sooner was Molly seated and Julie handed her a sheet of paper. Without looking closely she could see it was one of the department's log entries, essentially memoranda documenting whatever real or imagined sins had been committed. For the past ten years it seemed like she got one a week and often joked to Carrie they should use them to paper the outhouse at the local riding stables. Carrie—since leaving Mr. Merle's Molly hadn't thought much about her missing roommate.

Mentioning that Carrie'd disappeared wasn't the kind of thing Julie would see as a big deal. After all, if it wasn't one of her twenty-something, blonde haired, leg spreading, squealing dispatchers, it wasn't worth mentioning. In the six months Shannon had been with the department it hadn't taken long for her to see that it was the skinny, younger blondes who got the dispatch jobs and the over thirty brunettes especially if they had some meat on their bones, got the records jobs. Molly had been the right age when she started, but the wrong hair color and weight. That and she wasn't promiscuous.

"I don't know what to say about this, Molly. This is such a disappointment."

She tried, inconspicuously, to see what had been written on the paper. Julie, however, guarded the contents of the log entries as if they were the crown jewels until she was ready to spring them on her victim. On the heels of Carrie's disappearance, Molly so wasn't in the mood for Julie's antics. "It might help if you told me what this is about."

"That attitude alone tells me you don't begin to understand the gravity of this situation."

There was a reason they called Julie the Red Queen, "What situation, Julie?"

"You failed to complete an essential task before you went off duty Tuesday morning. By time we realized your mistake it was simply too late to do anything about it."

The woman may as well have shouted "off with her head" for all the sense she was making. She'd give the woman one more chance and then she'd ask for a union rep. It was looking more and more like she'd need a witness to whatever it was that Julie was harping on. "Julie, I'm trying to figure out just what the problem is."

"What's done is done. It's too late now and there are a stack of reports left over from the past three days. Maria and Sally have been incredibly busy and with her back problems, Shannon just doesn't pull her weight so you need to get out there and catch up on that paperwork. If you'll just sign this you can get to work."

"First, I'm not signing anything that I haven't read. Second, I would appreciate you explaining to me why it is incumbent on me to finish all incoming paperwork on my shift but they don't have to on theirs."

"I'm offended you think you have to read a counseling memorandum from me. After all, with the gravity of this situation it could have and might still, lead to an internal affairs investigation. As to the incoming paperwork, Maria has considerable extra responsibility because of her bilingual skills and her lower back problems. Sally has, well, I don't think you realize how busy we are here during the week. You probably think we have it as easy as you do nights and weekends."

"Julie, I'm not going to bother with the fact that if Maria speaks Spanish at all it's to her husband on the phone. However, have you ever sat and counted the reports that come in on Friday and Saturday nights? We average fifty to sixty each night."

"But you don't have the walk in and telephone traffic now, do you? Except for the past few months, you haven't worked days since you got off training ten years ago."

"And I wouldn't have had the opportunity if Sally didn't need a special schedule due to her multiple schedules and the department needing coverage during day shift."

"I cannot discuss another employee's health problems with you. I had hoped that your time on days would show you just how busy we are."

"I only had a glimpse because generally Maria and Sally will not work weekends."

"And that is their privilege because of their seniority."

The woman made no sense, as usual. It occurred to Molly she'd be better off in a washing machine, going in reverse during the spin cycle than trying to have a conversation that consistently turned in convoluted daisy wheels with the other woman. "Maybe you should have them work a few weekends so they can accurately report to you what does go on then."

While tempting, telling Julie about Kris' sexual antics during her shift or how the blonde badge bunny closed out calls that she didn't feel merited an officer, that would fall on deaf ears. Hands down, Kris held most favored status in Julie's little kingdom. No one dared to say anything negative about her. The two people who tried ended up in internal affairs investigations that cost them not only their jobs, but Julie and Captain Berger made certain they would never work in law enforcement again.

She reached for the counseling memo, "I'll just take a minute to read this."

"You'll sign it."

"Not without reading it."

"I don't think I need to remind you, Molly, your review is coming up."

"Are you threatening me, Julie?"

"Of course not. I'm merely pointing out that insubordination will get you a bad review."

"Just a moment." Molly rose and went to the door, "Sally, can you come in here a minute?"

"Sure, what's up?"

"Julie wants me to sign something without reading it first. She seems to think wanting to know what I'm signing is insubordination. For all I know she is accusing me of causing Lt. Jeffman's car to crash."

"There is no need to be dramatic, Molly," Julie spat. "That poor man is now a paraplegic and poor Kris almost lost her looks in that crash."

Under her breath Molly told Sally, "guess having your head in a guy's lap is the safest place to be in a car."

Sally shushed her then asked Julie for the paper. Her eyes popped open as she read. "Julie, this says that Molly intentionally omitted sending in the DUI stats at the end of the weekend."

"Exactly. She was supposed to have them in between seven and eight in the morning."

"Julie, Molly wasn't even on duty that day. This is her first day back on swings. She left Monday afternoon about five. Unless she was working overtime till Tuesday morning, she wouldn't have been here to do this at the designated time. Molly, did you work overtime Monday night?"

"No. like you said, I was off at five . . .in the afternoon."

"There you go, Julie," Sally laid the paper on the desk, "if the stats were due between seven and eight Tuesday morning, there was no way Molly could do it before she left. Maria is the one who missed the deadline. Hopefully you saved this on your computer so you can correct the misspelling on the name."

"Maybe you need to be reminded who is the manager around here, Sally. I'll let it go this time, but in the future, Molly, please make certain you complete all the tasks assigned to you and if for some reason you can't, leave me a memorandum about it."

"Sure, no problem." Molly shook her head and started out of the office.

"That's a good reminder for all of us, Julie," Sally told her. "Dispatch could use it too."

"Dispatch has enough on their plates without having to write memorandums about why they can't get to something. They *do* pass information on to each other during briefing."

"That reminds me, any movement on records staff

attending briefing? It would certainly help keep up with things." Sally probed.

"If there wasn't so much paperwork to complete I'd agree with you, Sally. Speaking of which, the two of you have goofed off long enough. You've already lost almost an hour of time and poor Maria most likely has had to deal with more than her share."

Outside the office Sally followed Molly to her desk. "Sally, what was that about?"

"It looked like the *Avoid the Fifteen* program we do every year."

"We do?"

"Uh huh. This year, however, there was a decision made to share stats." She put her hand up to stop Molly from speaking, "The only reason I know about the stat sharing is I had dinner with one of the dispatchers from county last night and she mentioned it. In past years we participated, but no one ever kept stats. I'm curious though . . ." she walked over to the arrest ledger and read through the bookings from five Monday evening through seven Tuesday morning. "There were four DUI arrests from five in the afternoon through eight Tuesday morning."

Molly glanced down at the ledger, "Ten arrests and bookings from six p.m. to seven in the morning."

"More than double. They wouldn't have shown up in the stats and from what I understand, the timing of the arrests as well as how many are important for patrol purposes."

"Are you going to tell the Red Queen?"

"Why? It won't do a bit of good." With that Molly headed to dispatch to pick up completed reports, Sally to the front desk to pick up counter reports citizens had left with Shannon already manning the main phone position and Maria bid them all a good weekend on her way out the door.

A collective sigh of relief sounded through the records area about a half hour later when Julie left for the weekend as well.

After Sally logged off for the weekend she sat on the other side of the desk Molly worked at entering arrest data into the computer. "You looked a little worn when you came in today and I don't think it was just Julie."

"It was that obvious?"

Sally nodded.

"My roommate kinda moved out."

"Carrie? No way."

"Way."

"Did you two have a fight?"

"No. Remember that guy she met a few months ago?"

"Blake something?"

"Yup. He had to, ah, move back to his home a bit ago. You know, family things. Carrie decided to move back there too. It was kind of sudden."

"What about her job?"

"Uh. I'm not sure what arrangements she made." *But I'm going to have to check it out first thing Monday morning.* Maybe she could get in touch with Carrie's supervisor over the weekend and explain better what was going on. Good one, she thought, explain what? That Carrie ran off to one hundred and sixty years into the past? Right. That would end her in the padded cell next to Dean, Carrie's old boyfriend. Still, she needed to explain why Carrie wouldn't be coming back to work. Unless she showed up over the weekend anyway.

"Are you going to look for another roommate?"

"I hadn't thought about it. She uh, Carrie only left a few days ago, and it was pretty sudden. Why? Know someone looking for a home?"

"Maybe."

"You and Mike are doing okay, aren't you?"

"Oh yeah. My cousin, Rita, you know, the singer, mentioned something about moving to Napa or Solano. Keep my posted."

"Definitely."

"Well, I'd better get going. You guys have a good shift."

"Thanks, Sally." Molly told her.

Shannon glanced up from the phone call she was on and waved.

Being in a few hours before Molly, the graveyard shift out on patrol, Shannon went to take her dinner break. For the first time since waking that morning, Molly finally had a few minutes to sit and think. It was going to be a long weekend.

CHAPTER SEVEN

The second Kris bopped off for a ride-a-long, *more like a suck-a-long*, with the flavor of the month, Molly decided to take advantage of a lull in work. All the reports had been compiled and entered into the computer, the arrest ledger updated, filing pretty much done — there would be time to finish it over the weekend if Shannon didn't get to it during her shift. At least with filing, Shannon could sit at the counter and pull files in a relatively comfortable position. Standing at the front counter seemed to be the hardest for the other woman. With a few minutes to herself Molly figured she'd make up a list of things she had to take care of with Carrie's disappearance. With the slow expulsion of a deep breath she wondered if she could trust that Carrie was truly safely in Black Eagle's village. What if what really happed was that Dean got out or escaped from the mental hospital he'd been committed to and kidnapped Carrie? After all, she and Carrie had photoshopped a picture of Carrie standing beside Black Eagle. Could Dean have managed to escape, print up a similar photograph on aged looking paper and somehow gotten it into the house? "Not likely. Still . . ."

Picking up a pen, Molly began a list of things to do given Carrie's departure. "Let's see . . ."

Check to be sure Dean is still in the nut house;
Call Carrie's work and see if somehow she left them a message, if not,
Make something up about how much longer she might be gone;

Call Carrie's bank;
Plan non-op her car;
Change utilities to my name;
Check her day runner and cancel appointments.

She chewed the tip of her pen thinking of other things she would need to take care of. "I never thought I'd see the day I'd say this, but it's a good thing you have no family, Carrie Taylor. A darn good thing because the last thing I'd want to explain is that you're a time traveler."

"Who's a time traveler?" Shannon asked, sliding into the chair beside Molly's desk.

"Who—ah, oh, a character in one of Carrie's books."

"She's a big romance reader, isn't she?"

"Yeah. I don't think there's one she hasn't read, especially time travels. They're her favorite."

"Did I hear you tell Sally earlier Carrie moved out?"

"For a bit. Her boyfriend had some family stuff going on."

"Are you looking for a new roommate?"

"That's what Sally asked. Not right now. Want me to let you know if I do?" Not that getting a new roommate was going to be high on her list of things to do. After all, what if there was a vortex or something in the house that made Carrie time travel and not . . . not what? She quickly jotted down to have a long sit down with Mr. Merle. Like Black Eagle, Molly had no doubt the kindly old gentleman knew more than he let on.

Moments later the police radio came to life with calls coming in fast and furious. There were the usual Miwok Friday night calls of noisy neighbors, loud parties, a few calls for medical assistance and officers pulling cars over for moving violations. Shannon went off duty about midnight followed by two of the officers reporting in they were on their way back from booking two DUIs at the county jail. Not a minute later a silent alarm code came in from one of the local banks.

Molly listened to Janette in dispatch give out the address

of the bank and assign the officers. More often than not, cleaning crews set off the night time alarms. When that happened generally one of them would call into the station and give a pre-determined all clear code. Then they'd all step outside to wait for the officers who would still drive by and check things out, but it wouldn't be with lights flashing.

And then, there were the exceptions. From the sound of things, tonight was going to be one of the exceptions. Going to a secured channel Janette directed officers to the bank. She tried twice to raise the car Kris had gone out riding along in, but there was no response. No surprise. If this was the real deal, Janette would need solid back up in dispatch.

In preparation for the officers' arrival, Molly went into the dispatch center and logged on. First she brought up a graphic of the bank's internal phone numbers. Even though it was the middle of the night, protocol mandated they try the number to see if by some chance an employee was inside or, if there was a suspect, that they would pick up the phone.

Next, she brought up a diagram of the inside of the bank and began to notate possible hiding areas, the vault and other key points inside. With no common wall with any other business, there were fewer locations for the officers to stage. "Janette? Unless things have changed, there are two dumpsters in the back parking lot. They look about oh, ten feet away on one, fifteen on the other. There's a clump of bushes fronting the back door, two trees on the street by the front."

"Thanks. And thanks for plugging in. I wish I knew where Kris was."

"Probably flat on her back somewhere."

"Not what I hear."

"No?"

"She's into riding on top and mouth work."

"Nice. Vault's on a timer so there's no getting in there till morning unless they plan to blow it. If anyone is inside that is."

"Unit 11 on scene," the first officer called in.

"E 7 on scene," the shift sergeant announced his arrival.

Two other units reported in. After the sixth unit arrived the sergeant positioned the officers for best visual survey of the bank. While the officers set up, Molly ran the stats on the bank, times and dates of prior break-ins, number of silent and audible alarms, number of actual as opposed to accidental. The information wasn't needed right then, but may be a factor later on.

After a few minutes of radio silence the sergeant called in, "Make the call."

Molly dialed the bank's main internal number and waited for an answer. If there was an employee inside, they would be asked to step out. Generally, suspects didn't pick up the phone and confirm their presence. If they had a wit of sense, they would and say they were employees and things were just fine. They weren't that smart.

Not surprisingly the phone rang and rang. After fifteen rings Molly disconnected and shook her head. A moment after Janette updated the officers that two of the SWAT team members who were working graves, reported they were at the back door, while two other officers advised they staged to the front. A fifth reported in as being across the street, using his car for coverage. The rest, along with several county deputies who had been in the area, took up other strategic positions.

Janette sighed, "I can't believe all the fire power out there when it's just the robbers, if that's what it is."

Molly turned to her, surprise lacing her tone, "You mean besides the fact that they have little to do so everyone's come to the party?"

"Yeah."

"Well, we don't know for certain there are no hostages. For

all we know they've been in there since the bank closed. You know, like if one of the employees was somehow stuck in the vault or the suspects arrived right before closing and managed to hide until everything was shut down. Then they wait until all the businesses in the area shut down and meanwhile the employee only makes it to the alarm now. And we don't know how many there are. Remind me again how long you've been here." Molly tried to keep the derision she felt out of her tone while taking in the thin blonde's low cut blouse and tight jeans.

"A little over a year. I just got off probation."

"Hmm, that's right. Well, over the years there have been times it's been one suspect who didn't know what he was doing and blundered around inside by himself. There was another time, about six years ago when there were nine or ten of them inside the bank, loaded for bear with automatic weapons and tear gas. They did have one employee held hostage and we didn't know it until they exited the bank. We got lucky, the civilian got out without a scratch and we arrested all the suspects and got a solid conviction. These kinds of calls can fall anywhere in between. You never know what you are going to find once you get inside so it's better to have a little too much than too little."

"Too bad about your age, you would have made a great dispatcher."

"Excuse me?" This was so not the time to bring it up, but how often did she have the chance to sit in dispatch and get the 411 on what the scuttlebutt they heard?

"You are always on top of things, anytime there's a hot call you have the run maps up on the computer, the contact histories of not only the address we're responding to but the other houses in the area, as soon as we have suspect and victim information you have them run out along with any other related people. I could go on, but you know better than I do all you

43

do from just the outset of a call."

"I know what I do. I want to know about the age crack."

"Oh that. I asked Kris one day why with how good you are you weren't in dispatch. She said it was your age, that older women can't keep up with the radio traffic."

"O-o-older women? Janette. I'm thirty-one. That's not exactly old."

"But you are over thirty and Kris said that once you turn thirty you lose whatever you had to make it in dispatch. If you are in here before then, Kris said, you're okay because you get the tempo down. After that though . . ."

"Janette, I've been here ten years. I've been trying to get into dispatch for ten years. I wasn't born thirty."

"I didn't know that, but Kris said that, well, don't take this personally, okay?"

"Kris, like she's the bible of police dispatch. Just what did *Kris* say?" It was starting to sound like Kris was the voice of the department's moirés.

"In addition to age, women who were over weight couldn't move fast enough to keep up with radio traffic."

"O-o-over weight? I may have a few extra—oh hell." Molly shook her head and turned back to her terminal, "Did she happen to mention how many officers you have to sleep with to pass probation?"

"Sleep wi—uh. Well not how many, but . . ."

"That was a joke."

"Molly, you aren't fat. You are curvy and I'm not exactly a bean pole myself."

She decided to be gracious. After all, she *did* have to work with the twenty-something twit. "True, if you stood sideways and stuck your tongue out *you* wouldn't look like a zipper."

"Zip—oh my god, the zipper! It's Kris you all joke about, isn't it?"

"I can't believe I said that." She was so screwed. If Janette so much as breathed a word of it there'd be a major IA. While it was just fine for Kris to say whatever popped into her mouth, provided it was empty of man parts at the time, the same didn't hold for anyone who wasn't part of her in crowd. Things were sticky before Kris arrived simply because Julie felt she could say whatever she wanted any time she wanted. She'd tell the staff it was her privilege as the manager.

Kris though took insulting to a whole other level. Molly challenged the decision to hire Kris into the dispatch job she had been promised. Sally clued her in that during the background process Kris started sleeping with the admin hiring sergeant. It more or less guaranteed her the job. On the heels of that revelation Molly applied, for the first time, to County. When she didn't get the job at County, thanks to Julie's input during the background, she started to apply to every other department in the area. Except for Napa. There was something just wrong about working in your home town. Especially if the job consisted of arresting former high school and college peers.

"Don't worry, your secret is safe with me. I can't wait for the next rotation so I don't have to work with Kris anymore."

"I don't want to burst your bubble but no one likes working with her. You'll see everyone else bidding any shift that will avoid hers."

"Thanks. That is not what I wanted to hear. Isn't there . . ."

After almost fifteen minutes of radio silence it crackled, "11 to E-7, I've got three inside."

"E-7 to 11, copy three inside, dispatch copy?"

Janette cleared her throat and keyed down, "Copy. Description."

Molly was already reaching for the hot sheet that listed known suspects with one hand and clicking through with her mouse to bring up a database of recent robberies.

"Dispatch, 7. It's pretty dark inside, all three are in dark body suits, dark what appear to be ski masks, gloves and boots."

"7, dispatch, any sign of weapons?"

"Dispatch, 8," one of the SWAT team members answered up, "They appear to be semi-automatic rifles."

"Dispatch copies."

A series of clicks sounded over the now still dispatch center, alerting Molly and Janette that the other officers on scene were aware of the guns.

"Dispatch, Unit 17."

"17?" Janette responded.

"I'm 1015, one in custody."

Janette sat, frozen, looking at the console.

"Janette?" Molly called from across the room. When the blonde didn't respond Molly keyed down, "Copy 1015. Any available unit?"

One of the deputies answered up he was enroute to secure the suspect.

Janette seemed to wake up. "17 is on the perimeter. How did he catch one of them?"

Molly turned away from the radio to look at the other woman, "I could be wrong, but that suspect was probably driving the get-away car."

"Oh shit! If he had a gun . . ."

"Yeah. That's another reason why we send so many."

"Am I ever going to get it?" Janette all but sobbed.

"Janette, you didn't do anything wrong. They're out there and they know what they are doing. We're inside and our job is to have information ready for them if and when they want it. Yes, we have to anticipate what they are going to be looking for, but there's no way we can know if there are suspects sitting in cars outside the site."

"Mol, I would have sent one unit and a backup."

"And your sergeant would ask you for however many

more he thought you needed. You're doing fine."

"I don't think so. At least Kris isn't here."

"Who was she riding with?"

"John Lively I think. Will she be in trouble?"

"Only if E-7 wants to make a stink about Lively not answering up. Or maybe he's on scene and didn't tell you, which is a total no no as well, only not as big a one as not showing up. Complete breach of officer safety protocols. The only way Kris will get in trouble is if E-7 says something about it and since he's been in her pants, or mouth, himself . . . did I say that in my out loud voice? He's not about to diss her."

"No. But he might do her."

"Goes there. Does that."

CHAPTER EIGHT

Between periods of radio silence and officers repositioning Molly ran out whatever information was available on the bank, the suspects and whatever else she could think the officers would need for their reports. Neither she nor Janette took a break, eating at the dispatch console. Rather than do what Kris and her ilk would do and pull out a book—well actually Kris wouldn't pull out a book, she'd start some internet shopping or fussing with her makeup—Molly pulled some of the easier paper work from the records area to complete.

Janette did, in fact, pull out a book which prompted Molly to tell her, "You probably don't want to be doing that on duty. I don't care, but if Kris comes back in and sees you reading, especially when she needs to divert attention from the fact she wasn't here when all this went down she'll make sure you're written you up for it."

"Thanks." She closed the book, "Which reminds me, I thought when I was in training I was supposed to have a senior dispatcher or a trainer with me at all times, at least for the first two years."

"You are. But you really don't want to interfere with Kris' sex life, you know."

"But this case tonight is huge."

"Yes, it is."

"So what happens when the D.A. pulls the tape and hears only my voice, or yours, going out over the air? Won't that raise questions?"

"Minor ones. The defense attorney will be more interested in where the officers may have screwed up. If they get wind that one of the arresting officers was out messing around, well we don't know where he is and as long as he doesn't submit a report it shouldn't be any big deal. What they'll probably tell you to say is that she was here, guiding you the whole way."

"But that's not true!"

"Welcome to the world of Miwok PD."

Janette turned to stare at her, mouth gaping.

"You can't mean to tell me you haven't noticed that before."

"That's not . . .how many . . .do you?"

"No idea if you're trying to ask me how many she's done. I'm a stickler for facts and the truth. You might even hear some chat around here that I'm so by the book there's no need to open it. I won't lie, not for anyone. But I'm not on probation and I will tell you, early on I was asked to lie during an internal affairs investigation. I almost lost my job because I wouldn't lie. I went through an entire Skelly hearing before they realized I'd keep telling the truth and some of their more sordid secrets would come out. Now they pretty much leave me alone. Well except for Julie. Get on her bad side and the Red Queen never forgets."

"I can see that."

"Don't you love how she comes out with these pronouncements and if you don't follow what she wants she keeps coming at you over and over and over again. She'll put me through an IA every year or so just to keep my record muddied so I can't get another job."

"But if she doesn't like you . . . ."

"As long as I work here there are things that I can't disclose. Remember that loyalty oath you signed when you took your oath?"

"Yeah."

"Can't discuss department business. The day I leave is the day I can talk about what goes on here. And police departments, they not only don't like that you've participated in an IA, they don't like it if you divulge department secrets. If you do it at one they think you'll do it at another. From Julie's perspective, it's better to keep you here, stuck in place, then to let you out there on the world with your stories. Besides, she gets her jollies making lives miserable. That's mostly why *she* prevents me from promoting. It would give me something I want and she's about dangling what you want in front of you more than doing what would really make you happy. Once you have it, she doesn't have anything on you."

"I can see why you wouldn't like working here. Isn't there anything else you'd like to do? Can do?"

"Actually, I do like just about everyone else. There's a strong camaraderie here. A lot of good people. As to what I'd like to do? I've always wanted to be a dispatcher. I like sitting at a computer terminal and doing something to help people, make a difference. I don't particularly like talking on the phone — and some of the world's biggest whiners call the police department because we basically have to listen. Of course there's real calls, serious calls and even the craziest person in the world can have a crime committed against them. But the day in, day out phone calls. Nu-uh. And I hate doing paperwork. Ten years of those reports, yeech. My roommate, well former roommate right now, worked for an insurance company and more than once offered me jobs there. It would have been doing paperwork."

"So where did your roommate go?"

Molly chuckled, "Back in t . . .back to her boyfriend's home. I don't think I've ever seen a couple more in love than those two."

"Sounds like she just up and left."

"Not really," Molly thought about her statement that she wouldn't lie. This was about to be a whopper. "I knew she planned to be with him as soon as she could. She's there now."

"Where's he from?"

"Um, Wyoming or South Dakota or one of those states."

"You don't know?"

"South Dakota. He has family in other places."

"I've never been to either state, have you?"

"No."

"Just think, you'll get to go now."

"Go there?"

"Yeah. To see, Carrie. That's her name, right? You can go visit her."

"Um, maybe." First she'd have to figure out how to time travel. No, first she'd have to find out if she could time travel and make it back to her own time. There was no way she was going to give up her lattes, microwaves and in door plumbing. And aside from that photograph, did she really know Carrie went back in time? What if Black Eagle's people were right and Carrie was trapped . . . *I'm getting tired and deluded. If people got trapped in photographs I would have been trapped as a baby with all the ones my folks took of me. I'm better off wishing for one of King Arthur's knights to come riding in and rescue me.*

"Why wouldn't you go?"

Before Molly could answer, which she took as an omen from above, the radio crackled, "Miwok, E-7, 1015 with three in custody."

Janette starred at the radio until Molly prodded her.

"Miwok copies, 1015 with three."

"Janette," Molly called, "Ask their names. We need to run them."

"Right. E-7, Miwok, names and dates of birth."

As one of the officers called off the names, Molly started to run each felon, forwarded the text to Janette and then printed out the information. Several officers stayed behind to secure the scene and begin investigating what had happened in the bank while three separate units escorted the prisoners to the jail to join their comrade who had already been booked. Moments after the sergeant called out a code four and announced the remaining units were back in service, he acknowledged Janette work, "Nice going dispatch. Great job."

Janette beamed, "Miwok copies."

When he entered the station a few minutes later he spotted Molly leaving the dispatch booth. "Picking up a few tips, Nichols?"

"Not exactly. I was backing Janette up."

"Backing . . ."

"You told Kris she could ride along tonight with Lively or one of them, remember?"

"And she came back in when the call went out, didn't she?"

"Was Lively on scene?"

Hand to his jaw he considered the question. "Now that I think of it — good thing you were here."

"Thanks. You're okay signing my overtime slip, right?"

"OT? Damn, what time is it?"

"Almost five. I was supposed to be off duty at three, but since Janette was alone it would have been wrong to leave and I wasn't about to interrupt you on that call to ask permission." She'd see if he would decide to pick up on the fact that Kris should be in trouble for leaving Janette alone, especially with a hot call. And then, if he'd so something about it there would be some justice. Mentally Molly shook her head. She knew exactly what would happen. The sergeant would corner Kris, ask her about missing from dispatch almost all night and she would ask him to ride along with him. She give him a few blow jobs, come back in and no one would know a thing. At least no one who would or could do anything about her.

"Sure, I'll sign it. See you tomorrow."

"That would be later today, Sergeant," Molly smiled.

Pulling out of the parking lot Molly yawned a jaw cracker of a yawn. "Man, I am tired. That was a long assed day."

By time she pulled into the garage and walked into the house, all that she could focus on was laying her head on her pillow. Carrie and Black Eagle were the last things on her mind. She managed to brush her teeth, tug off her pants, top and bra and fell on the bed. Oddly, it wasn't Carrie or Black Eagle or Taister who visited her dreams. Images of the blond haired man in Mr. Merle's shop flitted in and out of her dreams. In each he wore a suit of shiny silver armor and rode a big black horse, like a knight in shining armor coming to rescue his damsel in distress.

CHAPTER NINE

The alarm's shrill ring jarred Molly awake all too few hours later. "Damn, just as I was getting to what Carrie would call the good part." She rolled out of bed and staggered into the bathroom.

Standing in the hot shower, doing her best to wake up, memories of the dreams she'd had surfaced. Images of Gareth in knightly garb or Gareth lifting his helmet's visor, bright blue eyes looking her up and down with appreciation were interspersed with fleeting kisses. His smile slow and seductive made her tingle. Vaguely she remembered one where she rode behind him on the big black horse, holding on with one hand on his waist, the other on his chest. The beat of his heart beneath of her hand somehow felt real, as if it really happened. Just the remembrance of *that* dream turned her on.

Her shower done she wiped the steam off the mirror and studied her face. No one had ever called Molly beautiful. Cute, sweet, yes. Pretty even. Definitely not beautiful. But the big blond in her dream called her beautiful. That much she remembered.

"Okay, Nichols, time to get real. Those are Carrie-esq dreams. Not Molly dreams. Your dreams are about being lead dispatcher on the radio during an exciting code three call. Kind of like last night's except, by default, you were the back up. It should have been me on primary! I should have been there, calling the codes. And look where Carrie's dreams got her. Back in some dusty old Indian village. No coffeemakers, no refrigerators, no microwaves. Not the life for me. And no more thinking about that guy in Mr. Merle's shop. With his suit of amour, which is probably where that dream came from, he is a bit too out of it. That Gareth-guy is, was, Carrie's type. Not mine."

She snapped her fingers, "Damn, I forgot to look for . . ." She glanced at the clock, "No time now. Hopefully I'll get out on time tonight and can look to see if there's a note or something from Carrie. Or a clue in the house. Why did she have to time travel when I have to go back to work instead of on the last day of my shift?"

She grabbed an apple and shoved a frozen dinner into her back pack and ran out to her car. If she hit the lights just right and no CHP were on the road, she would make it to work in time to snag coffee and a scone before going on duty. At least Julie didn't show up too often on weekends.

Creepy Captain Berger would be in. He loved to slime in on Saturday afternoons, but it would be after she was on duty for a bit. Mostly he ignored her, after he looked at what she was working on and made sure she did nothing but work, work, work. Heaven forbid she glance at a magazine, even the dispatcher's magazine. Well that would be wrong in his and Julie's puny little minds anyway because according to them, that magazine was for dispatchers, not records clerks. But since there was no records drudge magazine, what was wrong with knowing about dispatch? After all, the senior records people were expected to know how to dispatch even though Julie had implemented a non-dispatch classification for newbies in records like Shannon.

Still, she'd have some quiet when she got in. Shannon would have been there a few hours before her and once she left about ten she'd have even more time to just enjoy being alone. Maybe tonight she could finish her list about things she needed to do about Carrie's disappearance. Well, not really a disappearance. Not for the first time Molly wondered if she was doing the right thing trying to handle it by herself and not filing a missing person's report. The fact doing denial kept her from even looking in Carrie's room wasn't up for discussion.

Luck was on her side and she slid into the parking lot with just enough time to grab a latte, breeze past the new serial killer posters and make it inside to pop in her headset on the dot.

"You sure cut it close," Shannon greeted her.

"Sorry. I didn't get home till almost seven this morning."

"Heard you guys had a hot call last night. I've been working through the reports all morning."

"It was pretty cool."

"Let me take my break and then I want to hear all about it."

Shannon scurried back into the records area while checking to be sure no one else was around. "Bergtrol," she giggled as she sat in the chair across from Molly.

"Good one. I like that."

"So tell."

"Not much to tell really."

"I read the reports that have been turned in so far. There is plenty to tell."

"Not from inside, it was pretty standard stuff."

"Uh huh, talk this morning was Kris missed out on it and was pretty pissed she did."

"What did she have to be pissed about?"

"Even I've seen how much she looooovvveeessss working the hot calls."

"You mean when she screeches over the air?"

Molly chuckled, "There is that."

"Does she have any idea how awful she sounds on the air? She sounds like a cow giving birth."

"Heard a lot of cows in labor have you?"

"Not really. But I have heard nails on a blackboard and that voice of hers isn't too far off."

"You got that right."

"Soooo, why wasn't she on the radio?"

"Why do you think?"

"Maybe the correct question should have been who was she doing last night?"

"Lively this time."

"Anyone say anything last night?"

"Not last night. At least not before I left. Things were hopping up until then. What's the word today?"

"Just that she wasn't in the station during the call."

"I can't wait to see Julie turn that one around so I'm in the wrong."

"Can you imagine if she *were* here? With her no victim no crime decision making analysis she would have decided not to send an officer in the first place."

"Talking about our favorite badge bunny?" Sasha Connolly, one of the female officers, asked when she entered the records area.

"Now why would you say that?" Molly smiled at her friend.

"Locker room talk is they're glad she wasn't on the radio last night because they needed to concentrate and her wailing over the air would have been a total distraction."

"The guys still love her."

"It's not love, Mol. It's not even lust. She's an easy lay and none of the guys wants to be the only one that hasn't done her. At least that's what was going on. Mitch Toyos, Kyle Sanchez and Rich Kennedy all have herpes."

"Herpes?" Shannon looked from Rita to Molly. "Are they sharing . . . what? Soap? Poor potty habits?"

"Oh they're sharing all right. But no hygiene products," Rita grinned at her.

"Then how . . .oh. Really?"

"Yup. Kris has the gift that keeps on giving." Molly nodded.

"And giving and giving and giving." Rita told her. "You can tell who she's slept with and who's waiting in line by who's taking antibiotics. Sad thing is, the guys all know about it and even when they clue each other in, they still can't keep it in their pants."

"But I thought . . ."

"What?" Molly shook her head, "That she only does blow jobs? Those are just the warm up."

"You know this how?" Rita parked her butt on the edge of the desk.

"You'd be surprised at how much people say in front of the records staff. Thanks to Julie's attitude, the rest of the PD thinks we're no more than moveable dummies. I've had officers have whole conversations in front of me telling each other about things that could get them into an IA if they weren't careful. There hasn't been one yet who thought what he did with ole PBL should be kept private."

"PBL?" Rita winced.

"Peanut butter legs. She's so spreadable, she's incredible."

Rita stood and saluted Molly, "Gotcha. That sounds totally right. Thought about what you are going to say when they ask about her being out of the station last night?"

"The truth. I'll tell whoever she went on a ride along and didn't come back in before I went off duty — at six this morning."

"You go girl. Anyway, I gotta hit briefing. Any progress on getting the records staff permission to go?"

"It'll never happen as long as Julie's the manager. We'll never be more than paper pushers as long as she's around." Shannon groused.

"Don't let her hear you say paper pushers." Molly clued her in. "I've gotten written up for saying it."

"Yeah, but she writes you up for everything." Rita told them. "One time didn't she try to write you up for an officer missing range day?"

Molly burst out laughing. "Damn, I forgot about that."

"What happened," Shannon looked from one to the other.

"Julie actually went on a vacation one time and while she was gone brass let this officer, hmmm, what was his name, Mitchell or Hilton or something, go. He wasn't cutting it so they cut him loose. The day she came back was range day and she's the one who hands out the passes to the shooting club. Hilton or whatever his name was didn't pick up his pass so she tried to write me up. Then, when one of the lieutenants told her he'd been fired she went ahead and wrote me up for not telling her about it. Thing is, had I told her he'd been canned, she would have written me up for gossiping."

"What did you ever do to make her so out for you?"

"I wouldn't lie."

"Gotta go." Rita sauntered out of the office area and back toward briefing.

"Maybe when Carrie is settled you can apply for a job there. You said she moved out of state, right?"

"Maybe." Like that would happen. Not that Carrie or Black Eagle would turn her away. She so wasn't going back in time. Life with Julie in it might suck the big one. Living in a teepee and cooking over an open fire so wasn't her thing. "We should probably get to work on these reports, huh?"

"Right."

Between the phones, paperwork and meal breaks the next few hours flew by. Surprisingly Berger didn't pop in and Kris parked her fanny in dispatch and didn't come out except to go to the bathroom a few times. No one said a word about her disappearance the day before. It wasn't until an hour or so after Shannon left for the day Molly had a moment to herself to think about the situation Carrie had left her with. That and to acknowledge the real reason she hadn't looked for the desk or a note this morning was because if she did, then it would all be real and the last thing she wanted, was for Carrie's disappearance to be real. Not that she begrudged Carrie her happiness. If anyone deserved to be happy, it was her roommate.

Carrie loved her romance novels, especially the historical ones. They were a good balance for each other. Carrie fantasized that she was the heroine in each story. Molly had her feet firmly on the ground.

When Mr. Merle gave Carrie the picture with Black Eagle in it, her roommate admitted that just like in junior high, she'd kissed the man in the picture. The surprise wasn't her engaging in what most people would think a childish behavior. It was the man in the photograph turned up in Carrie's bed. Nothing like that would ever happen to Molly. She was too grounded and practical to have a man travel through time and wake up in her bed.

Fortunately Carrie didn't have any family that needed an explanation of what happened. If it really did happen. "I gotta get out of here on time tonight so I can look at that desk in Carrie's room and call Mr. Merle in the morning. Hopefully that Gareth guy won't answer the phone and get my mind going where it shouldn't. Reality check, Ms. Nichols. Why on earth would tall, blond and buff answer Mr. Merle's phone? He's not the kind of guy who would find you attractive. Take him off your radar. Nope. Not at all. He might go for Carrie, let Kris suck him off, but I'm not what would be high on his radar."

Still tired from the night before, when Molly got home she only took a moment to look in Carrie's room to see if the desk she remembered was still there. Nodding to herself she went off to bed, acknowledging to herself the real reason she hadn't walked into Carrie's room and looked for a note or some sign Carrie was back in time was because there were just some things you really don't need to know. Right now she wasn't ready to consider the fact that Carrie may never come home.

Once again images of Gareth flitted through her dreams. Twice she woke to find herself holding her pillow as if it were the blond haired man beside her. "Gareth you are spending too much time in my mind. Go back where you came from, would you?"

CHAPTER TEN

When she woke before the alarm the next morning Molly took it as an omen that she had to face reality and check for some sort of communication from Carrie. Padding into Carrie's room Molly shook her head at herself. Looking for omens was something Carrie did. If she saw or heard something three times Carrie was certain it meant she was supposed to do something about it. If Carrie had a dream about someone, she'd call them the next day.

Molly always prided herself on being reality based. It was black or it was white. No gray areas in her life. Sure, she'd go along with Carrie's plans and schemes. Someone had to keep an eye on her friend and make sure nothing went south or someone got hurt. That was Molly's job. Although Gareth, if Gareth weren't in one of his weird costumes, nah. With his oddball talk and clothes he was the epitome of a Carrie-guy.

She paused at the threshold of Carrie's room and drew in a deep breath. "Now or never. No more avoiding her room."

Molly took two steps in. Then another, before pausing to look around. She sucked in her upper lip and glanced around the room. Nothing had changed since the other morning when Carrie left her life in Napa behind. Drawing in a long, slow, deep breath Molly steeled her resolve. "Send a note from the past. Ha! Magical thinking, Mr. Merle. Magical thinking. If I had any sense at all, I would have filed a missing person's report first thing the other day. Time travel my ass."

With careful control, she surveyed the room, inch by inch. She nodded when her gaze fell on the antique desk. The old roll top was a favorite of Carrie's. Despite her carefree and giving nature, Carrie seldom, if ever, tapped into her trust account. The desk was one of the rare occasions she pulled funds out of the account her parents left to her.

"Well, there's the desk." She told the empty room. "Let's have at it, Molly. No, let's not and say we did. Walk out of the room, pick up the phone and call the police and file a missing person's report."

She was sure she headed toward the door. So how did she end up in front of the desk? "Oh yeah, I changed my mind, didn't I?"

Giving herself a moment she sat in the old wooden desk chair, another antique Carrie couldn't resist. It fit perfectly with the desk even though it came from a different estate sale. Molly looked over the tidy surface. A pad of post-it notes, old fashioned silver handled quill pen in a faux ink container, blotter, her phonebook was a reproduction of an 1800's leather bound journal and a picture of her family taken days before the car accident that killed the entire Taylor family except Carrie six years earlier. For as dreamy as Carrie could be no one could ever say she lacked order in her life. She prided herself on how her books were organized — by genre in alphabetical order by author. No mean feat for someone with over ten thousand books in their collection. "Something else I'm going to have to deal with, unless I suddenly start reading romances. Okay, enough stalling, Nichols. Start looking in the drawers."

Beginning with the top shelf Molly poked in each cubby, going through the papers neatly stuffed in each. Receipts for books, CDs, grocery purchases, Taister's appointment cards and some vet records, greeting cards for future birthdays and anniversaries, receipts for clothing she'd bought for Black Eagle. Molly stopped in her tracks when she pulled the last out. If there were receipts for men's clothing surely Black Eagle'd been real. If he were real . . .

She moved to the little drawers, pulling each out in order. One held an assortment of paperclips, another, rubber bands, a third stickers. "What a waste of time, I'm not going to find a letter from Carrie in here." Molly studied the last drawer, telling herself the roiling of her stomach was because she had to go to work today and not fear of what she would find. "Come on, Mol, Carrie's the one who believes in premonitions, not you. Open the drawer."

She slowly drew the tiny wooden structure out and with a gasp, quickly slammed it. She took in a breath and once again, pulled the minuscule drawer out. A yellowish piece of paper, its edges tattered as if worn from age lay in the drawer. Her hand shaking every so slightly Molly reached in and drew the paper out. Creased with age, it cracked ever so slight when she began to unfold it.

Dearest Molly,

I hope this letter finds you and finds you well. I'm sure my — sudden departure has caught you quite by surprise. I know it did me. I've been so caught up in the romance of my life here with Black Eagle I almost forgot about my life there in Napa. Until today when Black Eagle told me I needed to write you and let you know I'm okay. I'm actually better than okay. Mr. Merle's ancestor came by our home to say hello. Isn't it interesting that he knew I'd arrived here? Just like in a time travel novel where there's a character who knows what's going on. I didn't tell him I was from 2021. Well, I didn't actually meet him I don't want people to think I'm crazy and back now in the 1800's someone would think I was crazy. Anyway, I asked how did Black Eagle think I could mail a letter that would reach you almost two hundred years in the future. He told me in Mr. Merle's ancestor's shop was a desk that looked just like the one in my room. He said it might even be the very one that's there because it looks exactly like it. You know the little heart carved on the pull out shelf? The one on my desk? He said the same mark is on this one so maybe they are the same. If not, someone in the future is going to enjoy this letter, don't you think? Anyway, I hope it reaches you so you will know both Taister and I are here with Black Eagle and we're both very, very happy.

Molly, I've never been happier. Even without lattes, life is beyond wonderful. This is the life I have longed for. I hope you are well and Molly, I know you don't believe in anything you can't prove or explain. But Molly, love doesn't always fit in a neat little box. When you meet the right man, and trust me, you will, hold on to him with both hands. Love makes magic real.

Take care. I'm not sure if I'll be able to write again or even if this letter will find you.

Love,
Carrie

Molly studied the worn page. "This has got to be a joke. One huge joke. But who would play one this mean? Dean? He's in the asylum, right? Julie? Nah, she doesn't even know about Carrie and Black Eagle. Well who? Mr. Merle? He's not mean."

She rose and walked over to the bed and sat. "It has to be a joke. This just can't be real. Can it?"

She read the note again. It was definitely Carrie's handwriting and the talk about love and time travels epitomized Carrie's thinking. "The newspaper! I can go to the library and bring up old newspapers from then and see if there are any pictures!"

Molly glanced at the clock, "No time today. Let's see, I'll call Mr. Merle from work—no. If he's playing a joke I don't want to let him know I've found a clue. Tonight at work! I can log on at work tonight! During my dinner break when it's all quiet I can do it. And screw Julie if she gets on me about using the department computer. What's she going to do? Write me up? Or Kris might go on another suck-along tonight and I can log in on her station so it's under her ID. She can do whatever she damn well pleases. Yeah. In fact, I'll even suggest to Lively he ask her to ride again. Man, first I know about Black Eagle's fake ID that wasn't really fake and now I'm planning to use Kris' ID. What next in my life of crime?"

Pleased with her plan Molly dressed in a favorite navy blue turtleneck and black jeans and headed out to work. Maybe by tomorrow morning she'd know if she could be happy at Carrie's note or not.

For a change, luck was on her side. Molly didn't even have to suggest to Lively to take Kris for a ride. Ole PBL decided she was going before Molly showed up. As soon as Shannon left for the day Molly headed into dispatch and sat down at Kris' terminal. Janette glanced over her shoulder, "Looks like you sitting with me is becoming a habit."

"Seems that way, doesn't it? You busy over there?"

"No. Typical Sunday night. Zero to none in traffic."

"Cool. I've got some research I need to do so give me a holler if you need me."

Within seconds Molly was logged into the library's newspaper archives. One of the plusses living in the Bay Area was the Link program with the library where she could access all kinds of obscure information including old newspapers. Not that they were obscure. They simply weren't anything most people would dig through. Especially to find out if their best friend was now living a hundred and sixty years in the past.

Scanning through her choices Molly finally found the paper she was looking for. Speeding through page after page, quickly checking each picture she was about to give up when a picture of an Indian holding a black cat appeared on the screen. There they were, Black Eagle, Carrie and Taister. All of them were smiling, even Taister if you knew his different expressions. In the photograph he was wearing his "I just had steak" look, one of his heavy duty purr times. "Damn, it is real."

"Huh?" Janette rolled her chair over to Molly's console. "Say, isn't that your roommate? The one who moved away?"

"Um, uh, no. Actually it's a great-great aunt or something. Carrie emailed me to tell me she found this awesome picture of an ancestor of hers. They sure look alike, don't they?" Molly carefully moved the page down just far enough to hide the print below the picture.

"They sure do. Of course I only met your roommate at the department picnic last summer. From what I remember though they sure do look alike."

"Yeah. They sure do." Molly maneuvered the mouse to the print icon and clicked to have the news article printed out. Between the old photograph at home, the note in the desk and the news article she couldn't deny Carrie had done the impossible. She'd traveled back through time. At least now Molly knew for sure what happened and what she would have to do. Her next few days off would be spent setting Carrie's life in 2021 to rest.

CHAPTER ELEVEN

Glad the longest four day work week of her life finally
ended Molly practically ran to her car when she got off
duty Tuesday morning. The next three days would be spent
settling Carrie's affairs. That, and a long sit down with Mr.
Merle to find out just how much he knew about what had
happened. She had no doubt he knew something about how
Carrie got back in time. The question was just what did he
know and how much did he have to do with it? Black Eagle
had been certain Mr. Merle and his ancestor had been one and
the same. Mr. Merle's nephew, Gareth guy, called the old fella
Merlin. "Well if he *was* Merlin that would explain everything
now, wouldn't it. Merlin, right. And who's Gareth? One of the
Knights of the Roundtable? Of course he is. Just ask him?
With his suit of armor and funny language. Sir Gareth? Right
up Carrie's alley."

On her days off Molly normally never set an alarm. Today,
however, she set not one, but went snagged Carrie's and set
that one as well. No how, no way would she sleep in and have
to wait another day to talk to Mr. Merle. She told herself she
wasn't hoping to see Gareth. She could have sworn she heard
her own little voice calling her a liar.

Surprisingly she fell right asleep.

Not so surprisingly, once again dreams of the strawberry
blond man flitted through her sleep. In each he rode up to her
on a big black horse, a warm smile on his lips when he'd raise
the visor of his helmet. The time periods seemed to keep
changing though. One time they were on what looked like

Tara, the plantation from *Gone With the Wind,* another the backdrop resembled the one in the town where Carrie might now live, followed by him sitting outside her house. In between there were snippets of a castle in the background, complete with colored flags and a moat. Clearly this business with Carrie disappearing sure created havoc in her ordinarily pretty staid imagination. Despite the dreams she woke refreshed, moments before the alarms sounded. A quick breakfast of toast and coffee and Molly headed into town.

When she arrived at Treasures, several customers were poking through the array of offerings. Thinking back on what Carrie had once told her, the first Tuesday of the month Mr. Merle generally took in a shipment of new items. It stuck in her mind because new shipment day was generally one of the highpoints of Carrie's month. That and the day the new romances arrived at the bookstore.

Book day, as Carrie called her other favorite day, consisted of a spending lunch at the bookstore and the evening organizing her new books in the order to be read. While Molly enjoyed reading as much as the next person she wasn't quite the four to five book a week reader Carrie was. Then again, Molly didn't have quite the imagination her roommate did and despite her solid and practical lifestyle, she did have a fairly busy social life. She wondered just what Carrie was doing these days for reading material or, if living her own romance novel filled the need the books took care of.

This month's shipment to Treasures seemed to include some old west items. If she knew anything about Mr. Merle, they were the real deal, however the gun one of the men held up to the light to examine appeared to be almost new. *Maybe Mr. Merle time traveled to get the gun for this month's consignments. Yeah, right.*

The elderly gent was chatting with a pair of women over an egg shelled colored pitcher and bowl circa the same time period as the gun from what little Molly knew of the old west.

"Molly! Take a seat, I'll be with you in a minute," he called and gestured to a bench under the glass case holding the old sword.

She'd barely sat down when she heard the rattle of the beads that separated the shop from the proprietor's little kitchenette. The clack of the colorful beads drew her attention and brought an odd combination of a smile and a groan to her lips.

"Didest I hear my fair Lady Molly is here?"

"Gareth. Hi!" This time he was wearing a plain brown tunic that fell to about his knees and what looked like black tights. A low slung leather belt girded his hips just above where his . . . right, she was so not going to go there. At least he wasn't wearing a sword this time. The man sure was into ballet dancer costumes.

On the plus side, it appeared he'd trimmed both hair and beard, the shiny blond locks were a dramatic contrast to the deep blue of his eyes. On the other hand, she felt woefully underdressed without a bit of makeup, grubby jeans and an old sweatshirt.

His stride across the room to her side reminded her of a panther she'd watched stalking another big cat at the zoo one time. She could have sworn the blue of his eyes darkened even more when he looked at her. What devastated her though was his smile. The man knew how to turn on the charm with just a look. *If he'd only get himself some decent clothes. And aren't I a fine one to talk with my current garb. How'd you like that? I'm calling it garb.*

"Lady Molly. I bid you good day!"

"Rehearsing for another play, Gareth?"

"Play? Tis my morning dress, dearest lady."

"Right." She admonished herself there was no reason for her cheeks to heat up as much as they had. They outright felt like they were on fire. Why should she blush when he was the one making a fool of himself?

"Truly, my lady. I have missed you. Were it not for the wizard I would have sought you out and seen the entertainments of your village."

"Wrong time period, Gareth. Remember I told you today we'd be showcasing western items." Mr. Merle came up behind him.

"Western?" Perplexed Gareth looked down at his garments. "I know not this wes . . ."

"Of course you do, son." Mr. Merle widened his gaze and raised his hand which caught Molly's attention. Carrie and Black Eagle had talked about the movements the elderly gent had made with his hand over Black Eagle's picture. Was he really a wizard like Gareth called him? Nah. *That* was Carrie magical thinking. Not Molly real life practicality. Still . . .

Gareth turned to Molly, "Dost thou liketh this western garb, Lady Molly?"

"Huh? Oh sure. Yeah, I like cowboys. Say, could you like call me just Molly?"

"Cow . . . I would be pleased to call you just Molly."

"Yipee ki yay, git along little doggie and all that." She stood and brushed the back of her jeans. "I've really gotta run, I'll see you later, Mr. Merle."

"Molly, please stay. I'll just be a moment. Gareth, please, take Molly in the back and make her a pot of tea, would you?"

"Would you like that, Lady Just Molly?"

"Really, I'd like you to drop the lady business and call me Molly. Just Molly."

"Of a certainty. Molly Just Molly, would you care for some tea?"

Mr. Merle nodded to her.

"Sure. Why not?" Without the sword he was probably safe, well except for the knives in the kitchenette that was. As they left the room she heard Mr. Merle explain to the customers that his nephew was big into re-enactments and was getting ready for one of the most popular ones. At least two of the women tittered about how good he must look in those old Richard the Lion Heart type tights. Molly shrugged to herself, that explained the lady business.

The beaded curtain had barely settled when Gareth reached to shut the door. "I knoweth not why Merlin hath both the noisy bangles and a door." He looked genuinely perplexed.

"Listen, Gareth . . ."

He turned and gave her a small smile. In that instant, he looked so sweet and innocent. Like a little lost boy. Molly found herself fighting the urge to reach out and cup his jaw.

"Yes, tis Gareth. And you are Just Molly."

"No. Molly, *just* Molly."

"Ah, Molly *just* Molly."

"No. Just Molly."

"Yes. Just Molly."

"No. It's. My name is Molly. Molly Nichols. There's nothing in front of the Molly."

"Nothing. I see. You are no lady?"

"Ah, not the kind of lady they had way back when."

Confusion clouded his eyes, lightening the blue to a rich turquoise, making him seem somehow endearingly vulnerable. Poor Mr. Merle, for as normal as Gareth looked, something wasn't quite right about him. That had to be it. She was probably safe with him. Even with the knives in the kitchen. She just needed to not think about the way he appeared in her dreams.

"You do not appear a light skirt."

"Light skirt?" That sounded like something out of one of Carrie's historical romances. Then she got it. "Now wait a minute. I'm not a prostitute either."

"I did not mean to offend. Truly Lady Just Molly, I only wish to please you."

"Then how about you just call me Molly and leave it at that. You know, like your name is Gareth. Just the one name, right?"

"My true name is Prince Gareth of the Orkneys, second son to King Lot and Queen Morgause."

"Right." *King Lot? Queen Morgause? Holy round tables, did he just tell her his mother was King Arthur's sister? The man truly was delusional.* Sadly he looked so proud when he told her his lineage. "Listen, I really do need to get going. I have some things I need to get done today so if you'll just tell Mr. Merle . . ."

"Merlin."

"Whatever, just tell the old man . . ."

"Wizard."

To her own surprise, she stamped her foot, "Would you shut up for thirty seconds so I can get my message out?"

He smiled. That sweet smile. The one that made him look vulnerable and sweet and plain ole delicious. "Shall I tell you the secret of silencing my words?"

"Sure. Go for it."

His smile broadened. "Better I show you!"

In a flash he had her in his arms, her back against the wall, one hand tangled in her hair, the other around her waist and that sure as heck wasn't his belt buckle poking her tummy. The smile went from sweet to sensual as he lowered his lips to meet hers. Softly, gently, he feathered the tinniest of kisses along her upper lip. Agonizingly slow, drawing out each movement of is softly kissable lips. Time stopped. She forgot to breathe. Her arms hung limply at her side. Her heart began to race at the moment he began the sensual assault on her lower lip. Someone moaned followed by her lips parting. His tongue slid into her mouth, and with achingly leisurely movements he caressed her tongue with his own. His groan joined her moan of desire when she slid her hands up to hold on to his arms. Her hand barely covered half of his bicep. In the recesses of her mind Molly told herself to push him away. Her arms, however, seemed to have formed a mind of their own because instead of shoving him to the other side of the room, one of them snaked up to entwine in his hair and the other held on to one heavily muscled arm.

The rattle of the door handle began to pull Molly from the kiss induced lethargy. Slowly she pulled away and looked up at the tall blond man.

A look of wonder flitted into his eyes a moment before he asked, "Do you like the way to silence me?"

"I, I, you *kissed* me! I let king of the nut cases kiss me! Oh my god."

"I am no king, but simply a prince and knight my lady. Yet any man who holds you would feel himself a king."

"Uh, look. I, ah. That was so not . . ."

"Merlin told me to make you tea. Sit and I will make it. Have you seen one of these wondrous boxes or this water trough? You turn this device and cold water, ice cold water like that of a mountain stream, comes into your cup. You see?" He stuck the kettle under the spigot while watching her to see if she'd ever seen such a thing.

"Yeah, it's a faucet."

"Faucet. Yes. That is what Merlin said. And this box. You turn this handle and it brings heat to the top. In minutes the water will be hot enough for our tea. The wizard says tis not magic yet if it not be magic, what is it?"

"Refrigerator. Modern technology. Everyone has ovens, stoves and running water. Well almost everyone. There are still some countries where they aren't as up to date, but here, in Napa, we all have it. Most of us have microwaves and cof-feemakers too. Where are you from that this is news to you?"

"I told you. The Orkneys."

"Where are these Orkneys?"

"Part of the united Britain. Twas Arthur's dream." A flash

of confusion brought a frown to his lips, "Arthur."

"Arthur? Is that your brother?"

"Arthur? Nay. Arthur tis my king. My brothers are Aggravain, Gehris and Gwain."

"Aggravain, Gehris and Gwain? Weren't they knights from King Arthur's story? Yeah, I remember. We had to read something about it in school, English Lit and Carrie read a few books about them."

"Carrie, is that not the woman who came with you when I first arrived?"

"I think so."

"She reads? How rare."

"We all do. All of us here mostly. Look, I'm all for getting into character, but this is getting a bit old. Could you shift gears and let go of the knight in shining armor business?" Even if she could so use one to fight her personal dragon right now.

Before he could answer the tea kettle whistled, startling the blond haired man. He looked at the pot a moment as if remembering what he needed to do. As he reached barehanded for the handle Molly swatted his hand away, reached for a pot holder and poured the boiling water into the tea pot Gareth had already prepared. At his troubled look she told him, "You would have burned your hand."

He nodded, "I recall. Thank you, Molly."

He smiled, that winning smile, one that told her he hoped she was pleased he called her only Molly.

"No problem."

A moment later Mr. Merle entered the room and looked from one to the other. "I see you got the tea going all right."

"La ... Ju ... Molly helped me. I forgot the handle can burn."

"Thank you, Molly."

"Is everyone gone?" She asked looking out the door into

the shop.

"For now. Tuesdays are busy days."

"That's what Carrie told me. Mr. Merle, I need to talk to you. About Carrie."

He nodded toward the table, "Of course."

"Ah, just you. I'm not sure your nephew could help much, you know?"

"I see. Gareth, why don't you run upstairs and enjoy your tea up there?"

"No."

"No?"

"No. My lady is here. Tis impossible to court her if I am apart from her."

"Absence makes the heart grow fonder. Go upstairs and put on some of the new clothes you Aunt Vivienne purchased for you."

"I do not wish to."

"Fine. I'll send you outside as a toad."

Gareth's eyes widened and he paled ever so slightly beneath his trim beard when Mr. Merle reached for one of the frog salt and pepper shakers that sat on the little table. "Nay. Molly, I will return when you are done with the wizard."

"Thanks." She watched him bound up the back staircase to what she presumed was Mr. Merle's upstairs apartment. Did Mr. Merle just say Vivienne was Gareth's aunt? Whatever, the man was an enigma. When he was out of earshot she turned to elderly gent, "I'm so sorry."

"For what?"

"Your nephew. It must be so hard on your family to have someone mentally ill living with them."

"Gareth isn't mentally ill. He's as sound as you or I." He elderly gent sounded completely shocked.

"Mr. Merle, the man thinks he is one of Morgause kids. You know, Morgause, King Arthur's sister? The one who slept with him and you know, had Mordred? He thinks he's one of her kids and that he was one of the knights of the round table. He's not playing part. He *really* thinks that."

"He told you that?" The elderly gent appeared completely caught off guard by that admission.

"Yes. That's why I said it must be so hard on your family."

He turned away from her and shuffled over to the stove to pour his tea. As he sat he told her, "I can assure you, Molly, Gareth is not insane by any means. He *is* quite passionate about history, particularly Arthurian history. I'd say that is the reason why he goes about as if he were indeed one of the knights of the round table. If he could pick any place to live but this one I'm certain he would have chosen Camelot. He's quite an authority on the time period."

"That may be so, but Mr. Merle, doesn't he realize most people think it's a little nutty to walk around in a suit of armor or those tights?"

"Trews."

"Huh? Does he own that suit? It must have cost a fortune. Even if he's renting those clothes all the time," she waved her hand in front of her face, "but it's none of my business. I came to tell you about Carrie."

"Yes? Did you hear from her?"

"I think so." She pulled the worn piece of paper from her back jeans pocket, handed it to him and watched in silence as he read the message.

"This is good news, Molly!"

"You think so?"

"Of course. She knew to write you and to let you know she is happy and well in Black Eagle's village."

"For now."

"What do you mean?"

"What if things go wrong? In a few years, in her time now, the Indians will start to die off or be put on reservations. And

Taister. There are no veterinarians back then, are there? What if he gets sick? The little guy is almost fourteen. What if she decides she made a mistake and wants to change her mind?"

Mr. Merle sipped his tea a moment before answering. "I think, Molly, I think if Carrie became unhappy she would write you another letter."

"Became? Oh my god, she's dead, isn't she? Carrie's dead!" Molly rose, fist to her mouth and staggered over to the sink.

"Molly, it's not like you to be so dramatic. She not dead. At least not in her time. Molly, she traveled back in time. Whatever age she was when she went back."

"Thirty-one."

"Well then. She was thirty-one when she went back in time. She would continue to age the same as if she were here, now. If she was still alive, well goodness, she'd be almost two hundred years old. I would say she is alive and well in her time. You see?"

Molly collapsed into one of the wooden ladder-backed chairs, "I hadn't thought about that. I thought, that is. And if I'm being dramatic I'm a bit out of my element here, you know? Gee, Mr. Merle, I've never thought about growing older, you know?"

"Yes, dear. I do. Now, tell me. Now that you know Carrie is alive, well and happy, what will you do?"

"Do? Well I was thinking, if I stuck my own note back in the desk, would she get it? Maybe we could keep in touch that way, you know?"

Mr. Merle seemed to consider the idea. "You could try it. Keep her up to date on your life and she on hers. And you know, if you did periodically check the desk you could see if she was unhappy."

"I could. But how would I get her back home? Mr. Merle if I came to you and told you she wanted to come home, would you bring her back?"

"Molly, Molly, you still think I was behind this time travel?"

"Yes. I think—"

They were interrupted by hurried footsteps descending the back stairs. A moment later Gareth, dressed in a white cotton button down shirt and stone washed jeans that made Molly's mouth water, re-entered the room. "Here now, Wizard. I hath donned your modern garb."

The simple of act of putting on those jeans turned Gareth from a good looking guy to down right damn-studley, gorgeous one. Molly was pretty sure the bulge beneath the fly buttons wasn't an athletic cup but the man's very own nicely wrapped package. Now if only he'd stop with the old fashioned talk. Man he was hot.

"That's good, Gareth. Now remember we talked about you ceasing to play the knightly part while you are visiting here."

"I agreed to no such thing." He turned and headed toward the back door.

"Where are you going?"

"Out."

"Out? Gareth, I do not think it wise."

Molly looked from one to the other. Good looking or not, she wasn't going to get in the middle of this family discussion. If asked she would have agreed with Mr. Merle his nephew should stay inside under someone's supervision. She still wasn't buying into the guy acting a part. "I guess I'll get going. Thanks for your advice and support, Mr. Merle. I'll keep you posted."

The white haired gent turned and gave her a weak, yet genuine, smile, "I would appreciate that, Molly. Have a good week."

"I will. Thanks and again and Gareth, you have a good week too."

"But, what—" he sputtered. "I was only stepping into the

yard for a moment. Where do you go?"

"Me? Home. See ya later." She hurried out of the kitchenette and into the shop. She heard the beads rattle behind her, but it was the sword on the wall that caught her attention. If asked Molly would have sworn it glowed a bit brighter. Just for a moment it seemed to flash, like an old fashioned camera going off.

The sound of the men's footsteps hurried her to the front door. After the week she had between Carrie's departure and work, the last thing she needed was to be involved in whatever the Merle family was up to. And despite his protestations, Molly knew to her toes Mr. Merle had something to do with Carrie's disappearance. He just knew too much about what to do, like looking for the note, and how to do things. Still, if her friend were happy, who was she to interfere?

After the studied dimness of the antique store the bright fall sun momentarily blinded her. Next on her list was to stop by Carrie's old office and make some sort of explanation to them. Then she had to change the utility bills to her name. She started off down the street, mentally checking off everything she had written down to take care of with Carrie's moving away. Yes, if she thought of it as just moving out of town she could cope better with all this time travel business. While not a fan of romantic fiction, maybe reading a few of Carrie's smut books would be a good idea. Heck she might as well dig out her copy of *Morte De Arthur* if Gareth was going to hang around much longer.

She'd just started across the cross walk when the loud squeal of tires a short way up the street stopped her in her tracks. Several other cars came to a screeching halt and loud voices raised with some rather colorful language before she saw the cause.

Gareth stood in the middle of First Street, turning ever so slowly in a tight circle. Even from half a block away she could see the look of sheer terror in his big blue eyes. If the set of his jaw was any indication, he'd be reaching for a weapon in nothing flat.

"Get out of the street, asshole," one driver yelled.

"Trying to get yourself killed, numb nuts," another shouted

"Damn tourists," came from a third.

Several drivers got out of their cars, a couple with fists raised, fortunately not directed toward Gareth. Although he was probably the reason two cars had collided, explaining the loud boom she heard just a minute before she spotted the blond. Without another thought she headed down the center of First Street to grab him.

His "What wickedness this?" spurred her on. If he started spouting that King Arthur business in the middle of downtown Napa the cops would take him off to Napa State in nothing flat.

"Gareth!"

"Molly! Beware the demons the wizard hath unleashed!"

"Oh cut out the wizard shit! Come with me." She grabbed his arm and dragged him to the other side of the street calling back to the drivers, "He's not from around here. Sorry. We're really sorry. I thought he was home. Sorry." Over her shoulder she saw Mr. Merle on the sidewalk in front of his shop, clearly as confused as Gareth about what to do. Well screw the old guy. If he couldn't keep an eye on his nephew someone had to.

Molly pulled Gareth on to the sidewalk and down Main, "Not another word from you. Not a one."

"But."

"Not a word until I say you can talk." She paused briefly to look at him and the look of confusion that clouded his gaze was oddly reminiscent of the way Black Eagle looked when he first arrived in Napa. A few steps down Main she stopped in front of a coffee shop. "How about a coffee? Huh?"

"I may speak?"

"Yes, you can speak."

"I rather an ale."

"Since I have no idea what meds you are on or if there should be one that you aren't taking, screw the ale. Here, sit down." She pulled him inside a low metal fence that surrounded the front of a favorite coffee bistro.

"The moving boxes, Molly. They, the sounds. Where are the horses?"

Before she could tell him once again to stop spouting his medieval ideas she studied his expression. The blue of his eyes all but disappeared with the widened pupils. A slight tremble in his lower lid clearly indicated his fear was real. "Let's have a seat, all right. We'll have a nice latte and talk. How does that sound?"

He swallowed and looked up at her with hope in his eyes as he nodded.

"Good. You just sit here and I'll get them."

He moved to stand.

"*Sit*. Do not move a muscle or I will drag you back into the middle of the street and leave you there. I'll have, I'll have Mr. Merle freeze you in place there if you move so much as an inch."

"Molly, please. May I shift to sit a bit more comfortable? This garment" he gestured to the jeans, "doth not allow for me to sit suddenly. They pinch my manhood."

It did no good to tell herself the heat in her cheeks came from the sun. Without a doubt she blushed from ear to ear judging by how fast the flame spread across her face. "You can squirm around on the chair as much as you like. No getting up and walking around. Got it?"

He breathed a sigh of relief, "Yes. Thank you."

She waited a minute while he settled in the chair, all the

while his gaze moving up and down the street. Fortunately, Main wasn't quite as busy as First and he looked normal enough sitting at the patio table. Now if only he'd keep his mouth shut no one would think anything odd going on. Molly hurried inside and ordered their drinks. While she waited for their coffees she paced back and forth to the window where she could look out and keep an eye on Gareth without him knowing she watched. And the boxes thing. He didn't see them from inside the shop? Gees.

"Fraid your guy might bolt on you?" One of the customers asked.

"What? Oh no. He's not from around here and sometimes forgets to tell me when he's going to look at something."

"Say, is he an actor? That why he's looking around like everything is all new? Are they going to be doing a movie up here or something and he's scouting out locations?"

"Um, no. He's just a friend."

Molly smiled when she walked out with their drinks and Gareth moved to stand and then immediately sat, "Molly, you make it exceedingly difficult to be chivalrous."

"Chiv — guys don't much stand for women any more." She set their drinks down. "I got you a peppermint mocha. Try it and if you don't like it, I'll get you something else."

"Peppermint?"

"Mocha. Carrie told me once Mr. Merle really likes them so I thought being his nephew you might too."

"Thank you. Vivienne conjured one for Merlin had one not long ago but I did not partake." He pried back the lid and peered inside. "What is this?" He stuck his finger into the drink and drew it out coated with whipped cream.

Oblivious to the sounds of passing traffic, an occasional blast of a car's horn, Molly told him, "It's whipped cream. Try it."

Gareth swept his finger back inside and drew it out with a

dollop of the fluffy white cream on his finger. The look of sheer pleasure when he tasted it once again reminded her of Black Eagle and how enthused he was about trying out Carrie's favorite foods and drinks. Could Mr. Merle have brought another man through time? Thinking that this one would be perfect for her? He couldn't possibly have known she'd been wishing for a knight in shining amour to deal with Julie.

"Oh no." Molly groaned.

"Did they forget your cream?" Gareth leaned over to peer at her cup.

"Cream? No. I have a latte."

"I hath had one. From Vivienne."

"That's nice. I just realized what's going on. Mr. Merle. He brought you here, didn't he?"

"Yes! So you *do* know he is a wizard!"

"Not a wizard. No. Everyone knows they are made up. Fiction. But he does move people through time. He's got a machine or something to make people move through time. Maybe that funky old mirror or that sword on the wall. That's how he brought Black Eagle here and now you. Maybe he does it with his camera. I wonder . . ."

"Yes?"

"Do you know if, well is he with NASA or Homeland Security or something like that?"

"NASA? Security? He is Arthur's man. His councilor."

"Who's Arthur? Oh no, don't start that again. Reality check here, okay? King Arthur and his Knights of the Round Table are a story. A good story made up by this guy Mallory hundreds of years ago. He wasn't real and neither were his knights. I'll admit some of things they did like being into chivalry and all that were cool and we should have more of it now, however the guy and his buddies weren't real."

"Not real? Here. Take my hand. Take it."

A light breeze gently lifted the hair that brushed along

Gareth's collar, catching Molly's attention. Without realizing it, Molly let him grasp her hand in his larger, warmer, slightly calloused one.

"Does that feel real to you?"

"Of course it does. *You're* real. It's the character you are pretending to be that isn't. It's interesting though, if you are a time traveler how you'd know about King Arthur? Unless. When are you from? What year?"

"Four hundred twenty."

"Four hundred twenty? Not long after the Romans left Britain."

"Yes. They left the country at the mercy of the Saxon dogs. Arthur, along with the other Knights, his companions, united the country."

"Please, cut the Camelot stuff, huh? Just for a bit and focus, okay? I've got a lot on my mind, tons to do and just can't take on any other weirdness."

Gareth nodded and took a long swallow of his mocha.

"You like it?"

"Most assuredly. Not as good as ale, but tasty."

"Good. Now, let me ask you. Is Mr. Merle really your uncle?"

"No. He is Arthur's uncle." He raised his hand to stop her from telling him once again not to bring up Arthur. "Please, let me finish. The man you call Mr. Merle is Merlin, advisor to Arthur Pendragon. Merlin's father was Aueralius who was High King a short time before his death. It was Aueralius who united Britian before his death. His brother, Uther, then ascended the throne and held the kingdom until his son, Arthur, came of age to rule. Uther was Merlin's uncle, Arthur is his relation. Arthur is the warrior king, Merlin the magical advisor. My mother is Morgause, Arthur's older sister by their mother's first marriage."

"Yeah, yeah, Uther fell in love with Ygraine and snuck into

her bed and then killed Gorlis, her first husband, who was Morgan and Morgause's mother. That's all in Mallory's book."

"If you know all this then why do you ask me?" He leaned back in his chair looking slightly affronted.

"I know the story of King Arthur. It's you and how you know Mr. Merle I want to hear about."

"I am telling you."

She reminded herself not to buy into his delusion if in fact that was what it was. "Do you know what a camera or photograph is?"

"No."

"Great. You're older than Black Eagle. A camera takes your picture. Like a portrait."

"Ah. My mother had my brothers and I painted."

"Well like that. Did you ever see Mr. Merle with a box he pointed at you and out came a picture?"

"No."

"No? The how did he get you here?"

"What do you mean?"

"This is going to sound crazy so bear with me. My roommate, Carrie, was real big on reading romance novels. You know, books about people falling in love. Ones from other time periods, historicals were her favorites. Mostly she liked time travel novels that went back in time. Books where someone falls in love with someone from another time and one or the other moves to the new time."

"And you do not believe this is real?"

"No. Well, I didn't until she met Black Eagle and I think Mr. Merle was behind that. You see Carrie had bad luck with guys. She was smart, caring, good-hearted."

"Why do you say was. Did she die?"

"No. Not now. She's not here in Napa anymore. Like I said, this is going to sound crazy. Carrie was the best kind of person. A truly good person and sometimes people took advantage of that. She'd met this guy, Dean, who was a total asshole to her."

Taking drink of her latte Molly missed the look of surprise Gareth shot her at the use of the word asshole.

"He cheated on her with other women and then when she dumped him he kept coming around again. It seems that the only way he could make partner in his law firm was to be married and have a kid and he thought Carrie would be easy pickens."

"Partner?"

"A boss. Someone in charge."

"She was going along, just living her life and one day she went to Treasures and came home with a photograph of this Indian. A way old photograph. Carrie was always a romantic, always off reading those books and in high school we'd joke around about getting a picture of a really hot guy and when you couldn't kiss him you'd kiss the picture."

"Then we must procure a picture of me for you."

"Huh? Why?"

"Till we wed you may needs kiss me. If I am not beside you the picture will please you."

"Uh, yeah, right. I don't think so." She couldn't believe he was talking about being married. It was either part of his delusion, which about now, with telling him Carrie's story, he must be thinking the same of her. Or, he was messing with her. A guy who looked like that, positively gorgeous, wouldn't be interested in a woman like Molly. No how. No way.

"Anyway, back to Carrie. She was obsessed with this photograph and the next thing you know the guy from the picture turns up in our house. Not just our house, but the day he arrived she woke up to find him in her bed! He came from 1850 or '60 or something like that and a lot of the things you are doing, like the cars, reminds me of how he reacted."

"Cars?"

"You know, in the street."

"The metal boxes that move."

"Uh huh, those. So anyway, at first we thought someone was playing a joke on Carrie. Like maybe Dean, her old boyfriend, got a friend of his to act like a nineteenth century Indian just to mess with Carrie. Then we realized that smarmy little Dean wouldn't send an absolutely tall, dark and gorgeous guy into Carrie's life cause who wouldn't fall for him?"

"You prefer dark-haired men." He ran his fingers through is own light colored locks. "Perhaps Merlin can change . . ."

"Your hair is fine. A little long maybe, but fine. The beard's a nice touch too. I'm just saying, for Carrie Black Eagle was mighty fine. We thought about it and Mr. Merle was the only link because you see a few days before this Mr. Merle's ancestor took Black Eagle's picture in 1860 and the next thing he knows he's here in 2021. Kind of like you except you say you came from 420. We went to talk to Mr. Merle about it but he suddenly went on vacation."

"Vacation?"

"Yeah, you know, when you leave town for a few days of fun?"

"When did he take this vac-va-vacation?"

"About six months ago."

"Six months, before Beltane. Yes, I saw him about then. Go on." For some reason the time frame clicked over something in Gareth's memory.

"While we waited for Mr. Merle to come back we took Black Eagle around and he and Carrie fell in love. It was pretty clear they were made for each other. When Mr. Merle came back Black Eagle was certain that his Mr. Merle and ours was the same man. That couldn't be though because if his Mr. Merle was as old as ours is, why shit, I mean shoot, he'd be like four hundred years old."

"He was old in 420 as well."

Molly snapped her fingers, "So we were right! He is the same guy and for some reason he's snagging guys from way long ago and bringing them here to match them up with what he thinks are lonely women. But something goes wrong."

"With Merlin, always."

She chose to ignore that. "Actually I don't know if it always goes wrong. I just know with Carrie, Dean kept bugging her and it was Black Eagle who took care of him. Dean's now in the house of padded walls for a long time to come."

"House with padded walls?"

"I guess what you'd call an insane asylum."

"Asylum?"

"A place for people who aren't right in the head."

"Ah. We thought they were possessed and either the Druids or the church, depending on which faith a town followed, would take care of the person."

"We don't have any more Druids, at least like that, and the Catholic church may do an exorcism now and again, but not like way back when. Now though we know that people who don't think like the rest of us may have a mental health problem and they are put in places that can help them in a humane way. Dean went on a rant that Black Eagle was a time traveler and that Mr. Merle was behind it."

"What he declared was true. They put him away for speaking the truth?"

"Look, Dean needed to be put away somewhere. The guy was bad news. And reality check, who believes in time travel?"

"You do."

"Maybe. At least I've seen evidence of it."

"What happened when this Dean went to the land of padded walls?"

"Next thing we knew, and this happened around the first time I met you, remember? Carrie and I were in Mr. Merle's store and you came out in your knight clothes?"

"I had just woken."

"You sleep in that heavy armor? Isn't that kind of hard?"

Gareth looked confused, "We all sleep or slept in our armor. When the great sleep came over us we had no time to change."

"Uh huh. Right." She so wasn't going down that road. "Anyway, we woke up one morning and Black Eagle was gone and oh yeah, I forgot about this. You know how he was in the photograph?"

Gareth nodded despite the look in his eyes letting her know he was struggling to follow.

"Well when he popped up in Carrie's bed he was in the room and was gone from the photograph. Poof," She snapped her fingers, "Just like that. One minute on the Kodak paper, the next in bed with Carrie. The night he disappeared, one minute he was there and the next he was back in the picture."

"What did you do?"

"First we went to Mr. Merle. That was useless. So we went home and photo-shopped."

"Photo . . ."

She shook her head, "I'll explain it later. Basically we played with the photograph and put Carrie and her cat, Taister, picture in there only nothing happened. She was still here and Black Eagle was back in his time. Then last week, the second time I saw you — did you just wake up again?"

"Wake? No. Since I woke I have lived at Merlin's."

"Sure. When you saw me again was right after Carrie disappeared and suddenly she was in the photograph, the original one, with Black Eagle. She went back in time to be with him. I'm sure Mr. Merle has something to do with it only he keeps denying it. And here you are. A guy from the past, suddenly here in the present. Has Mr. Merle introduced you to any women?"

"Only you."

"Well watch out if he introduces you to someone because I bet he's brought you through time to be with some lonely woman who hasn't met a man from this time."

"He always was an old meddler."

"I'll say."

"Are you lonely?"

She decided to ignore that. "So you liked the mocha?"

"Yes. Very much. If I sat still would you procure me another?"

"Sure. No problem. Gareth?"

"Yes?"

"You're all right. You listened to my story without once looking at me like I was the crazy one."

"Tis not you who are bedeviled. As you said, Merlin has long meddled in people's lives. I have no doubt he is the one who has disturbed my slumber."

CHAPTER TWELVE

She sat back down. "What do you mean he disturbed your slumber?"

"He means," Mr. Merle came up behind them, "I woke him early this morning so he could help me move some things around in the shop, isn't that right, Gareth?"

"No. I mean you woke me from my eternal rest." He turned to Molly, his look grave. "You say Arthur and his knights are but a tale. Do you know the legend of his return?"

"Um. Carrie said something about it or it was in one of her books. Something about some day they're all going to be back."

Gareth took a swallow of his mocha and nodded. "The legend says that in the time of the world's greatest need King Arthur and his knights will rise to once again make all well in the world."

"Sounds like a nice story. Unfortunately it's a little late for those guys."

"Late?"

"Yeah. We've had some bad times since they were around. Wars like the Revolutionary and Civil wars here, World Wars One and Two, famines, plagues, all kinds of bad things happened. If he was going to get up and ride again it would have been for something big like that."

"Or maybe those things were not enough. Maybe it would happen with the world needed chivalry to return. From what I have seen of your time there is little care for women. You labor, your men treat you badly, you . . ."

"It's not just men that treat us badly. My supervisor at work makes the Queen of Mean look like a sweetheart and I have to admit I wouldn't mind a knight to come galloping in and take care of her. Or better yet for her to end up in one of the creepy serial killer posters we've got up at work now. But that's not going to happen."

Gareth started and moved his hand to his hip as if going for a weapon. Realizing no such device sat on his hip he settled into his chair, "Where doth this Queen of Mean live?"

"Molly is using only a figure of speech, Gareth." Mr. Merle told him while signaling for the waitress. "I'd like a peppermint mocha, please. Would either of you care for a refill?" He looked to Molly and Gareth.

"I'd appreciate a refill on my coffee." Molly told her.

"Another of these peppermint mokes," Gareth gestured with his mug. "A rare treat these."

"Mochas. Yes, they are good." Mr. Merle agreed.

"Now, this Queen. Where do I find her?" Gareth returned to the subject at hand.

"She's dead." Merlin flatly informed him.

"One of my brothers hath already arrived and dispatched the wench?" Gareth looked up and down the street as if someone he knew had appeared.

"Wench, that's a good one," Molly chuckled. "No, the Queen of Mean was this woman, Leona Helmsey, who had this major bad attitude toward the people who worked for her. She didn't pay her taxes and said that taxes were for the little people."

"Tis true. The king levies taxes for the keep of the kingdom."

"Not anymore. Nowadays almost everyone has to pay some kind of tax and kings and queens are figureheads. They don't really have any power. What am I saying? This isn't news to you."

"Tis news."

"Come on, Gareth. I'm not buying into your story unless . . . I want the truth now. I'm going to ask this with Mr. Merle here and I want the truth. Are you from way back in time and did you see Mr. Merle with a camera where he took your picture?"

Gareth sighed, "I told you this did not happen, Molly. I hath known Merlin, your Mr. Merle for years. He hath no magical chest that would capture my soul and bring me to your time. What happened to your friend and her man is not what hath happened to me."

"Mr. Merle, is Gareth one of your time traveling buddies?"

Mr. Merle shook his head.

"Did you bring him here? To maybe do to me or some other woman what you did to Carrie?"

"No. Molly, Gareth is my nephew, come to visit for a short time, that's all."

"I am not . . ."

Molly cut him off. "Then why is he reacting to things the way Black Eagle did? When he walked into the middle of the street, why did he freeze and look around like he'd never seen a car before? Why didn't he see them from your store? And don't tell me he's Amish or something like that because they know what cars are. They live side by side with non-Amish and see cars all the time. In fact I heard they will make use of modern technology just not in their houses so that argument won't fly."

"Tis because I hath *woken*, Molly. For some reason I have woken in this time. Now tell me more of this Queen of Mean. Perhaps that tis why I hath come."

It was Molly's turn to shake her head. They called Leona Helmsly the Queen of Mean when she was alive. Now she's dead. My personal nightmare is Julie Prince. She's the manager of the dispatch center where I work and my personal nemesis."

"Strange times this. A woman a prince?"

"No, it's her last name. People have last names like King, Prince, Noble. Usually male names. Her last name is Prince and her mission in life is to make mine miserable."

"Who assigned this mission? How doth she do this?"

"I don't want to burden you with my problems."

"Truly, Molly, I would know. Mayhap I can help in some way. If not me, my eldest brother, Aggravain, knoweth some of our mother's magic."

"Gareth, I don' think . . ." Mr. Merle started.

Molly interrupted him, "Okay, cool it on the magic stuff. Both of you. But you know, sometimes I do just need to vent." She wasn't going to address the fact that she was glad of the chance to avoid dealing with Carrie's departure. The Red Queen is always writing me up for things other people do wrong. That gives her ammunition for not promoting me to a better job. Every time I apply for a better job she points out that I've done all these things wrong. The thing is, I didn't do any of them wrong. Like last week I went in and got in trouble for not sending some statistics off to the task force office. It wasn't even my responsibility. You know, we've gotten this display of serial killers and a few have them torturing their victims and man, would I love to see Julie stuck on one of those pictures."

Gareth stared at her, wide eyed, his lips parted. Either he didn't have a clue what she'd just told him or, was a consummate actor pretending he had no idea. "Can you think of a way I can I help you, Molly?"

He sounded so earnest, so kind, so genuine. She glanced at those lips of his and thought back to the kiss they'd shared. She should have been angry, offended, incensed. After all, who kissed a total stranger like that? Instead, she wanted Mr. Merle to disappear so she could have at the blond haired man again. Gareth whateverhislastname may be crazy as a loon, but the man sure could kiss. She glanced over at Mr. Merle to find him giving her a knowing smile. There was no way the old gent could know what she was thinking.

"Don't be too sure of that, Molly," he murmured just loud enough for her to hear.

"What?"

"Shall I share your thoughts with Gareth?"

"Absolutely not! Thanks for the offer, Gareth. I like what I do and most of the people I do it with. She just makes life there horrible. So I wait till right before she goes on vacation to apply for other jobs and hope no one calls her. One of these days the right one will happen. Meanwhile I need to deal with her."

"Did your Red Queen know the Queen of Mean?"

"She's not my Red Queen. That's just a name we use for her. I don't think they ever met. Julie isn't the kind of person Leona would have bothered with. Um, you know who the Red Queen is, right?"

"You said your nemesis."

"From Alice in Wonderland. You know, the Red Queen was the one shouting 'off with their heads'. That's our Julie."

Gareth gasped. "Your Queen orders heads to roll on a whim?"

"Not literally." Could he really have not heard of Alice in Wonderland?

"He's not mentally unstable, Molly." Mr. Merle murmured.

"Mr. Merle! Stop that! And no, it's just an expression. You two are weird. Plain weird." She took a last swallow of her coffee, reached for her purse and rose.

Gareth rose beside her, once again looking confused. "What troubles you, Molly?"

"Nothing. I've got some things to take care of. I need to go by Carrie's work and explain about her leaving and get her bills squared away." On top of the business with Carrie and the stress at work having him talk about his fantasy life as a knight was more than she could handle.

"I will accompany you."

"Ah, that's not necessary."

"It would be most discourteous of me to leave you to fend for yourself."

Molly sighed and sat back down. "Gareth, I've fended for myself for years. Carrie's not coming back and I need to set things right and then decide what I'm going to do. Right now it's one step at a time."

"Then tis time you had a man beside you."

"Uh, yeah. Right." She rose, "Mr. Merle, you explain it to him. I really need to get going."

"Let me know if you need anything, Molly. And please, don't be a stranger." Mr. Merle assured her.

"I'll keep in touch, Mr. Merle. Bye Gareth and don't play in the traffic." She started down the street and wiggled her fingers at them.

Gareth stood and moved to follow Molly despite her protestations against his company. Mr. Merle laid his hand on Gareth's arm to stop him.

"My lady is leaving."

"Gareth, my boy. Molly is not your lady. At least not right now. Who knows what the future holds? You and I need to have a bit of talk."

Gareth settled in his chair, arms crossed over his chest, a glower in his gaze. "About what?"

"This time."

"So you admit you hath done something to wake me? It hath taken long enough for you to speak the truth."

"I'm not admitting anything. However, to tell the truth, I

don't know why you suddenly popped up here. Neither Vivienne nor I made a summoning, yet here you are."

Hands on the arms of the chair, he leaned forward, anger tingeing his voice, "You do not mean to send me back?"

"Would that I could. If it were possible either she or I would have sent you back to your rest as soon as you arrived. It does not seem that is about to happen. Whatever woke you seems to have planted you firmly in this time and that, dear boy, could be a problem."

"More of a problem than your meddling?"

"*I* do not meddle. The problem is the world is sixteen hundred years older than when you walked you walked the paths of Britain. Much has happened, most which students in school know something about."

"Tis simple. Tell me what these students learn."

"It's not that simple. First of all your language. No one has spoken like that for centuries and no amount of magic will completely change your vocabulary. At least we've got you dressed for the times."

"Ah, yes, these trews are most snug. I hath no doubt the Lady—Molly could readily see my desire for her."

"And since when has *that* bothered you?"

"You confuse me with Gehris. He and Gawain are the ones always seeking female companionship."

"You were never one to turn it down."

"True, yet I do not seek as much as they did and I am the most selective of my brothers. Well, perhaps Aggravaine is a bit more so. Yet tis his role as the eldest to set our ways."

"Trust me, women of today are rather fond of tight jeans on a man, especially in the posterior. As to teaching you what every day school children have known for years." He sighed. "My boy we have work ahead of us. Much work."

"Then you believe I am here to stay?"

"It would appear so. Between Vivienne and I we will do

our best to teach you. We think, with our combined magic, we can give you some of the knowledge you will need. One thing though, my boy, twould be best you do not speak of Arthur and Camelot."

"Arthur tis my liege lord. Camelot is my home."

"Not anymore. Arthur sleeps, Camelot is no more and Napa in 2021 is your home. If you speak of times gone by, make certain you do so as if it twere from a school memory."

"And Molly?"

"Ah, yes, Molly. We will see what we can do to help her. I know of this woman who causes her such strife."

"Then we will go and deal with her."

"That is one of many things that is done differently these days. Molly knows what she has to do and should she wish help, she will ask for it."

"What sort of men live these days that they do not help their women? Any woman? Tis against our code, Wizard. You cannot ask me to sit by and let my lady be wronged."

Mr. Merle sighed, "Gareth. Modern women have modern problems and their own ways of dealing with them and I'm not sure a knight in shining armor is what they want or need."

CHAPTER THIRTEEN

With a major headache brewing Molly walked into the dark, silent house she'd shared with Carrie for years. Her footsteps echoed loud enough to wake the dead, which made her chuckle. "Guess that's what woke Gareth up. Yeah, that's it. My uber loud footsteps woke him in the middle of time. One of King Arthur's knights my ass."

She turned on the hall lamp, kicked off her shoes and trudged into the kitchen. After standing in front of the open refrigerator for several minutes she shook her head, remembering where she was. The leftovers weren't quite at the science experiment stage and the pizza looked pretty good. "Nothing like cold pizza. Nope nothing except a hot kiss from a time traveling guy named Gareth." She slapped her forehead. "What the heck is wrong with me? I'm starting to sound more and more like Carrie."

She brought the pizza box over to the counter and looked out the window before reaching for a plate. Her reflection showed her a bone weary young woman who suddenly felt all alone in the world. "Maybe you need to start believing in something, Molly Nichols. Maybe you need to step out of the box you've built for your world and start living. You don't have Carrie around anymore to plan outrageous outings. It's time to find a few of your own."

Pizza in hand she headed into the room they'd designated as the library. It was more Carrie's room than Molly's. With floor to ceiling bookcases on three of the four walls, Carrie's books filled almost every shelf. She considered digging out her own copy of Mallory's *Morte de Arthur* than then decided what she really needed was to escape and read a total fantasy. "Who was that author Carrie was talking about before, before she left? *Her Knight*, that's it!" Her mission clear she headed toward the fantasy books and finally found the book she was looking for.

The plate holding the pizza on her lap, book in hand, she sank into the deep piled brown corduroy sofa and put her feet upon the heavy wooden coffee table. What a day. She was exhausted. Her conversation with Mr. Merle was okay although it didn't solve her problem. Make that problems.

And Gareth only complicated things. "And what was that about with him in the middle of the street? He couldn't be. He just couldn't be a time traveler. He was as confused about it as me."

Changing over the names on the bills and settling Carrie's accounts was fairly easy. Her co-workers were sad she'd left and at the same time were really happy for her. To a person they assured Molly that Carrie deserved every bit of happiness coming her way. The rest she'd deal with as it came up.

Chewing a bite of pizza she began reading *Her Knight* only to find her mind returning again and again to Gareth. Molly wasn't a prude by any means. She dated often enough. There was never anyone who really caught her attention. If she gave someone a thought after a date it quickly passed. Even Vincent, her last boyfriend who dumped her after taking Black Eagle to a baseball game, didn't amount to much of a loss. It didn't have anything to do with Black Eagle. Nope, not at all. He told her outright it was because of her constant work problems. She didn't talk about them, but they did cloud a lot of her waking moments. Out of sight, out of mind. So how come Gareth kept popping into her mind?

"Probably because he's the first guy you've met who didn't fall all over himself trying to make the world see what a catch he is. And he's nuts. Yeah, that's it, I just feel sorry for him. Man though, he sure can kiss."

Her pizza done Molly tried for the umpteenth time to read the same page. Two hours after sitting down and she'd only gotten to page ten. The book seemed like a good read, she just couldn't concentrate. Carrie would have enjoyed that. Carrie who could read an entire novel in a night, who sat up till two or three in the morning to finish a book she started after dinner, and still had the energy to go to work the next day. To date Molly'd never found a book that compelling. Then again, she didn't read much fiction.

Giving up she shut the book and laid her head back on the couch. A surprise tear trickled down her cheek at the thought of Taister. The little guy loved to sit and eat with the women and if there was a free lap in a room he felt it was clearly there for him. Every little sound seemed to echo in the old house. It was the first time since Carrie left that Molly was awake and alone with her thoughts. Not even Taister was prowling up and down the hallways. "Man, I miss you."

Eyes closed she tried to picture the village Carrie had gone back in time to. Instead images of a castle, colorful banners flying from stately turrets kept edging into her mind. At first Molly told herself it was the Castello di Amorosa situated down the road in Calistoga that drew tourists from all over the world, that played in her mind. After all, for the past few years it was the go to place in Napa Valley. Only it wasn't a British castle. No, the castle she saw wasn't the Moorish structure up the valley from her home. This one was older and clearly English. "What the heck is wrong with me? It's gotta be that Gareth and his weirdo notions on being a knight combined with Carrie going back in time."

She rolled over and punched her pillow as if that would drive the sensations of being in the old castle from her mind.

Before sunrise the next morning Gareth stole down the stairs, through the darkened kitchen and into the quaint little antique store. The fast moving metal boxes, those cars, had unnerved him the day before, as had many things in this new world Merlin had led him to. He was certain something the wizard had done to wake him. The long ago legend said that in time of the world's greatest need Arthur and the knights would waken once again. He'd gone to his rest beneath the Tor believing this. Yet if it were time for the knights to wake, where were his brothers? Where was Arthur and the others? Why was he the only one to find himself in the village of Napa without his friends, his horse, his king?

The shop's contents took on a spectral look in the glow of a full moon spilling into the room. A shard of the pale blue-gray light fell on the old sword encased on the wall. For a moment it seemed to glow with inner light. Not all that different than when Arthur wielded it in battle.

"Excalibur?" Gareth walked to the wall and ran his hand along the glass. The coolness of the glass anomalous with the reddish gold glow from within the case. "Am I to rescue them? Are my king and brothers held somewhere nearby and await me? Or tis it Lady Molly who needeth aid?"

He stood peering into the plain wood and glass box a few moments as if the sword would answer him, guide him. A creak from the kitchen drew his attention and he froze, willing himself to blend with the wall. He knew with certainty the steady thud of his heart must be heard in the other room. When no one appeared he released the breath he'd been holding and stepped away from the glass-enclosed sword. Twas not his. No, it belonged to someone greater than he could ever be. It was meant for the man he followed wherever his king was.

During the past two weeks Merlin had done his best to

teach him of this time. The view from the windows, the little Gareth saw, held many strange and wonderful things. It seemed all the women dressed to entice or to mimic the men with their coarse blue trews. The food presented a constant temptation to his palate and despite his thirst for an ale, their beverages were tasty, especially those peppermint mochas he'd discovered yesterday. Not having to wait for the cook fire to prepare his meals was a treat. He was so enthralled with the many delights that came from the small black glass-like box that sat on the counter that by time he realized its foreignness, fear of it meant nothing.

Vivienne popped in and out each day. At times Vivienne disappeared for days. Each time she remonstrated Merlin to send Gareth back or to answer what had brought him here. For once it seemed Merlin did not have an answer. That could mean either the old wizard was merely older or, perhaps his mother had once again worked her magic in yet another nefarious scheme.

Molly must hold some of the answers as to what brought him here. Else why would he feel so drawn to her? Therefore, he must seek her out and together they would solve the puzzle which was what woken him. And mayhap, in exchange, he could solve her problem with the Red Queen. Indeed providing protection against the troublesome queen may be the very reason he had woken at this time. It was Molly who found him in the street where the cars sped around him. Clearly the dark-haired woman held the key to his future!

Hand to his jaw Gareth surveyed the room. "I needs go to her. But how?" He surveyed the shop considering how to find Molly. "My Lady Molly knew Merlin through her friend, Carrie. Merlin said they share a home. If Carrie sought Merlin's wares, he would have a record of her purchases. Where?"

His gaze lit on a small wooden box near the larger metal one that held the coin of this time. From the beaded doorway he'd seen Merlin write on some parchment and place it in the small boxes. Despite his aversion to book learning, Gareth did learn something of written language so he made his way to the box. Gently raising the lid he peered inside to see a series of cards with single letters printed neatly on top of them. He thought back to his letters, "Carrie, Carrie. Cee? Kay?"

The headlights of a passing car illuminated the room and made Gareth momentarily freeze in place. A passerby might question someone standing in the darkened shop in the middle of the night and Merlin had warned him about the authorities of this time. They, like Molly and the customers, apparently would not understand he was a knight of the realm and need not defend his entry to any building. When the car moved on, he returned to the box, finding a card with the name "Carrie" written on it in Merlin's spidery hand. Taking it, Gareth strode quickly to the front door, turned the lock and handle and to his relief, the door silently opened. He stepped outside and drank in the cool night air before taking off at a trot up the street. Giving quiet thanks that Vivienne had shown him a map of the town, he had a vague idea of how to find Molly's abode.

When another set of headlights reflected in a storefront window Gareth slowed. Running in the dark of night was a sure sign someone was up to no good in any time. If the knights of this time stopped him more like than not they would react as Molly did if he told him his identity. Merlin had spoken of identification, something he did not possess. Better to stroll along and hope the modern knights did not stop him. What did Vivienne call them? She'd warned him of these men . . . and women . . . when he first woke. Poles. That was it! "No, it was po-po-lice. Po. Lice. No. Police! Yes! She called them police! And best I avoid them." Gareth smiled to himself. Spotting a group of trees a short walk away Gareth realized it must be a parkland. If he remembered the map correctly, Molly's street lay just beyond the park.

Luck was with him when he saw the numbers on a house that matched Molly's. A low gray metal fence edged the front yard which was covered with lush green grass. A large oak tree, the kind a youth would enjoy climbing or a young man would murmur poetic endearments to his beloved, sat on the right hand side. On the other grew an apple tree with a few ripe red apples ready for the picking, provided additional shade. Ringing the front porch were flower beds with an array of blooms, a most picturesque welcoming to a weary traveler. The wrap around wooden porch held a bench hung from chains and boxes with yet more flowers sat below the windows. A pad of sorts with the word "WELCOME" sat before the doorway. The bounce of a leaf across the porch in a light breeze caught his attention, moving him to the door. Merlin often arrived on a breath of air. To have made it this far, only to be caught by the old wizard, would be dismaying at the very least.

He raised his hand and knocked at the wooden portal. Silence reigned so he knocked once again. When there was no response head hung, hands on his hips he studied the door. There was nothing to do for it so he turned to walk to the hanging bench. No more than three steps later the door opened ever so slightly. In the crack he could see a rather disheveled Molly peering out.

"Oh no." She pulled the door open a bit more. "What are you doing here in the middle of the night? How did you find my house?"

"I wanted to see you."

"In the middle of the night?" She opened the door all the way to reveal a hallway of highly polished wood, a table holding a vase of flowers on one side, a tall staff with smaller branch like stems stood on the other, a coat and softer looking woolen wrap hung from two of them. A shard of pale morning sunlight streamed into the hallway from a room on the left. He tried not to notice her wearing only a large shirt, the kind which Merlin had called a t-shirt and insisted he wear instead of his lawn shirts. On Molly the garment was most appealing, revealing firm high breasts beneath words about some festival in Napa and long, tanned legs. She seemed not in the least bothered by her near nakedness, something none of the women of this time bothered about.

"Tis morn, Molly. Day is well nigh upon us." Gareth gestured toward the street behind him.

"Not if you work graves, it's not." She grumbled.

"Then I shall wait till you have had your rest." He turned to walk to the bench.

"No. It's okay. Come on in. You came all the way over here so I might as well make you a coffee. I wasn't sleeping that well anyway."

He followed her down the hallway, past a welcoming sitting chamber and into the kitchen. Molly's was larger than the one at Treasures. A table with four ladder backed wooden chairs sat in the center of the room. Plump cushions with purple violets against a white background covered the seats.

She had one of the large white chests Merlin called the refrigerator along a wall, a sink with the devices to bring water inside, a smaller black chest that resembled what he understood was called a microwave on the counter next to a series of glass holders in the shape of red apples. Words on the side proclaimed them to be flour, sugar, tea and coffee. Beside them sat a machine that resembled what the wizard had called a coffeemaker. It was to the coffee machine Molly turned, pulling the container marked "coffee" with her. With methodical movements she measured the rich dark powdery substance into a holder, poured water into the top and pushed a button to start the brew. Without speaking a word, she opened a cupboard and pulled out two heavy mugs and set them beside the machine before going to the refrigerator and pulling out what he'd learned at the shop was milk. At first it intrigued him that the people no longer needed to milk cows daily to have their cream. And twas not merely cream. They had such odd varieties such as low fat and whole.

"Hungry?"

After her silence since his arrival the single word startled him. "Pardon?"

"I asked if you were hungry. Would you like some breakfast?"

"Yes. That would please me. Most assuredly."

"Then have a seat. Let me throw on some clothes and I'll make up some bacon and eggs. How does that sound? Bacon, eggs, toast?"

"Wonderful."

She yawned and padded out of the kitchen. Gareth craned his neck to follow her progress down the hallway. When she returned a few minutes later her long brown hair was pulled back with cord, she'd pulled on a heavier shirt and the trews called jeans. Furry shoes with what appeared to be pink rabbits encased her feet.

"Now how did you find my house?"

So much for her forgetting the question.

Rather than stop to hear his answer she moved to the refrigerator and pulled out the items for the meal.

"Did I truly break your rest, Molly?"

"It's okay. I work from five in the evening till three in the morning and pretty much stick on that schedule on my days off unless I need to get up."

"I apologize."

"No need. If you've never hung out with a shift worker you don't know what we do or how we do it. I haven't been sleeping that well anyway. How did you find me?"

"Merl—my uncle keeps a box with parchment where

customer's names are written. I found your friend Carrie's name so I walked through the parkland and found you. Tell me, Molly, do you not sleep because you miss your friend?"

"In part. The house is a lot quieter with her gone and Carrie's cat, Taister, could carry on to beat the band when he was awake. Quite a character. No, it's my job."

"Where is this band now? You do not send them home?"

"Huh? Oh, beat the band is an expression. It means he meowed and meowed like crazy or to drive us crazy. He had opinions on everything."

"I see. Why do you work? Have you no father or husband to care for you?"

Molly chuckled, "Man, you must have been living in a cave. That's not quite the way things are done nowadays. Hasn't been for years. Women have worked, gee, ever since World War II we've gotten better and better jobs. Ones that used to be done by only men. So no, no one paying my bills."

Not a cave, but sleeping under an old hill hidden in the mists, he thought. "What is this work you do, Molly? What do you do for your Red Queen?"

The coffee bubbled its announcement it was done brewing and Molly turned to pour their drinks before turning and placing their bacon and eggs on the table and sitting herself. "Eat up."

"It smells very good."

"Thanks."

"Tell me then, your work?"

"That. I normally try not to think about it on my days off. I work for a local police department, over in Marin."

"You are the law?"

"No. I'm not an officer. I'm a paper pusher. Julie, my manager hates it when we refer to the job as that, but that's what it is. In Records we basically push paper around and never miss a chance to call it paper pushing when she's not around.

It's necessary. What we do is important. Don't get me wrong. It's only that I don't like doing it."

"What would you rather do?"

"I'd rather dispatch."

"What is that?"

"Dispatch is pretty cool. At least to me it is. What you do is pretty straight forward. Someone calls the police for help or whatever, you get their info and then send an officer out. Or an officer out on patrol and sees something. They radio it in and you get the information. I guess it comes down to a dispatcher merely making sure information is passed on to the right person in the right way. You don't embellish or leave parts out. Just get the news from one person to the other."

"Something like that would have been most helpful in Arthur's time."

She shrugged, "I'm sure it would have. Unfortunately for those guys they didn't have radios or other electronic stuff."

"This job, does the information make you unhappy?"

"No. My boss does. She plays favorites, pits people against each other, won't promote you unless you are a cute little blonde who sleeps with the officers. She's always riding my ass."

The mention of cute little blondes combined with thoughts of riding her set Gareth's mind off in several directions at once. The idea of riding the voluptuous brunette, now that appealed beyond compare. From the look on her face though, being bedded 'twas not what she meant.

"Do you wish to speak of this woman's actions?"

"I used to bitch to Carrie about Julie all the time. It didn't make the situation any better, but I felt better when I did. Sometimes. Most of us in Records bitch about Julie every chance we get, comparing stories of her latest outrageous actions."

"Does she cause you physical harm?"

"No. She mostly annoys me. Like I told you yesterday, it seems like every week I go in to work she has some other, what we call log entries, written up about me. They detail what she thinks we've done wrong. I seem to get more than anyone else. I'm a favorite target because she'll do just about anything to keep me from leaving. That way she has this huge paper trail to prove I don't deserve to move on to a better job. This badge bunny, a woman named Kris, started the same time I did and Kris is one of those cute little blondes I mentioned. Sleeps with every male officer that comes along. Doesn't matter if they are married or not. What Julie does is if Kris does something wrong she finds a way to pin it on me. So Kris continues to get everything she wants and I get zip."

"What would you like to happen?"

"You mean aside from getting into dispatch? I'd like to see Julie get hers. You know how I told you Carrie met Black Eagle because she saw him in a photograph? Well I'd like to see Julie stuck in a photograph where she's miserable for eternity. I'd want her to have mental pain and anguish rather than physical pain. In the best of all worlds I'd see her stuck in this nasty situation every day I walked into work. Or better yet, as a victim in one of those serial killer posters we recently got in. I know that doesn't sound very nice, but as we sit here today, you and me, that's what I'd like to see happen to her. Too bad Mr. Merle isn't really magical Merlin like you think he is and he can't change her into a toad or stick her in a nasty picture."

Gareth studied Molly. Maybe if he helped her with this Red Queen Julie, Molly would see he spoke the truth, that he really was one of Arthur's knights, woken to right wrongs in the world.

CHAPTER FOURTEEN

"So, I've talked your ears off. Sorry you came by this morning?" In reality, instead of feeling sorry she'd dumped her feelings about Julie on Gareth, she was glad she had someone to listen to her. She might never see him again, but venting about things at work helped her feel better.

"No, Molly, I wanted to see you. I am glad I came and heard your troubles. That is what friends do, yes? We listen to and try to help each other?"

"Among other things. Friends also do fun things together. So do you have plans the rest of the day?" She gave herself a mental slap. Gareth was a total stranger, had weird ideas about being a knight from way back when and showed up unannounced and uninvited on her doorstep. For all she knew he was a serial killer posing as a confused warrior from another time and only waited for the right moment to kill her. Then again, being Mr. Merle's nephew, could he really be a serial killer? Wouldn't the older gent know if his nephew killed people on the sly?

"No. I do not."

"Then how about this. I won't complain about my job and you won't talk about being an old knight and we'll do something fun?"

Clearly the situation with Carrie had affected her more than she thought. Asking a total stranger to do something fun? And what was fun? Carrie'd always planned their outings. She was the one who found tours and events in magazines or saw ads on TV for fairs, festivals and other shows.

Their annual vacations to places like Oceana Naval Air Station, Disneyland and Disney World, Mt. Rushmore and way back when to Chippendales in Las Vegas were all Carrie's idea. Now that she thought about it Molly couldn't think of one idea she'd ever come up with so what could she be thinking asking Gareth if he wanted to do something fun?

"I am in agreement. What would you like to do?"

"You are the guest here. What would you like to do?"

"Whatever you like to do for fun."

Great. Whatever she liked to do for fun. Sitting at the computer reading crime reports were at the top of her list. Not exactly high on most people's list for best in entertainment. She noticed he looked at her expectantly, waiting for an answer. Just wonderful. Carrie would know what to do. She would have had something right there that she'd been thinking about doing for weeks. Not tag-along Molly. Mentally she snapped her fingers. Carrie! Of course. She'd had all kinds of things she'd planned with Black Eagle. They both enjoyed the day out at the ocean. Maybe Gareth would like that.

"How about we head out to the coast? We can pack a picnic lunch, hang out at the shore and maybe grab dinner out there. They have some great seafood restaurants. You like seafood, don't you?"

"Very much so."

If the look in his eyes was any indication, he had no idea what a restaurant was. Or at least that was what inns were now called. He had to be another time traveler and if she found out Mr. Merle had brought the guy here for her she'd have something to say about that. Molly had enough problems without dealing with some time traveling guy from merry old England. Great hair, sexy accent and toe curling kisses aside, she didn't need to be explaining his presence to anyone. So why did she plan to take him out to the coast instead of dropping him back and Treasures with instructions not to come knocking on her door again? It couldn't possibly be that kiss he'd planted on her lips yesterday. Nah. And she didn't hope for another one either.

"Terrific. Let me grab a shower and get dressed for real and we'll go."

"Of course."

She glanced over at the dishes. "Let me get these cleaned up first. I'm not a fan of scraping dried eggs and gunk off dishes after the fact."

Gareth stood. "I will wash them. You take a hold of your shower."

"Hold my . . . oh yeah, grab a shower . . . are you sure?"

"It is the least I can do."

"You're on. Be back in a flash."

She headed to her room and started to peel off her jeans, stopping just as they reached her hips. Nice as Gareth seemed she couldn't take any chances. Not that taking a total stranger, ax murder, serial killer who could kiss her senseless out to the coast alone added up to smart. After all Ted Bundy was purportedly a hottie. She quietly turned the lock on her bedroom door, followed by the bathroom door when she walked inside. A hot shower and teeth brushing later she stood looking in the bathroom mirror while she dried her hair. Hopefully he'd enjoy himself out on the coast. It'd been years since she'd gone herself. Molly'd meant to go time and again over the years. Something always seemed to come up or she didn't have the energy to go. Nuts or not, maybe knowing Gareth would be good for her.

She walked over to her dresser and pulled out a sweatshirt in case the weather turned chilly. She paused before closing the drawer thinking about Gareth showing up with just the clothes on his back. Not that he had planned to do anything after chatting with her. "We'll just swing by Treasures and he can pick up a jacket or whatever." She grabbed her fanny pack and headed back to the kitchen.

"Gareth?" She looked in the room and saw he'd left it neat as a pin. "Gareth?" Maybe he left, which would be just fine.

"In here, Molly." He called from what she and Carrie'd deemed the library.

Walking into the book lined room she saw him holding several of Carrie's paperbacks in his hands.

"Whatcha got there, Gareth?" Molly walked over to join him and almost choked. Yeah, she knew they were Carrie's paperbacks, but why did he have to pick up the most salacious ones her roommate had? Half naked men, women with flowing hair in total dishabille in compromising positions were not the kind of things you wanted to show to a new guy from the git go. His wide eyed look, those blue orbs of his near to popping out of their sockets told her he felt just about the same. "Ah, those are Carrie's. She's an avid reader, mostly of smut, ah, romance novels."

"Your people need books to tell them how to be romantic?"

"Not how to be. Well maybe. These look like her historical ones." Molly glanced at the books in his hands. "Yup, historical."

"Molly, this man wears a semblance of my garb, but I would never walk about thusly. And the woman! A light skirt to be sure. Why would your women wish to be thought of as — as — as, well thusly?"

"Now those are good questions. I can't say I've ever read any of these. Not my kind of book. Carrie devoured them, reading three or four a week and she'd fill me in on what they were about. From what I understand the authors spent hours and hours on research, making sure the language is correct and at least in the writing the way they describe the clothing is spot on. They just make the covers hot to entice readers to buy them."

He held up one that depicted a man with long, dark hair,

amazing green eyes, magnificent chest bare and from the waist down a few discretely placed leaves covered his privates. "This is enticing?"

Molly studied the guy on the cover and she had to admit, the title *His Eyes*, definitely went with the vivid green of the guy's orbs. His chest was certainly an eye catcher. Would she want to get up close and personal with him? Sure. Definitely. What red-blooded woman wouldn't?

"Molly? Does he entice you?"

She glanced up, quickly. "Nooo. Not really. More likely than not the picture is air brushed, he probably shaves his chest and is gay."

"What is wrong with a man being happy?"

"Right. No. He's cute, but not my type."

"But he appeals to other women?"

"Sure. They wouldn't have him on book covers if he didn't."

"He's on other books?"

"Probably. Modeling is big business. Anyway, we should get going. Do you want to stop by Treasures and pick up a jacket or anything?"

"It turns cold there?"

"It can. Besides, we should tell your uncle you've got plans for the day."

"I see. Then we shall stop."

"Fine. Let's grab some picnic stuff and head on out." They walked into the kitchen where Molly pulled a picnic hamper out of the pantry and then packed it with cold cuts, bread and drinks. Snagging some plastic utensils and napkins they were ready to go. Without a word Gareth followed her out to her car and sat quietly while they drove toward Treasures. A few minutes later she pulled in front and Gareth jumped out.

"I will tell Merlin what we are about. You will wait for me, yes?"

"Of course. It wouldn't be any fun without you."

A few minutes later Gareth strode from the store, a heavy sheepskin jacket and sweatshirt in hand. Mr. Merle hurried out behind him.

"Molly, good morning."

"Hi, Mr. Merle."

"Gareth says you are going out to the coast. Are you certain you want to do this?"

"Sure. I've been wanting to go and playing tour guide to take him is a great excuse to go."

"Well call me if you have any problems."

"We'll be fine. I promise to return him in one piece. He told you we're going to have dinner out there, right?"

"Yes. I'll leave a light on in case it turns out to be a late evening."

Gareth climbed in the car and together they waved good-bye to the elderly gent.

They'd just turned on to Route 121 when Molly told Gareth, "Here's a cheap thrill for you. I can show you the route I take to work in Miwok and we can head out to Pt. Reyes going through there. We won't stop, but I can show you police department headquarters where I work."

"That sounds good, Molly. Your Napa is a pretty village now that I finally see some of it."

"Hasn't Mr. Merle shown you around? Gees, you've been here what? Two weeks? Hasn't he taken you anywhere?"

"No. We spend our days in his shop."

"Wow. You'd think he'd be taking you all over the place. I can't believe you'd come all the way here from England to just sit around in that store with all that old stuff. I know he can be busy, but just a few months ago he went on a vacation for two weeks or so and he could certainly close down for an afternoon and take you up to Sattui's or into the City for dinner or something. I bet you'd love a bay cruise. Maybe we can do

Regan Taylor

that sometime. How long are you here for?"

"Indefinitely."

"Oh. You're thinking of moving here?"

"Maybe."

"Then if you want, if you have a good time today, maybe we can go into the City next week and do a dinner cruise on the bay or something." *What am I thinking? I don't know this guy from Adam. He could be a serial killer or an escapee from a mental hospital or might just not want anything to do with me. Maybe I have serial killers on the brain. What if he thinks I'm coming on to him and it turns him off? But then he was the one who kissed me, right?*

"That sounds most appealing, Molly. Yes, let us plan on this cruise."

"What?"

"The cruise, I would like to go."

Holy Moly, a cruise . . . moonlight, romance, kisses. From an ax murderer. Right. Well if I make it home tonight I'll know for sure whether or not he's a slice and dice kind of guy. "Fantastic. I'll look into the tickets or whatever."

The way he said it sounded almost as if he had no idea what she was talking about. Then again, what did she really know about cruising on the bay? Carrie never planned a trek out there so it never entered Molly's radar. What she wouldn't give right now to have her friend there to give her some direction what to do with Gareth.

"The fields remind me a bit of my home," Gareth told her as they drove along past the famed Napa vineyards.

"Do they? I've always found it relaxing to drive this route. There's another way into Miwok, but it usually has more cars and isn't as pretty. Driving 121 gives me a chance to let my mind drift a bit and coming home from work, even though it's dark at three-thirty in the morning, there's a kind of peaceful out here that let's me shake off the tension from my job."

"I understand. Many is the time I would mount my horse

118

and give him his head, letting him decide what direction we needs go. Often times the machinations of my family, the conflicting demands, made my head ache. My mother, with her continual questing for power, my brothers as well as myself now and again falling into her intrigues, power hungry outsiders vying for my king's ear, plotting within the court to discredit the queen are but a few of the things that would make my head spin. Riding out, alone, would give me the peace that I thirsted for."

Molly wasn't quite sure how to respond to that. The guy still held to his belief that he was part of the Arthurian drama, yet much of what he said made perfect sense. How could he be lucid one moment and delusional the next? Making a mental note to pull some of the abnormal psych books they had at work out for a look see when she went back to work she addressed the rational side of Gareth's arguments. "I hadn't thought about horseback riding out here. Gees, I haven't ridden since high school. That does sound like fun though. Say! If I remember correctly, they have some stables out in Pt. Reyes. Maybe we can rent some horses. They don't let you gallop along the water or anything like that, but we can still ride. How does that sound?"

"Wonderful. Tis been too long since I have ridden."

Molly smiled to herself, pleased she'd come up with the idea to go riding on her own. It was all her own plan. Maybe she could do this romantic, dating thing after all. Gareth's sharp, indrawn breath brought her mind back into the car. "Gareth? Are you okay?"

"Y-yes. I never thought carts could move so quickly. The land seems to blur as we fly past it."

"Uh huh. I'm only going fifty-five. I can't really slow down much because we have to keep up with the flow of traffic."

One hand grasped the arm rest of his door, the other, white knuckled, gripped his thigh. Fortunately the distance from where they pulled on to Route 37 to where they headed into downtown Miwok didn't take long to travel. Instead of taking the exchange to the 101 which would have kept them on the freeway longer, Molly took the first exit which would take them through a residential portion of Miwok. From the corner of her eye she noticed Gareth visibly relaxed and began to breath normally.

"Welcome to Miwok," she told him.

"Thank you. It looks a bit different than Napa."

"Mmm, yeah, Napa's older. We have a lot of Victorians. Miwok has mostly modern houses. Not that they're modern like built in the past twenty years or so, just not as old as Napa's."

"It seems your people like to live close by each other."

"I'm not sure it's a choice. When you have a lot of people wanting to live in one area and there's only so much space, you make do. I guess you never lived in a city in England."

"I suppose our castles are like your cities."

They stopped at a four-way stop and spotted a patrol car prompting Molly to wave, "One of Miwok's finest. They're at shift change. If you look down there you can see the flag on top of the police station."

"You do not wish to show me your work?"

"I could drive by, but I don't want to go in. Julie's there during the week and I'd rather not wreck my weekend by seeing her."

"Another time then."

"Sure. Miwok's an interesting city. They've got a few big office buildings, a lot of suburban housing and then, just a mile or so from downtown you run into a totally rural area. While Napa has all those wineries, Miwok has dairy farms. It's a nice little town. Actually it's a city, but it has a small town atmosphere to it. If I hadn't been born, raised and loved my home in Napa I'd live here. Even working for the police department, I'd live here."

"What would be so wrong to live where you work?"

"It's not so much living where you work as much as the police thing. People don't come into the station because they're having a good day. No one calls to say 'hey guess what happened to me' and have good news to share. And we aren't popular with the criminal element. If you are dumb enough to commit a crime, you aren't the sharpest crayon in the pack when it comes to expressing yourself to the police. I've been threatened any number of times just because I work there."

He shifted in his seat to face her, "Someone told you they would do you harm?"

"Not like they were going to kill me or anything like that. Well one or two suspects did, but they were either drunk or high on something. But you arrest someone or tow their car they will focus on the first person they see or speak to. That would be us women in Records. So living here where you are dealing with people at work in a not happy situation can be a bit difficult. And I do like living in Napa."

Just then they crested a small rise. Molly slowed the car to safely take a curve and Gareth drew in a sharp breath.

"You all right, Gareth?"

"Yes. That was a sound of delight. *This* is very much what my home looked like. You see that lake there?"

"Uh huh, Stafford Lake. We have festivals and such out there during the year. Pretty, isn't it?"

"It reminds me of an inlet where we fished as boys."

"In England?"

"The Orkneys, yes."

Molly slowed the car a bit more so they twosome could enjoy the rolling hills. With their myriad shades of green interspersed with browns and clumps of bushes and low growing trees it was as they'd left one world and entered another.

"Amazing, isn't it," she told him, "you drive over one little hill and poof you are in another world."

"Is this Merlin's magic or one your people share with him?"

"No magic. Sorry. Same planet, same city, different area. That's what I like about Miwok. It's pretty suburban in areas, almost bordering on urban and then you have this whole rural area. Something for everyone I guess."

"While in my village we do not have your metal vehicles, your cars, our cities and farmlands are much like yours." He considered his words and muttered, "Or they were. Do the people out here sleep in caves?"

"Caves?" Molly chuckled, "No. Houses. Unless someone's homeless they pretty much live in houses or apartments, condos and such."

"Then your homeless live in caves?"

"Cave dwelling isn't seen too much these days. At least not in the U.S."

She brought the car to a stop at an intersection, looked both ways and turned to the left. They passed a firehouse a bit before turning into a series of buildings called The Cheese Factory. "This is one of my favorite places."

"This?"

"The Cheese Factory. It was started in 1865 and is one of the oldest continually operating cheese factories in the United States."

"The grounds remind me of the fairs from home."

"I like it cause you can have an impromptu picnic lunch by the lake. When you get out this way it seems like you're miles and miles from home, or Miwok but it's like fifteen minutes. What say we pick up some cheese and bread and have a little snack before we head out to the lighthouse?"

Inside the small shop Gareth looked over the assortment of cheese, commenting to Molly he didn't know there were so many choices. With some rosemary flat bread and a few selections of cheese they found a picnic table near the lake and sat and ate in companionable silence. When a few geese approached Molly fed them some of the flat bread.

"It seems you have made friends and they have invited their friends," Gareth smiled as he whispered to her so as not to disturb the birds.

They snacks finished the pair headed back to the car.

They'd gone only a few miles with neither speaking until Molly glanced over to her passenger. Gareth gazed out the window, azure eyes framed by dark tawny lashes open wide as he took in the passing scenery. For a moment Molly was taken back to Black Eagle's first time in a car and how the vehicle terrified him. Gareth, however, seemed perfectly at ease in her old Jeep CJ-7. She chanced a look at his hands and took in the soft blond hairs covering the upper side. He had strong hands with tiny scars crisscrossing here and there. There was no doubt he was a man who worked with his hands. Sensing her study of him Gareth turned with a small smile on his face. "Tis lovely country, Molly."

"It is, isn't it? Does it still remind you of your home?"

"Yes, it does, especially the cows, only we have more. I wonder though, where are the people?"

"What do you mean?"

"At home, this time of day, people would be about, heading to the market, to their chores."

"I guess most every one's already at work. Farming's a lot different than years ago. I guess in the valley they're more labor intensive, but not up this way. There's a cut out a bit up the road, want to stop and get out and walk around?"

"Yes, I would like that."

A moment later Molly pulled into the cut out behind another car. It appeared they had stopped to let their dog, a large yellow lab, out to take care of its business and have a quick run. Molly inhaled deeply and savored the salty sea air. The slight tang electrifying her senses, somehow making the ocean seem bluer, the wave caps whiter and the air crisper. When the breeze shifted ever so slightly the scent of the cows carried over the low rise near where they had pulled over.

"Know what I love about this?" Molly turned to Gareth, arms wrapped around her waist as if to shelter herself from the lightly blowing breeze?

"What?"

"It's energizing. I feel so alive out here, especially when the wind picks up and you've got to almost fight against it to move."

"I too find the air invigorating. It makes me want to mount my horse and ride for hours on end."

"So is the ocean like yours from home?"

Gareth looked out at the waves undulating back and forth against the dark brown beach. "The power of it, yes. At home though it was a deeper green. More like dark emeralds."

They stood, watching nature at its best a few moments more and then climbed back in the Jeep to continue the journey out to the lighthouse. "We're getting close," Molly told him not too long after.

"You remember the way?"

"Sort of. There's signs and the road is narrowing. It's hard to maintain the road with the ocean spray and salt."

He didn't seem the least bit afraid. Absorbed in the landscape and the rolling fields and hills they passed, yes. Maybe a teeny bit awed, but definitely not afraid.

Sensing her perusal he turned to her, a small smile playing on his lips. "Tis a beautiful country you have, Molly."

"Thank you. I've heard the English countryside is positively gorgeous."

"It is. Have you ever been?"

"No, maybe some day I will. Carrie was the adventurous

one. Every year for vacations she'd come up with another great place to go."

"Gawain is the wanderer from my family. Sometimes I think if he had not made the decision to go to court none of us would have ventured there. Instead we would have grown old in the Orkneys and never know the evil that can happen in the world. Not that our home was without evil."

"Bad things happened?"

"When you mother is a witch, all manner of things you do not particularly like, can happen."

"You don't mean she flew around on a broom stick wearing a pointy hat?"

He shot her a look that clearly conveyed he thought her mind had been bent. "No. She did not fly although she could seem to disappear for a bit. Not like Merlin or Vivienne. My mother never learned their skill to move from place to place . . . what?"

"You're slipping into your play acting role."

Gareth shook his head, the light blond of his hair like yellow gold caressing his shoulders. "As my uncle said, I am most passionate about my acting. To answer you, no, my mother did not fly."

Molly slowed to take a curve a few feet before metal strips laid cross-wise in the pavement.

"What is wrong with the road?"

"Wrong? On the metal, it's for cattle, or to keep the cattle from going into the street. See there?" She pointed off to the side where several black and white cows lazed in the sun. "They lay there like they're all warm and grabbing a tan, but judging from the wind blowing I bet it's pretty chilly out there."

"We must be nearing the ocean. There is less fog and the water appears a darker blue."

"Not as blue as your eyes." She gasped and brought her

hand to her mouth.

"You think not? Molly! Why do you blush?"

"Because that's not the kind of thing you say to a guy you just met. It sounded like a come on."

"Come on?"

"Like I was flirting with you. I wasn't. Not that you aren't cute, actually really handsome and I'm sure women flirt with you all the time and . . ."

"Molly, the road." He said it calm enough, but his voice held a note of order.

"Oh shit." She steered the car back on to her side of the road. "Man, I'm sorry. I can't believe it."

"That you moved to the other side of the road?"

"No, that I said shit in front of you. Gareth, believe me, I don't say stuff like that."

"I am familiar with the word."

"Yeah, but you don't say it to a guy you're in—well that you're trying to show around."

"Were you about to tell me you would like me to court you, Molly?"

Dang, he was direct if nothing else, direct and single-minded when it came to his penchant for talking about his re-enactment business. She cleared her throat. "We're almost there."

She slowed as the roadway narrowed to one way. They pulled into the parking lot and Molly chose a spot that over-looked a path that appeared to lead down to the ocean. She fumbled in the glove box, taking care not to rub against Gareth's legs although the way he filled out those jeans had her wanting to do more than stroke her hand along his thighs, preferably sans the pants. From the depths of the glove box she pulled out a hair clip and quickly secured her long brown hair. From the cargo area she pulled out their sweatshirts and handed Gareth his. "It gets a little chilly out here."

It certainly came as a surprise when her mouth went totally dry at merely the sight of a narrow strip of skin between the top of his jeans and the bottom of his form fitting t-shirt. The man had at least one pack and she'd bet he was a full six under that t-shirt. The urge to bend over and flick her tongue along his waist almost blew whatever common sense she had. Almost.

"The bluster reminds me of home. I tell you, Molly, this Point Reyes is very much like my home in the Orkneys."

"It is pretty out here. Sometimes I forget just how wild and untamed it can seem. How beautiful it is, but I don't think I could handle the wind and cold on a daily basis. How did you manage? Or was it only sometimes this windy?"

"Pretty much so. We could hear the banshees scream there as well."

"Banshees? What do you mean? Aren't they like fictional?"

Gareth stopped, cocked his head and after a moment nodded. "There, do you hear them?"

Molly listened a moment and shook her head, "That's just the wind."

"The wind? No. Tis a siren's song. Don't you hear it?"

"That kind of high pitched roaring sound?"

"Yes."

"It's the wind, Gareth. Just the wind. See — " She took him by the arm and led him toward a guardrail at the overlook. " . . . how the shoreline curves in, making a little cove?"

He nodded.

"Well when the wind gets in there and it's blowing really hard like it is now, it makes that howling sound. There's no evil being out there waiting for some unsuspecting soul to land in its path and drag it off to some hellish place."

Gareth studied the coast line a bit before nodding. "I see what you mean."

"So you're okay, right? We don't need to leave or

anything?"

He smiled, that sweet smile that made him seem so innocent, "We do not need to leave. Show me your lighthouse."

They started up the path and had only gone a few steps before Molly stopped and pointed. "See it?"

"A fox."

"Yeah, isn't it cute? Oh look, he's posing."

"Posing?"

"Like for a picture. See how he's standing there? I bet he's so used to people coming up here he isn't afraid of us anymore and just sits and watches life go by. He probably thinks people come up here for his personal entertainment."

His smile broadened, showing pearly white teeth. "There is much about this time that is curious."

Molly opted to ignore that statement.

By unspoken agreement they continued up the dirt path. With heads bent they all but fought the wind as they continued up the low rise. When a particularly hefty gust blew down the hill without thought Molly turned toward Gareth at the exact moment he reached around her, pulling her into his embrace. It felt right to be nestled against his big brawny body. He brought with him a sense of safety and security. Not that Molly ever felt threatened. She simply felt a sense of coming home in his embrace. A little voice told her she belonged there in the shelter of his arms and found she liked the sound of that voice. That was something new and different. For some reason she felt as if she'd known Gareth a long, long time.

When another gust of wind blew its way down the hill Molly reached around to take hold of Gareth's waist. In their side by side walking embrace they made their way up to the hill's crest. Several other people made their way up around the couple, some smiling in greeting, others in their own little world. They stopped for a few minutes at the visitor's center and peered inside. "Let's check it out later. I want to be sure we see the lighthouse before it gets too dark."

At the very top of the summit they passed a corral like area with a number of encased placards. Beyond stood a fence with a sign board advising that there were one hundred and thirty steps down to the lighthouse, covering about a three story climb along with a caveat that before someone undertook the walk down the stone steps they needed to be certain they could make it down and back. Arm in arm they made their way down and spent almost an hour looking out over the ocean, spotting a few seals basking on the rocks and spying what Molly was fairly certain was a whale's spout.

Standing there looking out at the ocean Molly found herself absorbed in its breathtaking beauty. The myriad shades of greens, blues and white capped waves undulating beneath them were hypnotic. Beside her Gareth quietly described his home in the Orkneys and how he enjoyed walking along the shore, watching the gulls fly not all that different from what they saw here in Pt. Reyes. He didn't speak like a know-in-all or condescending the way Vincent did when they'd go somewhere. It wasn't until they broke up or rather he dumped her that she realized how boring the may really was. In truth, he did her a favor.

Gareth spoke with her, shared parts of himself and made her feel special with his little quips about his home and brothers.

Inside the lighthouse itself they had an up close view of the large Fresnel lens that cast its beam out on the ocean warning ships of their proximity to land. A particularly chilling gust of wind whipped through and without thought Molly stepped closer to Gareth. Without hesitating he pulled her into his arms and looked down at her. She half expected to see him smile, but instead he stared into her eyes as if memorizing every detail of her face. Never before had a man looked at her with such longing and it shot right through to her groin. She had a vague awareness of licking her lower lip just before Gareth bent to kiss her. There was a slight taste of salty sea spray in the kiss that enveloped her with warmth. He tasted of salt and sea and man and nothing could prevent Molly from tangling her fingers in his hair. Thoughts of pulling off his clothes or at least dragging down his pants and having her way with him tickled at the edge of her consciousness. She was just about to tell herself that such thoughts were highly improper when someone behind her cleared their throat. *Oh shit.*

"You're welcome to take that up top if you like, but right now we need to close off the stairs since the wind's picked up." The park ranger smiled at them.

"The wind?" Molly couldn't believe how dimwitted she sounded.

"Yeah, when it blows over forty miles an hour we need to close off the stairs because the helicopter can't land in those kind of gusts."

"Helicopter? Why are you bringing a helicopter in?" Molly knew a bit about the conditions needed for landing one from her job at the police department. They'd been brought in to pick up medical transports pretty much at least once a month since Molly had been with the department. She looked around, "Is there an emergency? I'm EMT certified if someone needs help till it lands."

"Oh no, sorry. We're not landing one right now. What I meant is that if there is a medical emergency the helo can't land in over forty mile an hour winds so as a precaution, if they blow harder than that, we close off the lighthouse."

"I see. How hard are they blowing?"

"Before I headed down it was at forty-three miles and hour."

"Dang. No wonder we had to work to get down the stairs."

They were almost half way back up the stairs before Gareth

asked what the ranger meant.

"If they need to bring in a helicopter they can't if . . ."

"I understood that, Molly. What is a helicopter?"

CHAPTER FIFTEEN

"You're kidding, right?"

"Kidding?"

"Making a joke about not knowing what a helicopter is. Slipping into your play acting thing, right?"

He nodded but she couldn't miss the confusion in his eyes. Despite his size and the roughness of his hands, there was something so vulnerable and endearing about him. Something that made her want to put her arms around him and protect him while at the same time, Molly wanted to feel his arms around her, holding her close and promising to never let her go.

Neither spoke the rest of the way up the stairs. After spending a few minutes going through the visitor's center they headed back to the Jeep. Driving out of the area a pair of deer crossed the path and stopped in front of the Jeep. Gareth leaned forward in his seat, "If only I had my bow."

"Your bow? What for?"

He looked at Molly like she had two heads, "Tis not often dinner walks up to you."

"Eeeuuuu. You wouldn't kill Bambi, would you?"

"Bambi?"

Before she could answer one of the cows who'd been lolling in the field beside the road ambled over and nudged the window with her nose. Molly giggled. "Check it out, Bessie wants to know what we're doing."

"Bessie?"

"Yeah, you know how they call cows Bessie. She must be

friends with the deer girls," Molly burst out laughing, "talk about a three way."

His brow furrowed brow, Gareth shook his head.

"Well that's good to know. I wouldn't want to have one myself but some people like them."

"You don't mean to share!"

"Don't tell me people in England don't have them. Man, I can't believe myself. I've never spouted out such crap to anyone before. What am I thinking?"

"I don't know, but the deer have moved. This might be a good time to continue."

Glad for the rescue, Molly put the Jeep in gear and slowly edged away from the animals. If that oddball exchange didn't blow things with Gareth nothing would. It occurred to her she'd never before made such corny sex-laced statements. Innuendo wasn't exactly her strong suit. If nothing else Gareth whatever-his-last-name-was brought out the lascivious side of her.

They retraced their way out from lighthouse and Molly opted to take the Shoreline Highway back inland instead of going back through Miwok. Driving along the coastal road, sometimes close enough to the ocean that at high tide it would lap at the roadway, the couple enjoyed glimpses of the various area wildlife.

Molly pointed out the quaint village of Olema and a campground she'd camped in years before. At the sound of a loud rumble from Gareth's stomach she decided the time had come to check out the Pelican Inn, a restaurant she'd wanted to eat at for a number of years but never took the time to go to. Carefully navigating her way down the mountainous highway Molly commented that the guardrails didn't look like they'd do much to stop a car from barreling down the sheer cliffs to the side of the road. Gareth swallowed but said nothing. The only evidence of how he felt was how he gripped the side of his seat to the point his knuckles were almost pure white.

A short while later they pulled into the Pelican Inn parking lot and headed inside where they were greeted by the soft sounds of a mandolin playing and the crackle of a roaring fire. The hostess seated them beside a fireplace that stood tall enough for even Gareth to stand in and brought some fresh baked bread along with a crock of fresh churned butter. They looked over the selections before deciding on the Shepherds pie. For dessert they shared a seriously large helping of trifle.

Over dinner Molly told him, "You know, I forget how pretty it is out there." Molly told him.

"Why?"

"Because I don't come out that often. In fact, it's been a few years. It's one of those things you always plan to do but somehow life gets in the way. There's always something else going on or to do. Before you know it, life has passed you by and you haven't done what you planned to."

"Maybe it is time to start doing the things you have always meant to do."

"You say that like there are things you missed out on and now you regret it."

Gareth sighed and a faraway look with a glimmer of remorse or sadness entered his eyes. He gripped the edge of the table as if needing to have contact with something tangible. For a time it seemed as if he wouldn't speak or, in truth, had nothing to say. When words did come, Molly heard a slight crackling in his voice.

"I would have liked more time with my brothers, settled down with a wife, had children. I would have tried to learn more from my mother so that I could use her knowledge for good."

"Being wedded to a career will do that to you. I've seen it with the police officers at work. We get short-staffed. Actually most police departments are short staffed and you can't just go out and hire a bunch of new cops. They have to go through a background, a psych evaluation, medical check out and then get trained. Anywhere along the way they can be told it won't work. Once they're on the street between their hours and the types of calls they respond to things can get squirrely."

"What do you mean?"

"Schedules are always changing. You pick your shift by seniority so the longer you've been there, the better your chances of when you'll work. Newbies get whatever is left at the end. A lot of officers pick their shifts to avoid a certain sergeant or dispatcher. I know I'd pick mine to avoid the Red Queen if I could. Actually my schedule works out just fine because the two women who are more senior than me like, in fact they insist, on having weekends off as well as wanting nights at home so they pick the day shifts during the week. If they started to pick the night or weekend shifts I'd be screwed because I'd have to be there when ole Jules is. But a new officer, bottom of the barrel. A lot of them are pretty happy at first if they end up on Kris' shift because early on they learn she's an easy lay and they figure getting some on the side isn't a bad deal. What they don't know is she has the gift that keeps on giving and . . ."

"You spoke of this Kris before. What is this gift she gives?"

"You've never heard that?"

He shook his head no.

"Herpes. You know, you get it and it goes dormant and then when you least expect it or at the most inconvenient time, bam, there it is. And if you sleep with someone when it's active, well you've just shared it. Then they sleep with someone and they pass it on and so on and so on. That's what Kris has done for about two-thirds of the men in the department and given them herpes. She's what we call a badge bunny."

"Badge Bunny?"

"Yeah, she hops from bed to bed and in her case passes her STD around."

"STD?"

"Sexually transmitted disease."

"Ah, the pox. You are certain?"

"Absolutely. A few Saturdays ago Becca, one of the other dispatchers was on with us and she came out to me to see if I had any antibiotics because the guy she's dating used to go out with Kris. Now the guy and Becca both have the gift. As if she didn't know it's illegal to share drugs like that."

"What did you do?"

"I told her no. I'm not about to get in trouble for someone I like let alone a bimbo badge bunny like old triple B herself, Kris."

"Then what happened?"

"I told Becca to tell whichever sucker fell for to get himself to his doctor ASAP and get checked out."

"And did he?"

"I have no idea. Trust me, hearing about other people's STDs is not high on my list of fun things to do."

Pleasingly satiated from their meal they headed on their way home.

CHAPTER SIXTEEN

"I suppose your uncle will be concerned we're not back yet."

"I am not ready to return."

"Well it's not like we can just pop into the shop like magic. We've got a bit of a drive to get back to Napa. I can understand him being concerned about you. After all, it's not like you know what's what around here, right? Even if he tweeted you on the goings on for months before you arrived, it's still a new place with new things."

"Tweet?"

"Yeah, Twitter, you know what Twitter is, right?"

"Yes. Of course. My uncle treats me like a child."

"I don't know as I'd say that. Course I'm not there with you twenty-four seven. From what I've seen though I'd say he's just more protective of you. Think about it, here you are, your first time in the states, right?"

"Yes."

"And unless I'm mistaken you come from a small town that didn't have many modern conveniences and such, right?"

"Yes."

"And not many cars either, right?"

"Yes."

"So if you were my cousin or nephew I'd be concerned you were all right. Stuff can happen. Sometimes bad stuff, like muggers. At the police department we take enough reports from tourists who are caught unaware, even in Miwok which is a pretty small town without a lot of crime. Anyway, I was thinking we'd take the coast route to get back. It will take a little longer to get to Napa, but it's a clear night and maybe you'd enjoy the view of the ocean with the moon over it, especially since it's almost full."

Gareth looked out the passenger side window and took in the bright white orb sitting over the dark ocean. "It is a lovely evening and I am in no hurry to return to my uncle's."

"Cool."

No, he was in no hurry to leave Molly's side. She was unlike any woman he'd known before. Then again, there was much to Merlin's modern world that was not like any thing he'd known before. But Lady Molly . . . she was kind, generous, she made him laugh, explained things to him and above all, kissing her felt like heaven. Kisses shared with other women were enjoyable, roused his manhood. Kissing Lady Molly filled him with a longing while at the same time filled his heart with completion. Twas as if she were a part of him only now returned to his soul. If this 2021 were to be his new home, surely Molly was a part of that home. Even with her other concerns, her missing friend, the evil Red Queen and the bunny, she still focused on him and what pleased him. Would the fates allow him time to please her.

They drove in silence for several miles without encountering any other cars on the road. As the moon rose higher over the ocean it lent a mystical quality to the night. Molly tried to think of the last time she'd driven and enjoyed the passing scenery even if it was in the dark. Go, go, go summed up her life. If it weren't for Carrie she'd never would have seen the things she did, done the things she had. Spending the day with Gareth, seeing coast through his eyes gave her a new appreciation for how much she'd missed out on. She cleared her throat, drawing the blond haired man's attention.

"I had a thought."

He shifted in his seat to look at her. "Yes?"

"Do you have any plans tomorrow?"

"No. Except to sit in Mer — my uncle's shop and see if he has anything for me to do."

"So no reason to rush home tonight and get up early?"

"No." In the dim light cast from the dashboard she saw his smile and it warmed her to her toes.

"Neither do I. I mean, I have a few things to do before I go back to work Friday, but nothing important or to rush to. Well I do need to wrap up the rest of Carrie's business, but that won't take all that long."

"What is it you wish to do, Molly?"

"I thought maybe we could drive over the Golden Gate bridge tonight. I haven't gone over it in a few years and even though you can't see much at night, the headlands and city at night are beautiful. Would you like to go that way?"

"Very much so. Yes. I want to see as much of your city as I can."

"Great. Listen, I know we've just met and it was a little rocky to begin with and I'm sorry about that. My life has been a little topsy turvy with my job and Carrie leaving and, and, well sometimes I just don't stop to see what I have in front of me."

"That's all right, Molly. I know how frenzied life can become."

"Whew. So like I mentioned earlier, next week, would you still like to do some sight seeing? If you'll still be here in California? I know we talked about doing on one of the bay cruises, but I'm thinking more. I have some vacation on the books. We can just see the sites up here."

"I have no plans to leave. I believe I will be staying here for a long time to come and yes, I would like to see your sights. When next week?"

"I work Friday through Monday so Tuesday? What do you want to see first?"

"It is your city. What do you recommend?"

"Hmmm. Let me think." She drummed her fingers on the steering wheel as she took the turn towards southbound 101 and the Golden Gate Bridge. "I know I mentioned the bay cruises. Um, hmmm, we'll be coming up on the headlands in a few minutes. If you look out your window when we get to the bridge I think you can see the lighthouse we were at. Actually, I don't know if it's that same one or another one but it's a sight to see."

She pulled into the slow lane and with few cars on the road slowed to barely a crawl so they could both enjoy the review. She snapped her fingers, "I've got it."

"Yes?"

"How does this sound. We'll start out with breakfast at the Cliffhouse. See those lights over there, way down on the coast?"

"Uh huh."

"That's Cliffhouse. They do a mean eggs Benedict, you like eggs Benedict, right?"

"Yes." Although from the way he pursed his lips she wondered if he knew what they were. No matter, he'd find out and hoped he'd like them.

"Then we'll come over here and walk across the bridge and then go over to Fisherman's Wharf. We can check out the shops, I've wanted to go to the wax museum forever and then in the afternoon, after lunch, we can take the Alcatraz tour. I heard it takes you out on part of the Bay tour and you get to hike around on the island. They did all this work on it a couple of years ago and apparently fixed up a visitors' center and have a great tour. If you're not too tired after that there are some things we can see in the city in the evening. Maybe catch dinner or something. Gees, I seem to spend a lot of time talking about food, don't I?"

"I like food. I like the food I've had here so far."

"Great. So what do you think? Does any of that appeal to you?"

He turned to look at her, the white of his teeth shining in the glow of the passing street lights, "Everything appeals to me."

"Good. I'll call for reservations and all tomorrow. Your uncle won't have any problem with it, will he?"

"No. He will think it wonderful to have me out from under foot for a day."

"Fantastic. This will be fun. I've wanted to go for a long time."

"Your city has many bridges," he observed when Molly pulled on to the Oakland Bay bridge.

"Seems that way until you go to New York. Carrie and I went there one time for a few days and they have 16 big bridges around Manhattan Island and something like two thousand bridges and tunnels in that area."

"New York? What was wrong with York that they needed to make it new?"

Molly chuckled, "That's funny."

"What is funny? That York needed to have something new?"

"York is in England, right?"

"Yes, the court is there."

"I guess. New York though is here, in the United States. When the first settlers came they named it after the city in England and called it New York."

"I see. Molly, is that your Gold Gate?" He pointed behind and to the left of them over the bay.

"Yup. I have an idea." She pulled off at the turn for Yerba Buena and drove under the Oakland Bay Bridge to pull on to Treasure Island and into a parking spot facing the bay and the

Golden Gate Bridge. "This is Treasure Island. Where we pulled off is called Yerba Buena which means good earth in Spanish. They built Treasure Island for the 1939 world's fair and instead of taking it down after they left it up. Over the years the military was here and now it's a multi-use area with housing and shops and such. And yes, that's the Golden Gate bridge. Isn't it and the city beautiful? There's something romantic about it. At least I think there is."

"Can we go outside and walk around?"

"That's a great idea. It'll be a little chilly, but yes, let's."

They left the warmth of the car and headed to the front and settled their butts on the hood. After a moment Gareth tentatively put his arm around Molly's shoulders and she leaned into him. "This is nice."

"Yes, it is."

The pair stood for several minutes and watched a few sailboats make their way past the island. The lonely call of a fog horn sounded off to the side. Gareth slid his hand up along Molly's shoulder and entwined his fingers in her hair. She turned to look up at him and surprised at her own actions, reached up to draw his head down for a kiss. His lips met hers and in short order they were lost in a kiss that curled Molly's toes. Long before she was ready for the kiss to end Gareth raised his head, "I see why they call this Treasure Island. Indeed I have found my treasure."

"Me too," she whispered. The play of headlights alerted them to the fact they weren't alone. "We should get going."

"All right."

Back inside the car, seatbelts buckled, Molly headed back out toward the Oakland Bay Bridge and the freeway that would take them to Napa. By unspoken, tacit agreement, neither spoke for a long while. Molly considered her actions. In the past twenty-four hours she'd moved faster in a relationship than she ever had before. Instead of it feeling cheap or uncomfortable it felt so very right. Maybe in his own way Gareth was her knight in shining armor. It wasn't until Molly took the turn that would take them into Napa she voiced what had been running through her mind. "Gareth, would you, that is, would you like to come back to my house for awhile? I know it's late and you're probably tired, but . . ."

"I'd like that, Molly. I am not ready for today to end."

"Great. I mean, I'm thinking coffee or hot chocolate. Nothing serious. Just something warm to drink and to, well, like talk. You know?"

She wasn't ready for the day to end either. For all Carrie's teasing, Molly didn't really up and sleep with any guy she happened to date. She certainly dated a lot and seemed to see a different guy every month or so. But she didn't share their beds and except for Vincent who she'd broken up with. Well actually he'd broken up with her because of her job issues.

Not that she was planning on having Gareth stay the night, although if he wanted to she was all over it. No, no she wasn't. If this was going to be a relationship she planned to take it slow and easy. And she wasn't going to bitch about her job. No how, no way was she going to lose another guy because her job sucked. She'd simply had a great time today and didn't want it to end. They'd have some coffee or hot chocolate and then she'd bring Gareth over to Treasures. Then she'd see if he'd call on her again.

On the other hand, if he asked to stay, well would he ask to out of a sense of obligation for her showing him around today? Or because he really wanted to go skin to skin with her? There was something to be said for the way they did things in the world Gareth said he came from. Dating these days sure was complicated.

Too soon she pulled into the driveway. She had more things to work out in her mind about just how far she'd go with Gareth. For some reason the simple act of the man taking her hand made her breath catch. It felt right to have her hand tucked into his larger, warmer one. When he smiled down at her for the first time in her life she felt petite and protected. At first she chided herself that came about only because of his re-enactment and renaissance faire activities. Then she reminded herself she deserved to feel desired and cared for. As Carrie used to tell her, these kinds of things wouldn't be in romance novels if they weren't real for someone or something someone wanted to happen for them. Molly'd just never thought of herself as romance novel material.

On the other hand, Gareth was right out of a love story. With his long blond hair, amazing sapphire blue eyes, sculpted body and warm personality he epitomized what Carrie would call a walking, talking romantic hero. At least for now he was Molly's hero.

They were only going to have a hot drink, relax for a few and then she would take him back to Treasures. Plain and simple. "Nice girls don't sleep with hot guys on the first date," she murmured.

"Pardon?"

"Huh?"

"I can understand why if a man is hot he would not need the body heat of another. This date, do you mean courtship?"

Molly chuckled, they were back to the play acting. "Yeah. Courtship. You don't sleep with a guy you're just starting to court with."

At the door with the porch light casting its soft glow over Gareth's features, Molly had to remind herself to breathe.

"Molly?"

"Hmm?"

"When do you sleep with that guy? How much courtship do your people require? Why is he hot? Is he ill?"

She turned the key in the lock and opened the door. Flicking on the kitchen light its warm glow flooded the room.

"Courtsh . . . sleep . . . ah, well that depends on the couple. And the hot part isn't like if you're cold or chilly. It means that you get hot looking at the other person."

"Then I will tell you, I have been hot thinking of you all day this day, Molly."

"Uh—"

Before she knew what happened he'd turned her to face him, lowered his lips to hers and he kissed her softly. His lips whispered across hers, a feathery light movement. For a long moment Molly felt suspended in time. Amid the sensual fog that caressed her, she had a vague awareness of Gareth drawing his arms around her, holding her close. The slow, steady beat of his heart pulsed against her chest as he bent to deepen the kiss. A little voice in the back of her mind admonished her to remove her hands from his deliciously tight butt. For some odd reason they didn't obey and instead those same hands continued exploring his posterior. Oh my his fanny sure felt good. What felt like perfectly rounded globes didn't exactly fit into her hands, but the tight curve of his ass sure felt right.

That same little voice told her to move away from his heavily muscled body. Her hips must have turned off their hearing mechanism because she realized her groin was rubbing sensuously against Gareth's. The hard ridge of his cock rose up hard between them but it was his moan of desire that made her permanently shush that annoying little voice. She held his one butt cheek tightly with one hand while with the other she threaded her fingers into his hair. Gareth returned the favor. The hard ridge of his desire against her belly spoke volumes more than his own soft moans of pleasure.

Her protest of irritation never made it quite the way through her lips when he broke off the kiss and gazed down at her a moment before telling her, "I needs stop this torment, Molly or I will ravish you on this very spot."

"If there's any ravishing to be done it'll be in my bed."

145

"Would you like to ravish me, Molly?"

"Oh yeah, majorly so." She paused, realizing just what she'd said. "Oh my God, I can't believe I said that! Man! Gareth, please don't think I'm like a floozy or loose or — we came for coffee, right?"

"I think you are a woman who knows her mind and does not fear to speak her desires. I would stay and make love to you Molly Nichols."

"Are you sure?"

Gareth laughed. His full-bodied, warm laugh that filled the room. He reached for her hand and brought it to his crotch. "Do you doubt it?"

Molly couldn't help herself. She laughed. "No, no doubt. Do you want something to drink or —"

"I want you, Molly, as soon as you will have me."

Her breath caught. No one she'd ever dated spoke quite like that before. Quite like that? Not even close. Even if they only had one night together it she knew to her toes it would be the best sex she'd ever had. She reached behind her and locked the back door then took his hand and led him out of the kitchen, turning out the light, before heading down the hallway to her room. She turned up the dimmer only enough to see her way to the matches and candles on her dresser and lit them one by one until the room glowed with the soft candlelight.

As if reading her mind Gareth turned off the shallow light. In two long strides he stood before her. "You are sure, Molly?"

"More than sure." So much for taking it slow. Heck, why not live for the moment? If he was one of Mr. Merle's time travelers he could pop out of her life as easily as he sauntered in. She'd never felt shy about unbuttoning a man's shirt before, after all, even though she hadn't been with that many guys it wasn't like she hadn't undressed a man before. Yet here with Gareth she felt so timid, as if she'd never been with a man before. He oozed sexual potency without even trying. Fingers trembling she managed to undo the buttons on his shirt. He, on the other hand, had hers undone in moments.

He backed her to the bed.

She toed off her shoes while he tugged apart the fly of her jeans. As she scooted back on the bed he kicked off his shoes and yanked down his jeans. Hot skin against hot skin he lay on top of her, capturing her head between his hands to hold her while he kissed her as if he were eating the most fabulous meal ever. Anticipation made her shiver. Molly ran her hands up over Gareth's shoulders, down his back, stopping momentarily to caress his shoulder blades and marvel at how perfectly they fit into the cupping of her palms. His muscles, taunt beneath her questing hands bunched and released sending a pool of moisture from her channel in welcome to the man lying on top of her.

Tentatively she allowed her hands to continue down the length of his torso, stopping again to cup his butt cheeks. She held pure satin covered muscle in her hands and couldn't hold back a chuckle of victory when he moaned in response to her touch. Her smile faded momentarily when he lifted his head, ending the hot kiss he'd been sharing with her, but the heat in his eyes told her that kiss was merely a prelude to what was yet to come.

"You like the feel of my body, Molly?"

"What's not to like," she managed, finding herself unable to keep her hips from shifting upward to rub against his groin.

He dipped his head, his gaze raking across her chest a second before he slid one of his hands down her neck, to her chest to rest lightly on her breast. A pulse, a second, a third light grasp of her breast before he traced the upper side of her lacey bra to the dip between her breasts. "Your corset doth not cover much."

She giggled, "No, it doth not."

Gareth rose up on his elbows enabling him to look down between their bodies. He dipped his head closer so he could lick along the lacey edge of the red brassier. Confusion momentarily crossed his brow.

"Is there something wrong?"

"Where art the ties that bind you?"

For some reason his tone, a blend of sheer desire and uncertainty sent another warm surge of liquid desire to her groin. "No ties, babe. Just this lit-tle ti-ny hook." She reached between them, making certain the backs of her hands slid across his chest and catching on his taunt nipples before reaching the hook that held her bra together. "Watch."

His eyes widened, a curious blend of desire and innocence, a combination that muddled Molly's senses, making her tread the fine line between blatant desire and a need to some how shield and protect this man. Not that he needed protecting, not in a physical sense. That much was obvious from his build and how he carried himself. No, this was a deeper need. Without a doubt this was a boyish charm that the man showed to few, if any others. Hands resting on the clasp she looked up into Gareth's face and saw a vulnerable younger man. She swallowed; maybe this wasn't the best idea.

When he squirmed just so, parting her legs so his hips nestled between her thighs, any thoughts that maybe this wasn't a good idea flew from Molly's mind. His hard penis strained at her channel letting her know the idea of removing her bra had all but left his mind.

"Like this . . ." she glanced down to the clasp and with slow deliberateness parted the two halves.

"Ah. I like this device." Gareth rasped before nuzzling against one breast and drawing the nipple of the other into his mouth. His tongue, warm, wet and softly sensual licked at her breast, drawing her nipple deep into his mouth and sucking just slightly short of pain, made her buck against him. The chuckled emitted from his throat was one of victory and male pleasure. When he raised his head, his smile was incongruent with the purity she saw in his eyes. The man certainly knew what he was doing when he lowered his head to the other breast. This time instead of merely concentrating on her breast, he shifted his hips so his groin rubbed against hers. Back and forth, up and down he rubbed against her mound.

At a loss for words Molly merely craned her neck so she could kiss his jawline, eliciting a sigh of pleasure from the blond haired man.

Without stopping the tortuous pulsing of his hips against hers, he lowered his head so his lips were but a breath away from her ears, "I must confess something to you, Molly."

Oh no, she thought, here it comes. He's either gay, married or he's got some awful disease. "W-w-what?"

"It must seem I fall into bed with any lady that comes my way. That is not so. While my body may respond quickly to any wench that passes my way, I would have you know I do not bed merely any who pass my way."

What did he just say? "Ah, you're telling me you aren't promiscuous?"

"Yes." His grin conveyed sheer joy that she understood.

Did he need to share that little tidbit now? Surprisingly his statement didn't end up a mood killer. Instead it made her want him more. Wow, who would equate an admission of celibacy, for lack of a better word, with a major turn on. "That's good."

"Yes?"

"Yeah, it means you understand that I'm pretty picky about who I share my bed with."

"And you do mean to share it with me, yes, Molly?"

"Oh yeah. Definitely." With a mental air punch Molly

turned her attention back to Gareth's lips which he was more than happy to share. She felt his hips shift ever so impercep- tibly, the tip of his penis a long, satin and steal shaft against her portal and thighs. Bit by excruciatingly slow bit, he slid into her. She'd thought she knew what a major panty splat was. Her body's response to Gareth showed her otherwise. The man knew not only how to turn on the charm in a major way. He knew how to play her body to bring her to heights she didn't know existed.

Suddenly he stopped. Mid-thrust he stopped. Just stopped.

Molly groaned in what she had no doubt sounded like ag- ony. "Gareth?"

"I don't want to hurt you, Molly."

"Hurt, hurt me?"

"I have been told I am a large man."

"Ah. Oh. I see. Trust me, I'll be fine. Just fine."

"You are certain?"

"Gareth, I'm so turned on by merely the thought of being up close, personal and naked with you that my body is more than ready."

"How could . . ."

Understanding dawned and she wasn't going to waste an- other minute wanting this man. She'd wanted him hot, hard and thrusting and not worried about breaching her maiden- head. It was sweet. Definitely sweet. It wasn't an issue. "I'm not a virgin, Gareth. Please, make me a happy woman."

"Not . . . happy."

She grabbed his butt cheeks and levered her hips up, draw- ing him deep inside. "Please, Gareth, I want you."

"Your wish is my command, my Lady."

He thrust into fully into her and sent ripples of pure pleas- ure through her entire body. Of their own volition her toes curled, her breath seemed to rip from her lungs and her legs wrapped tightly around his hips. Well not that tightly. The man could still pump long and hard into her. He let her set the pace and met her thrust for thrust, groaning his own pleasure when he climaxed a moment after her own shudderingly intense orgasm. They lay together, hearts beating in unison, legs entwined, arms slack yet not letting go.

Gareth's breathing had no sooner settled into an even pace before he asked, "Did I please you, Molly?"

She smiled against his shoulder, "Gareth, if you could bottle and sell what you have, we'd be billionaires. Pleased doesn't begin to describe how good I feel."

"Then perhaps you will wish to see more of me."

"Oh, trust me, I want to see *lots* more of you."

Chapter Seventeen

M olly woke to what she swore sounded like the tinkling of fairy bells, *if* fairies existed. From the safety of her bed, after all, she could duck under the covers right quick if someone appeared in her room, right? So why did it feel as if someone had been there? Someone besides Gareth that was.

Gareth? *Oh my God! I slept with Gareth whateverhislastname is! Holy hell.* She closed her eyes, tight, and listened. Yup, she clearly heard the soft, steady breathing of another person in her bed. Slitting her eyes open Molly confirmed Gareth was indeed sleeping, quite soundly in fact, beside her. Careful not to wake him she shifted ever so slightly to look at the blond haired man. Gorgeous didn't quite cover how he looked. His long blond hair, blue eyes and muscular build would send any woman his way. What made him extraordinary was how clear those sapphire colored eyes of his were coupled with a smile that somehow was an intoxicating combination of sexy predator and shy innocence. In sleep he looked pretty young, maybe early to mid-twenties which fit with the lack of artifice he exhibited. Yet that didn't jive with the aura of worldliness the popped out now and again. Gareth added up to a complex combination of a simple down home man and a sexually potent, worldly male.

Molly let her gaze trail down his body for the first time visually confirming that the bumps she felt here and there along his body were in fact scars. Some of them appeared fairly old, like the ones she had on her knees from falling on them countless times as a tomboy growing up in the Napa Valley. Most that she saw on him had jagged edges, almost as if he'd been cut by a rough edged knife. He wasn't stupid. That much was certain. But he didn't act like a college boy. Not that an education mattered.

Most of the cops she worked with had high school educations and maybe some college and on the whole they were good guys. Of course Kris did all of them.

Well at least all the straight ones and she certainly did her darnedest to get the gay guys into bed. On a few occasions she succeeded and while the guys snickered about her performance in bed, she said little. With her it was the idea of the notch in her vibrator, not the actual act that mattered. Giving the gay officers credit, even after a night in her bed or having her in their patrol car, not a one gave up his lifestyle.

With only a brief admonishment to herself that she shouldn't be thinking about other guys when she had Gareth beside her Molly couldn't stop her mind from drifting to a recent conversation the records staff had about Kris. Shannon had actually asked one of the lesbian females if Kris had ever made a pass at them. After Gwen stopped laughing long enough to come up for air she assured them no self-respecting woman, gay or straight, would be that desperate.

"Mmmmm," The man beside her sighed.

"Did I wake you?"

He blinked and turned ever so slightly to take in his surroundings. "Molly. I thought I dreamt I held you in my arms through the night."

"Are you sorry?"

"Sorry? While a dream of you tis most pleasing, having you beside me is more than I ever hoped for. I would wake beside you the rest of the days of my life."

Talk about living romance! "Well, you never know."

"I do. I knew the moment I first laid eyes on you, Molly, you were the woman I had waited my lifetime for. My brothers always said Gawain was the patient one. And that is so. Now I think perhaps because we all indulged him, as the youngest, he found it easy to wait for what he wanted because twas not a long wait. He had but to ask it he received. Being the youngest our mother fussed over him, until Mordred came to our home. Things changed after that and our mother did favor him. She said because he had no family and merely a fosterling with no home we needed to give him special care. We needed to make him feel wanted. Yet despite our best efforts he . . ."

"Mordred? His mother seriously named him Mordred? Like the guy who killed King Arthur?"

"One and the same, Molly."

"Gareth, I know you are totally into your re-enacting stuff, but this early in the morning?"

"Tis not a re-enacting, Molly. Tis what happened."

"Yeah, I know the story. King Arthur slept with his sister and got her pregnant. She had a son named Mordred which honestly, I do know it means something like fisherman or fisherman's son or something like that. They were going to kill him, but his sister, Morgan was it?"

"Morgause."

"Okay, Morgause, hid the baby away and had him raised somewhere else. When he got older, Morgause took him back and taught him to hate Arthur so he got pissed off and went and killed him. Only Arthur didn't really die, Merlin took him to Avalon and he's sleeping until the world needs him again. It's all a really cool legend, but don't you think that the world got itself screwed up enough times before all this to need King Arthur to come back and set it right?"

"You have an idea of what is right, Molly. And the legend does say when the world has its greatest need for us, we will wake. Twas not Avalon, but Glastonbury Tor, where he slumbers. It would seem that time of need is now since I have awoken."

Lightly she pushed against him. "Gareth, you don't have to play the knight in shining armor for me. Seriously. I'm hooked. I like you, or at least the you that's present in the here and now. You don't have to do the courtly play acting thing for me."

He studied her a moment. For a second a looked flashed in his eyes just before something clicked into place. He lowered his lips towards hers, "But you will play with me, yes?"

Molly smiled and shimmied closer to him. "Oh we'll play. Definitely we'll play. Let's see what comes up, huh?"

She didn't need to wait long to see just what did come up.

CHAPTER EIGHTEEN

A shard of sunlight spilling into the room woke Gareth a few hours later. Checking quickly to see if the bright light had also woken Molly he was pleased it had not. Now he could have some time to look at her, to revel in her beauty, without her knowing he did so. He'd met and known many beautiful women. In most of them, the beauty shined only on their faces. It did not reach into their hearts the way Molly's did. Unlike women of his time, she spoke directly. She did not seem to resort to artifice and merely stated what she believed and felt.

Yet for as honest as she spoke, she did not credit him with the same honesty. It seemed a bit unfair that she could speak to him of her friend, Carrie, and her journey back in time yet did not believe Gareth that he fought beside Arthur, the greatest warrior and king of all time.

He glanced over at the woman sleeping beside him and resisted the temptation to tuck the strand of hair that caressed her cheek. The last time he did that the woman woke and there went his chance to merely sit and watch her in the silence of that long ago morning. Thinking of that lady led him to thoughts of the others, mostly his brothers. Say what you would about Morgause, she loved her sons, all of them. True, she favored Mordred. Twas not out of love rather her partiality rose from the power she thought the son she shared with Arthur would bring. How wrong she was, about Mordred anyway. About having her sons bond together, she did right by them there. They played together, fought together and met their end together. At least it seemed that way. Didn't they all fall into the long, deep slumber at the same time?

From where he lay beside Molly Gareth looked out the window and the growing morning light. That day so long ago sat fresh in his mind as if it were but yesterday. He supposed in a manner of speaking it was yesterday for him. Well, not yesterday, but a few weeks past.

The fighting had been brutal. The air stank of blood and dirt and vomit. Men screamed in pain and cried at their last breath. Then, in the middle of the field, all saw Arthur and Mordred. The silence when they foisted their mortal blows a deafening roar. As Arthur fell to his knees, cradling Mordred's head, Merlin wove his way through the dusty air. Yet there was something amiss with the dust that swirled around the threesome. With Merlin came a dense vapor. Not a fog or mist. No, this miasma enveloped them, surrounding them with a cocooning warmth rather than the cold chill of fog. They trailed Merlin to the edge of the water and watched the wizard lift his precious burden into a barge and as they sailed toward Avalon. One by one the knights curled upon the ground and fell into a deep sleep. Unafraid Gareth curled up beside them only to wake not so many days past to find himself in standing in what he soon learned was Merlin's kitchen in this future time. When Merlin could not explain to him how he came to be there Gareth turned to Vivienne. She had no answer for him either. All the magical pair seemed to know was Gareth, and only Gareth, had woken.

Actually they knew a bit more, or so it seemed they did. Vivienne believed that somehow when Merlin brought the man, Black Eagle, to the present time he disturbed something called a continuum and somehow what the wizard referred to as electrifying Excalibur. The knights had been told the sword had been returned to the Lady of the Lake but it seemed Merlin kept it beside him all these years. Gareth had seen it himself when day after day the sword seemed to grow a bit brighter. Neither Merlin nor Vivienne could or would tell him if his brothers or the other knights would wake. With certainty Merlin said no, no one else would wake because if they were going to, it would have already happened. Vivienne insisted the old man had no idea whether the others would wake or not.

After all, she pointed out, it wasn't as if this sort of thing happened before. Gareth felt certain she probably had a better idea of where things stood than Merlin. That, however, remained to be seen. All Gareth knew for certain was he wished his brothers were here. If they were, even if it was only one of them, he wouldn't feel so alone. Vivienne and Merlin gave the best advice they could. It wasn't the same as sitting and talking with his brothers. What made things harder was that he couldn't really talk to anyone about them. Merlin and Vivienne treated any discussion of his brothers with suspicion. They acted as if he spoke of them Gehris, Aggravain and Gawain would wake and join him. And Mordred too he supposed and that probably wouldn't be such a good thing. Who knew what havoc the brooding brat would cause? And Molly, well every time he tried to talk about his family her eyes glazed and she looked at him the way one looked at a simpleton. It made no sense. She believed her friend traveled back in time. Why couldn't she believe he'd been asleep almost two centuries?

Molly stirred beside him. Her eye lids fluttered open and she smiled as if she had a special secret to share. "You're here."

"I am."

"You're really here. You didn't leave." She whispered.

"No. Should I have?"

She ignored his question, "And you aren't a dream."

"No. No dream. Should I be?"

She considered that. "No. I like the idea of you being a living, breathing man. And I really like the idea of waking up next to you. Is that way too forward of me?"

"I was just thinking how much I enjoy your forthrightness."

"You do?"

He nodded. "It is refreshing. Too many women hide behind words they do not mean or words with many meanings. I like that you are plain spoken."

"It's a lot easier to be honest. You don't have to remember what you told who."

"Would you like to know what else I discovered I like, Molly?"

She shifted and absently reached for a strand of his hair and entwined it in her fingers. Her gaze was warm and welcoming. "What?"

"Waking up beside you."

"Really? I bet I know what you'd like even more."

"What?"

"Well I can't say I know you'd like it more but I know I'd like it more."

"Tell me."

"If you gave me a good morning kiss."

"I would be pleased to give you a good morning kiss." He bent to kiss her.

The man certainly could kiss. Some how they weren't just a matter of lips on lips or even simply tongues entwining with each other. When Gareth kissed he lit up her entire body. Tiny electric shards of pure pleasure raced down her tummy, to her legs, around her toes and settled in her groin. Sex with him had been, in a word, amazing. She felt bereft when he raised his head to gaze down at her. In a moment of boldness Molly asked, "You know where kisses lead to, don't you?"

He smiled, the sizzling smile that zinged right through to

her woman parts, "To more kisses?"

"At a minimum." Molly twisted so she could wrap her legs around his hips. His eyes widened just before he kissed the tip of her nose. "Like that cutie?"

"I like. Do you like this?" He pulsed against her, his penis hot and hard.

"Mmm, I think I can judge better if it's a bit more up close and personal."

He slid inside, "Like this?"

"Mmmmm, exactly like that." His skin, warm and vibrant felt better than good beneath her hands. His growl when she raked her nails along his torso thrilled her. The guy had stamina and sure knew what he was about. He made her feel desirable and beyond sexy. The first two orgasms were intense, but no where near as powerful as the fifth one that rode over her. Her vaginal muscles were in mid-contraction when Gareth climaxed, groaning his own pleasure. It took long moments for the pair to catch their breath, Molly murmuring that she could easily get used to waking up beside him, followed by a mental slap. Girl-guy rules said you never ever told a guy that on the first date . . . then again, they really hadn't been on a date, date. Nope, no date. She took a guy who came to visit his uncle out to the coast, took him to dinner and royalty jumped his bones for most of the night and into the morning. But damn, she'd do it again if she had it to do over.

With that thought and Gareth's arms around her, she drifted into a sexually satiated doze. When she woke awhile later Gareth still held her while he leaned on one elbow studying her as if to memorize her face.

"Hey!" Molly uttered softly while she reached up to tuck a strand of tawny hair behind Gareth's ear.

"Hey." He smiled and it sent a shiver down to her toes.

She squirmed closer to him, "I guess I'm not the best hostess, huh?"

"What do you mean?"

"We have amazing sex and I fall asleep on you."

"We have amazing sex several times and we both fall asleep so we are rested enough to have more amazing sex."

She chuckled and scooched up against the pillows, "You know what? You have what Carrie's romance books call that self-satisfied male smile."

"Does it offend you?"

"No, actually I like it. It's kind of nice."

"I like being nice to you, Molly." Pecs bunched under warm satiny skin, his smile broadened and he leaned over to kiss her.

The kiss ended way too soon for Molly but as they sat, forehead to forehead he toyed with a strand of her hair. "Gareth."

"Molly."

"Are you um, a little hungry or want some coffee or anything?"

"You. I am hungry for you."

She giggled, "You have me."

"Promise?"

"Promise, but I do need at least a glass of water."

"Me too." He shifted away from her to stand, reluctance to leave her obvious in his eyes.

"And we should probably call your uncle."

"My uncle?" Unabashed and bare-assed naked he stopped in his tracks and looked over his shoulder at her.

"Yeah, you should call him? I mean, we told him you'd be home last night and we didn't even call."

"My uncle? Oh, yes, Merlin, Uncle Arthur. Yes. We should call him."

He took a step and turned again, this time giving her a positively fabulous full Monte. "What should we call him?"

"Not exactly what. We should let him know you're still here and maybe when I'll be bringing you back."

"Ah. I do not wish to go back to his shop today."

"That's sweet of you to say. That is, I mean, do you mean, you want to stay here with me?"

"Yes. We're a, what do they call it." He pondered the word a moment, "A couple!"

"We're a couple?" She couldn't believe she squeak in her voice.

"Is that the wrong word?"

She pulled up the top sheet and wrapped it around her, "Word for what?"

"For us. We are joined, yes?"

"Joined." Molly considered that and wondered if he meant what she thought he meant. "Do you mean you think, that you want, us to be like dating?"

"Molly, a man does not sleep with a respectable woman and not marry her. You call married people a couple, right?"

"M-m-married?" She squeaked. He had to be joking. Gorgeous, big, brawny, hunky blond haired, blue eyed men didn't marry girls like her. They married models and actresses and gorgeous women, not average, every day girls like herself.

"Yes. Married. What if you carry my child? I would not have him born a bastard."

"Oh that." She tripped by him toward the bathroom. Maybe a hot shower would clear her mind so she could have this conversation. Yes, that would do it. A nice hot shower and she'd wake up and find out she dreamt yesterday and the incredible sex last night and this morning. That was the ticket.

Gareth followed her into the bathroom and without a word joined her in the shower. "I like this falling water."

"Yeah, me too."

"Molly?"

She stood beneath the spray, the torrent of water reminding her of a sudden spring shower. The kind you'd see in a movie where a romantic couple found each other after a fight and time apart.

"Yes?" Her voice came out in a smoky hush that she was sure couldn't be her own voice.

"We needs wed."

"No, we don't need to."

"I told you, I will not have my child be born a bastard."

She reached behind him for the soap and began sudsing her wash cloth. "Gareth, I'm on the pill."

He looked down at her feet. "Does it hurt?"

She followed the path of his gaze. "Does what hurt?"

"The pill you are on? Which foot is it beneath?"

"I'm not like standing on the pill. I'm taking it. You know, the birth control pill."

"Birth control?" His brow furrowed in puzzlement a beat before he smiled, nodded and told her, "Of course, the pill."

Somehow Molly had the distinct feeling he had no clue what she was talking about.

"So we don't need to worry about me being pregnant and rushing into a marriage that may not work."

"Molly, of course our marriage will work. We will make it work. Since I am new here you will have to have your priest post the banns."

"My priest? Gareth, I don't have a priest."

"Ah. I am relieved. 'Tis good you follow the old ways. We will handfast as soon as our families can arrange it."

"H-h-handfast? You mean the year and a day thing?"

"That is the old way. I will tell you in all honesty, I followed Arthur's Christ because he ordered it but like my brothers, we still followed, and believe in the old ways."

"Ri-i-i-ght. Sure. So, um, here, turn around and let me wash your back, huh?"

He obliged, but before he turned to give her his back she saw an odd mixture of confusion and assurance in his gaze.

The man clearly believed they were going to be married. Something told her that belief wasn't part of his re-enactment play acting gig. Nope, the man really expected to marry her. Not that being married to a walking, talking piece of eye candy wouldn't be all bad. Then again, did he have a trust fund or a job he needed to get back to? They didn't really know the first thing about each other. Oh yeah, sure they talked about her job and what a bitch Julie was and he told her some things about where he grew up but they certainly didn't *know* each other. And she wasn't about to support some guy she'd just met.

They needed a serious conversation to find out what he really thought. After all, he *could* have been feeling like he'd taken advantage of her and had to say marriage loomed in their future. Guys were notorious for saying they'd call and then never call. So Gareth probably said they'd get married instead of the I'll call thing and would forget about it by noon or early evening since they'd already slept past noon and were well into the early afternoon.

Back in her room, after drying off she couldn't help but take in every naked inch of the man she'd spent the past twenty-four, give her take, hours with. Six pack abs, a chest that would make that butter commercial guy look like a wuss, toned thighs, really nice calves; the guy was walking sex. Even if he weren't the most gorgeous guy she'd ever laid eyes on, that body was enough to make her girlie parts sit up and take notice.

Gareth smiled. He knew. He totally knew she thought he was hot.

"So, um, coffee?" She managed.

"Yes. Coffee."

"Hungry?"

"Famished."

"Me too." As she started breakfast out of the corner of her

eye she saw Gareth pick up the phone and study the receiver. She couldn't tell if he was trying to figure out how it worked or debating making a call. He finally told her he meant to call his uncle but didn't have the number. Molly quickly found it on the list she and Carrie had posted on the bulletin board by the phone and handed him back the receiver.

"Uncle Arthur," Gareth sounded like he was laughing. "Yes. I am still with Molly. I'm fine . . . yes soon . . . we are breaking our fast . . . I have news . . . yes news . . . we are betrothed."

Through the phone Molly heard, *"You're what?* I'm coming to pick you up this minute."

"No, uncle. Tis done. I will return soon."

A moment later the doorbell rang. Molly glanced at the stove and back to Gareth, "Keep an eye on the eggs a minute, okay?"

Molly padded to the front door and after a quick glance out the peephole, confusion flitting across her face she pulled open the door. "Mr. Merle! What? How? You're on the phone? When?"

"Good morning, Molly. We stopped by to see Gareth, is he here?" Mr. Merle spoke quickly while trying to look past Molly into the hallway.

"Um, yeah. Ah, hello Vivienne. Sure, come on in. How did you get . . ."

"Cell phone," Mr. Merle told her while he looked around the hallway clearly seeking Gareth.

"Right. Ah we're in the kitchen having breakfast."

"Breakfast?" Mr. Merle looked troubled. "Is everything all right?"

"Oh yeah, everything's great. Gareth, look who stopped by."

Gareth turned from the stove where he'd been tending the eggs, eyes wide. "These are done, Molly. The coffee vat ceased its bubbling."

"Coffee vat—right. Vivienne, Mr. Merle, have a seat. Would you like some coffee? Something to eat?"

"No, dear, we're fine," Vivienne assured her.

"I'd like a coffee if you don't mind," Mr. Merle glanced over at his sister.

"No problem. Listen, I know you like mochas, I have some hot chocolate mix, would you like me to make you up one?"

"That would be lovely, Molly." Mr. Merle nodded.

"I would have this mocha as well," Gareth seemed to growl at them.

"Sure. Vivienne, are you certain?"

"Well, if it would not be too much trouble."

"Not at all. Are you sure you aren't hungry?"

"We ate earlier," Vivienne spoke up.

"Why hath you come?" Gareth had settled into a seat, slouching down with a hand resting on his thigh. While his position seemed to indicate relaxation, his tone and glare in his eyes clearly conveyed menace.

Despite their protestations of not being hungry, Molly put out a plate of cookies which Mr. Merle quickly reached to take one. She smiled thinking how Carrie had told her the old gent had something of a sweet tooth.

"These are quite good, Molly."

"Never mind the sweets, *Uncle*. What are you doing here?"

"Why my dear boy, we were concerned about you."

"Concerned? I'm not a boy."

"No, but this is a new place for you."

"And when in the past did a new locale daunt me?"

"Ah well, that's just it. Things are vastly different here, you know?"

"Because of cars, telephones and television?"

Molly placed a dish of food before Gareth and sat with her own, "You don't have those at home? Wow, that must be a heck of a rural place you live in."

Her three guests stopped mid-bite or sip to look at her. "What?"

None of them spoke.

"Well those Orkneys sound pretty rustic. They've got hard line phones in Pt. Reyes but cell service sucks. That can't be the only place in the world where things aren't major modern."

Gareth cleared his throat, "Yes, my home lacks many of the amenities you have here in Napa. Still, I fail to see why that would concern you, Uncle."

"Yes, well your aunt and I didn't want to see you end up in any kind of trouble."

"I'm fine. In fact, we have news."

"We do?" Molly held her coffee cup half way to her mouth, "What news?"

"As I said, we are betrothed."

Vivienne's cup rattled to the table.

Mr. Merle coughed on a bit of cookie.

Molly spit her coffee back into her cup.

Gareth continued as if completely unaware that the others in the room stared at him in total incredulity.

It was Mr. Merle who finally spoke, "So you said. And when did you decide this?"

"This morn."

This time it was Molly whose cup clattered to the table. "Well we didn't exactly decide to get married. The subject came up, but only generally."

Gareth looked at her as if she were a dense child. "No. Twas not generally. Surely you recall after we . . ." he turned his wrist in a circle.

"We what?"

"We agreed to wed."

Molly shook her head, "Ah that would be a no. You came

167

up with this cockamamie idea that because we, you know, that thing and then you got this idea that, that, that we had to get married. Oh my god, I sound like Carrie. I sound like someone out of one of her books and like she used to do when she sputtered and stuttered about a guy. Holy crap. Weren't you listening when I explained to you that we don't get married just because we, you know." She glanced at his aunt and uncle.

"Did you engage in martial relations without the bound of matrimony," Vivienne softly asked. While her tone oozed sympathy, her eyes were filled with delicious mirth.

"Gees, I can't believe I'm having this conversation." Molly rose and paced over to the sink and back.

"Why is that, dear?" Vivienne asked.

"You're his, his, well you're kind of like his parents right now, right?"

"I suppose you could say that," Mr. Merle nodded.

"And given you really don't want to know your parents have sex, it's not like they really want to know you do too, right?"

"My parents never hid their sexual activities from us. It is a natural act, Molly. It is not as if I had sex with someone other than my intended." Gareth assured her.

"I'm so not having this conversation. You have got to be the most confusing family I've ever met. We, I, had a great time yesterday. It was a blast and got my mind off the day job and Carrie being gone. Things were going great until, until, well until you came up with this idea." She sat down, defeated.

"Things were good until we arrived this morning, Molly?" Vivienne reached out and put her hand on Molly's arm.

"Tis not your fault Vivienne. I believe twas mine when I told Molly we needs marry. I think she thought I offered her marriage because I had to and not because I care for her."

"That's it. We're not having this conversation. This is way too crazy and I'm not going to talk about this anymore." Molly slapped the table top.

"I think," Vivienne began, "now that we know Gareth is doing well we should go about our business. Don't you agree, brother dear?"

"Gareth, are you coming?" Mr. Merle stood and gestured to Gareth to join him.

"No. I need to make amends to Molly and explain myself. I will return to your shop later."

"I think you should come now."

"No."

"Listen, Gareth," Molly broke in, "that might be a good idea. I have some things I need to take care with Carrie's business so why don't you go with your aunt and uncle and we can catch up later? Maybe we can go to a movie or something."

"Do you promise?"

"Sure. Think about what you want to see and we'll go. If it's all right with your aunt and uncle I'll come by about five and we can have dinner and go to an early show."

"That sounds like a good idea," Mr. Merle nodded. "We'll see you about five."

"Okay," Gareth looked from one to the other as if expecting a trick.

"Cool. No, that's okay, I'll get the dishes. I need to clear the kitchen anyway. I'll walk you out."

At the door Molly glanced outside. "Where's your car, Mr. Merle?"

"My car? Oh well that. It's around the corner. I wanted to get a bit of a walk in so we parked around the corner."

Molly nodded.

Gareth put his hands on her shoulders and looked into her eyes. She was sure she imagined it, but he looked almost afraid.

"I'll see you at five, I promise." She raised on tip toe and gave him a quick kiss on the cheek.

"Five." Gareth trailed Mr. Merle and Vivienne down the street.

CHAPTER NINETEEN

The threesome had barely cleared the corner of Molly's street before Mr. Merle turned and looked around them. With a nod to Vivienne they each took hold of one of Gareth's hands and in a blink were inside Treasures.

"I knew you did not have a car." Gareth groused.

"What were you thinking?" Hand on his chin, Mr. Merle paced back and forth in the bedroom he'd given to Gareth.

"I thought twas time for me to see my new world."

"I mean asking her to marry you. We would rather you had asked us what to do in this time before you did something like that."

"Speak for yourself, Merlin." Vivienne cut in.

"Oh, Vivienne, please. He has fifteen hundred years of knowledge to catch up on before he enters into a serious relationship."

"And you have given me much of that, Merlin."

"I?"

"Between your tel-tel-television and the Mirror of Time I have watched much of life's changes. Add to that the distillation of knowledge you and Vivienne have given me I am prepared for this time."

"Almost."

"Enough. I will admit there are things I've yet to learn. Yet isn't that being alive? To continue to learn? And there is something I would learn before this night."

"What is that, dear?" Vivienne sat on the edge of his bed.

"When I told Molly we would wed she disagreed."

"I'm sure she did," Merlin smiled at him.

"Well she did not say we would *not* wed. She merely found fault with my reasoning. Merlin, I will not bring a bastard into this world. My son, or daughter, will bear my name. When I told Molly this would be so she told me she was on this pill. I did not see her stand on anything. What did she mean?"

Merlin chuckled. "You see, there is much you need to know about this time."

"Then you should begin telling me now because I have a, a, a date! Yes, a date with Molly tonight to have a movie. What is this pill? Do I need to procure it for her?"

Gareth watched Merlin glance at Vivienne who smiled in response. "By all means, my brother, explain to our nephew about the pill."

"Well it's quite simple really. Back in the 1960's there was what the people of this time call a sexual revolution. People no longer felt the need to be married to engage in sexual relations. Free love they called it. Part of what made it so simple for them to do this was what they call the pill. It is, in fact, a pill. A mixture of chemicals or what are called hormones that prevent pregnancy, at least in most cases. Women no longer need be worried about becoming pregnant with a child they are not ready for. I suppose Molly told you she is taking it?"

"She said so. Then she brought me to her bed merely for pleasure?"

"Isn't that why you went with her?" Vivienne asked dryly.

"No! I care for Molly. I knew the moment I met her, that first day I woke, she was the woman I waited a lifetime for."

"Gareth, how can you say that? Think about it. You woke up in this time after almost two thousand years. All you knew from your old life were Vivienne and I. Remember how confused you felt? You were quite disoriented and we had to, well it became necessary to conjure a calming spell so we could explain to you what had occurred, or at least what we thought occurred. I will admit, my boy, it was quite a surprise to turn around and see you standing there in full war garb."

"I remember well. I did not need you to bespell me! I may follow the old ways, but that is no reason to bewitch me. And while it may have been a confusing time for me, a surprise, it does not mean my heart did not trip at the sight of the fair Molly. Now that I consider the matter more closely I know why I woke in this time."

"You do?" Merlin and Vivienne asked in unison, the pair leaning toward him as if he were ready to impart a most special secret. Perhaps even the answer to their own question about why he suddenly woke yet none of the others had.

"Yes. I am here to rescue Molly."

"What?" The pair asked again in the same instant.

"What other reason can there be for me and only me to wake at this particular time?"

The magical couple looked at each other and shrugged.

"Think on it. Molly works for a witch perhaps more evil than my mother. This woman causes her harm at every turn. The legends say we will wake at the time of greatest need. What if this is Molly's greatest need and she needs but one knight to save her? Clearly it is me. I will vanquish the Red Queen and Molly and I will live out the rest of our days in peace. She will cease this pill, we will wed and have many children."

"Merlin?" Vivienne softly asked.

Merlin stroked his jaw.

"You know I am right." Gareth nodded at them.

"Perhaps," Merlin slowly told them. "Perhaps. However, Gareth, you must know, Julie Prince is not a witch. Witches in this time are actually well thought of or at least they no longer engage in what we thought evil in our time. She is merely a mean-spirited woman who lacks the compassion to care for another person."

"They call them bitches," Vivienne put in.

"Yes, bitches." Merlin continued. "You cannot kill her. You cannot even consider harming her in any way. What you can do, however, is support Molly. I don't mean with money. I mean by listening to her and letting her know she isn't alone. From what Carrie told me, Molly's last boyfriend did not care enough to continue hearing about problems with her job and left her when she needed him most. That made her feel even less worthy for love." Merlin looked over to the mirror and sat contemplating the ancient device a bit. At long last he spoke, "You may be right, Gareth. This could be Molly's time of greatest need and perhaps you will be the one to help her."

"Of course I am."

"But Gareth, beware that once you have helped her, rescued her, you may fall back into that dreamless sleep. There is no way of knowing if you are meant to remain in this time."

"You are wrong, wizard. Believe me, Molly and I are meant to spend our lives together. She will be my wife and we will grow old together. You will see, ours will be a love that will burn brightly through all time and the poets will sing their praises to our devotion to each other."

"That sounds very romantic, Gareth. However, you are living in a real world."

"Vivienne, I cannot believe you of all people believe you cannot have romance in a real world." Gareth shook his head.

"Oh I believe you can. What I'm thinking of, however, is you agreed to take Molly to a movie tonight. Have you thought of which one you will go to? And how you will pay for it?"

"Merlin! I have a need for some coin."

Merlin smiled and with a flick of his wrist produced some money.

"And, what exactly is a movie?"

CHAPTER TWENTY

Shortly before five Molly walked into Treasures and called out for Mr. Merle.

"We're here in the kitchen, Molly. Come on back."

"Molly." Gareth stood.

When she saw Gareth in a cotton burgundy button-down shirt, stone washed jeans that left nothing to the imagination and a pair of suede cowboy boots Molly decided it she'd be feeling might-ty uncomfortable trying to sit through a movie and not climbing up in the man's lap and having her jolly way with him. Damn he was a sight for sore, weary and pure lusty eyes. She'd marry him in a minute if he asked while dressed like that. *Reality check. No marrying the re-enactor.* "Hi. You have a good afternoon?"

"Yes. You?"

"I got a lot done. Just a few things to finish up tomorrow and I'll be ready to go back to work on Thursday. So did you think about where you want to go for dinner?"

"Ah, Vivienne made dinner."

"Viv . . . oh she didn't need to do that. Don't you want to go out?"

"I made one of Gareth's favorites. Lamb pie."

"Um, sounds good."

"I hope so. I haven't made it in some time. At least since I last saw him. Let me let Merl, ah, my brother know dinner is ready."

"They really love you, don't they?" Molly asked Gareth when they were alone.

"Yes. They care very much for me. Right now they are the only family I have."

"What about your brothers?"

"They aren't here. I meant the only family I have here."

"I see. So what movie are we going to tonight?"

"One I hope you will enjoy. Uncle told me you enjoy history. There is a movie called *A Connecticut Yankee in King Arthur's Court* at the Uptown. Do you know it?"

"Yeah, that's an oldie. Mr. Merle's right I love the old movies. Bing Crosby, right?"

"Yes, Bing. You know this movie?"

"Uh huh, good choice. Um Gareth, Vivienne and Mr. Merle aren't planning to come with us, are they? I mean if you want them to that's cool but—"

"No! I did not even wish to come back here with them earlier today."

"But you do agree, do you not, nephew, it was for the best to return home for at least awhile today?" Mr. Merle asked.

Gareth sighed, "Yes. You are correct. If I had not returned with you how could I have planned my evening with Molly?"

"Exactly. Molly, are you certain you do not mind entertaining Gareth for another evening?" Merlin asked her.

"I'm looking forward to it. I had more fun yesterday than I've had in a long time. I'd forgotten how much fun it is to play tour guide."

" Please, do not forget, Molly, you promised to take me to see San Francisco at the island in the bay."

"I haven't. Maybe we can go on my days off next week."

"Perhaps we can wed there."

"On Alcatraz? You're kidding, right?"

"Yes. Kidding. What is wrong with Alcatraz?"

"It's not that there's anything wrong with it per se. You know it used to be a prison, right?"

"Of course, a prison, I remember."

"Well, if you two want to make that seven-fifteen show we'd better eat," Vivienne bustled them to the table.

When she thought about it later, if someone would have asked, Molly would have told them it sounded an awful lot like Mr. Merle and Vivienne were coaching Gareth on what to say and do when he was alone with her. He'd done pretty well on his own the day before. Better than pretty well when it came to sex. Dang the man knew what to do to make her girl parts happy. She was not, however, going to mention that to the older couple. No how. No way. After all, if every father's daughter was a virgin, the Merles didn't need to know their nephew took the word orgasm to a whole new level.

Vivienne had just offered dessert when Gareth looked at the clock, "We should go if we want to be there on time, Molly."

"Mmm, yeah. Thanks for a great meal, Vivienne."

"Come in for dessert when you bring Gareth back later."

"We will think on it," Gareth informed them as he grabbed their jackets.

Outside the shop Gareth told her, "We are not returning for dessert."

"But we'll have dessert, right?"

"Are you hungry?"

"Not right now. Um, you know dessert is more than something sweet to eat, don't you?"

Gareth looked at her, puzzling over her words a moment before he broke into a large grin. "I like dessert. Maybe we should go to your house and have some before the movie."

"Uh uh, movie first, dessert later. We'll call your uncle from my house after we get there. That is, I mean, if you want to."

"I like nothing better than to wake beside you."

"Me too."

Despite an occasional grumble or muttered "posh" or

"pooh" from Gareth throughout the movie Molly thoroughly enjoyed it.

They stopped at the Annette's Chocolate and Ice Cream Factory for some ice cream on the way home.

"Annette's is one of my absolute all time favorite places to eat. Another one of the best parts of Napa. Has Mr. Merle brought you here yet?" Molly told him.

"We do not leave the shop much."

"That's too bad, especially since Annette's is just up the street from Treasures."

"It is most busy in the shop and with just my aunt and uncle they would lose much trade if they closed."

"I guess. Well we're here now. What looks good to you?"

Gareth smiled. Molly felt a pleasant liquid warm move through her body. "To eat."

"Yes, to eat."

She playfully punched his arm, "I meant ice cream."

Gareth studied the menu. Taking the puzzled look that creased his brow to mean there were too many choices Molly suggested, "How about the banana split?"

"Banana split?"

"Or how about a hot fudge sundae? It's got ice cream, hot fudge, whipped cream and nuts. What do you think?"

"I think you make a good choice. Yes."

With their order placed Gareth looked more closely around the restaurant.

"It's not all that fancy, but the food is the best, especially the chocolates. We should buy some on the way out."

"I'd like that. I have found I do like your chocolate."

Molly studied him a moment, who didn't know about chocolate? "So, did you like the movie?"

"I did."

"Then what was all the 'posh' and 'bullocks' business? If you didn't like it, it's okay. You don't have to like everything

I do or everything we do. I like someone who speaks their mind."

"I will tell you what I did not like. Understand, I enjoyed your movie. It was most entertaining. But that was not Arthur. Not be any means. He was not that old and far more fit than the man pretending to be him. And do you really believe knights of the realm would fear the sun disappearing? Pooh! Little your movie beings know."

Molly digested that. "Sounds like you don't much like comedies."

"Ah! It is a jest! I like that. Are there other movies that do not show us as buffoons?"

She decided to ignore the "us" part of his question. "Of course, there are some really good ones. If you like, next week or so we can rent a few."

"Why not now?"

"Um, well first of all it's almost eleven o'clock and the video store is closed."

"Ah. Tomorrow?"

"Tomorrow I need to finish up Carrie's business and get ready for my work week."

"You shall have my help."

"Aw, Gareth, that's not necessary. I can . . ."

"Molly? Hey! It's Maria, from Carrie's job. I heard what happened. Did she really up and move to Montana?" Carrie's dark-haired friend approached their table.

"Maria, hi. This is Gareth. Gareth, Maria."

"Nice to meet you, Gareth. Maria studied the blond so closely Molly wondered if she was considering having him for a late night snack. "What are you guys up to?"

"We saw A Connecticut Yankee in King Arthur's Court over at the Uptown."

"I love those old movies! Are you a fan too, Gareth?"

"Actually I was discussing the errors I saw in the movie."

"Errors? You want to see errors check out some of those old Valentino black and whites from the 1920's. Now those are funny without even trying to be. So tell, what's the deal with Carrie? Is she really happy?"

"As far as I know she is."

"You have spoken to her? How?" Gareth leaned closer as if Molly was about to impact some great secret.

"Well not recently like today. It think, well it was pretty clear she and Blake were . . ."

"I thought his name was Black Eagle." Gareth searched his memory. "Yes, Black Eagle."

"Oh, ah, I think you misheard. Blake Eagleston. It sounds a lot like Black Eagle, doesn't it?"

"No. My uncle said . . ."

"Well, whatever he said, last I heard they were really happy and things are going good."

"I'm glad to hear it. If anyone deserves to be happy it's Carrie. And how about Dean—a what was it she used to call him?"

"Sir Dickless."

Maria snapped her fingers, "That's it."

"He had no shaft?" Eyes opened wide Gareth appeared truly stunned.

"Well, not worth mentioning. Not, not that I had first hand, ah, Carrie said that after they broke up."

Maria continued, "I heard the funny farm is going to be keeping Dean Dickless for a long time to come."

"One can only hope."

The other woman glanced at her watch. "O'dark thirty comes early so I gotta get going. Don't you have to work tomorrow?"

"Nu uh. I'm not back on duty till Friday at five."

"Lucky you. Although, are you still answering to the Red Queen?"

"Carrie told you about that?"

"You so know it. I know it's hell for you dealing with her, but she sure gave us a lot to smile about. Some of the things that woman pulled with you, man."

"We'll have to get together so you can hear the latest and greatest. Not that I enjoy talking about it. Sometimes you just need to vent."

"Exactly." She glanced at Gareth, "I didn't mean to leave you out, Gary?"

"Gareth."

"Gareth. Doesn't that sound like a name from one of Carrie's romance novels?"

"It sure does," Molly agreed.

"Let's get together soon, huh? Call me next week?"

"I will."

"Good to meet you, Gareth. See you Molly."

A moment later the waitress gave them their bill and the pair left. In Molly's Jeep Gareth asked, "Why do you call Carrie's man by a different name?"

Molly blew out a breath. "So we don't look crazy."

"Having a made up name is not crazy?"

"The name isn't. I mean there are Native American's who still use their cultural names. The whole time travel thing though, ninety-nine percent of the people out there would think anyone believing it is certifiable."

"Certifiable?"

"Nuts. Looney."

"Yet Carrie and her man did travel through time."

"That's the way it looks. But most people aren't going to buy into that so we have to act like she only moved away. That's going to be a problem though."

"What?"

"If people ask for her or about her. I don't want to be in a position of making up stories about her and at some point someone is going to want to write her. I'll have to figure something out that doesn't sound too out there. So, um, ah, do you want to go back to Treasures or did you want to . . ."

"I would have dessert, Molly."

CHAPTER TWENTY-ONE

"Do we need to tell your uncle where you are?"

"I probably should. I've no doubt he would know where to find me, but it is only right."

"Phone's over there. Can I get you a soda or coffee or something?"

Focused intently at the phone he merely uttered, "Something." He'd seen Merlin use the device and had a vague recollection of instruction on how to use it, but the how evaded him.

Molly walked over with a glass filled with a bubbly clear liquid, "Ginger ale."

"Ah. Ale. Thank you." He raised the glass to his lips with only a passing thought as to why the ale would have the tiny bubble and prepared to take a long, thirst quenching drink. The bubbles tickled the tip of his nose and vibrated along his upper lip. The taste, however, threw him. "Wha-what, is this brew dances on my tongue!"

Molly chuckled, "I never heard carbonation described quite that way."

"Car-carbon. What didst you call it?"

"Carbonation." Molly studied him, the look in her eyes questioning whether or not he was joking about not knowing the word. "You know, the process of putting air into a beverage to make it effervesce."

"Yes. Effervesce."

She gestured to the phone, "Are you going to call?"

"I forget the number."

"Oh, that's easy. Carrie had it here on our top ten list. It's 555-7718."

"555 . . ."

"7718. Here, she's probably got it on speed dial."

Gareth watched while Molly pushed two of the buttons followed by beeping tones coming from the device. She handed him the contraption just as a sleepy sounding Merlin said hello. "Uncle, 'tis I."

"Gareth, my boy. Where are you?"

"At Molly's. I will return on the morrow."

"Are you certain—"

"Most certain. Good eve." He handed the phone to Molly, making a mental note to have Merlin teach him how to use the contraption the next day. "'Tis done. Now, dessert!"

Molly giggled, "Follow me."

"Anywhere."

He walked just far enough behind her to catch the soft sway of her hips. There was no artifice in the movement. His lady possessed a seductive gait by merely placing one foot before the other. As she crossed the threshold to her room he reached for her and pulled his lady to him. "Molly." He whispered before capturing her lips in a kiss. Damn the woman could kiss! She devoured him like a fine wine and pleasing meal. When here fingers grazed along his shirt he thought he'd pop out of the jeans he'd worn. How modern men withstood such encasement eluded him, however that was a thought for another time. At the moment other, more delicious things, like Molly's breasts, pressed against him.

She backed toward her bed, fingers busy along his shirt and boldly dipping into the waistband of his pants. Determined not to disappoint Gareth returned the favor and tugged Molly's sweater over her head and tossed it to a chair across the room. She kicked off her shoes and he tugged at her jeans. Laughing she bounced on to the bed and pulled him with her. "Foreplay later, right now I want to feel you."

"That you shall, my Lady. That you shall."

The next morning Molly woke earlier than she would have expected. Spooned up against Gareth, her back to his chest with his arm around her waist felt incredibly right. With his chest almost double the breadth of her shoulders she felt warm and secure in his embrace. On work days she normally slept in pretty late, no matter what time she turned in. Making love with Gareth three or was it four times? Being with him and making love with him, seemed to energize her more than a quadruple latte.

Careful not to wake him she rolled within his embrace to face him. In repose he looked fairly young, maybe even too young to be out with a thirty something woman. With his long blond hair, slightly tanned complexion and way too long golden lashes, and almost too perfect nose and full lips. He reminded her of the lead dancer from when she and Carrie went to see Chippendales a few years ago. On closer inspection there were a few tiny scars scattered on his forehead and cheek, a couple of larger ones, almost as if he'd been cut with a wide knife blade, on his shoulder. A longer, white puckering of skin lay at the top of his rib cage on one side. He and his brothers must have had some pretty rough tumbles growing up. While she could lay there and ogle him all day that wasn't going to get anything done and there were things to do before going back on duty tonight.

Slowly she eased out from Gareth's embrace and slipped from the bed. On tip toe she made her way to the bathroom and turned on the shower. The hot water didn't quite replace the warmth of Gareth's arms. When she stepped back into her room her breath caught. The sight of Gareth sitting upright in her bed, his broad chest bared above the sheets made more than her mouth water. Gorgeous didn't begin to cover how incredible he looked. This wasn't the kind of man you wanted to share. His smile made more than her mouth water.

"Hi." *Man, that sounded lame.*

"Pleasant morn to you, Molly."

"I didn't want to wake you, did I?"

"No, but as I am awake, mayhap you will join me again in your bed."

"Sounds like a plan."

He pulled the sheets back revealing an impressive hard on.

"Is that for me?"

"All of it. Just for you, Molly."

"Yum." She giggled and ran for the bed, snuggle in close to him while he shifted to embrace and kiss her.

Waking from a light doze not long after Molly told him, "I could get used to this."

"And so you shall."

"I shall, however, next week. Right now I do need to get up and get ready for work. We've got time for a shower and some breakfast before I have to go. You want a ride home?"

"Yes, yes and no."

"No? You want to walk?"

"No. I will accompany you."

"Mmm, much as I'd like that, uh uh. Not a good idea. The Red Queen will probably be in and while ye old badge bunny can bring in as many men as she wants, not a good idea for me."

"Ye old badge . . ."

"Bunny."

"Ah, the hare at your work."

"Nah, it's just an expression. She screws like a bunny. Lots of dispatchers are like that so they call them badge bunnies. Like I said yesterday, they'll screw anything in a badge."

"Ah. I see. But you are not such?"

"Not just no, but hell no. They think they're oh so special but most of us think they're a major joke. The one I work with? The officers all joke about her behind her back. The only reason they do her is because they don't want to be the only one that hasn't. It's a guy thing, you know?"

"Mayhap. My brothers and I often competed. Mostly my twin, Gahris, challenged me the most."

"Are you a lot alike?"

"In looks, yes. We often passed for each other. He has more hair than I, on his chest. I am better endowed where it pleases a woman most."

Molly found she very much liked that despite the arrogance of his words, the look in his eyes appealed to her to tell him he did please her. "Your guy parts definitely do the trick. So how are you guys different?"

"Gahris chases more skirts than I. He has no thought to settle down whereas I long hoped for my king to choose a bride for me."

"Huh? Is that a nice way of saying you didn't really want to get married?"

"No. Not at all. I did desire a bride. Several ladies were offered to me, but none captured my heart. We have known each other but a short time, Molly, yet you quicken my heart more than any other has. Indeed, none made my heart feel it skipped till I met you."

"That has to be the most romantic thing anyone has ever said to me."

"If my wish is true, no other will speak such romantic things to you."

"Cut out the re-enactment and king talk and I'm your girl. Right now though, I gotta take off for work with just enough time to leave you off at Treasures."

They started for the door. Just before the portal Molly snapped her fingers. "I forgot something I meant to do the

187

other day. Hang on, I'll be right back."

She hurried down the hall and into Carrie's room. Grabbing a piece of paper she quickly wrote a note, *"I'm glad you are well and happy. I may have my own good news for you soon. Write me. Please."* She quickly tucked the note into the little cubby where she found Carrie's note and hurried out to Gareth. After the past few days with him she had hopes this next week at work wouldn't be a slice of Dante's inferno.

Chapter Twenty-two

Molly was barely in the door before being summoned into Julie's office. With an inward groan she walked in to find Sally already seated. In response to her brow raised in question her union rep shrugged.

"In the interest of time I took the liberty of having your union rep sitting in with us from the beginning." Imperious as usual Julie informed her.

"Okay." Molly shrugged and sat. Whatever happened the past three days had nothing to do with her.

Julie fussed with a document on her desk. "I tried to make this a basic log entry, but I'm afraid this is much more serious than a simple documentation of wrong doing."

"If this is about Kris not being around the night of the bank robbery I'm more than happy to give you whatever information you need."

"Actually this isn't about Kris. Do you remember taking a call two weeks ago from a domestic violence suspect two weeks ago?"

"Domestic . . . we had had a few domestics the past month." Molly puzzled over which one Julie was talking about.

"This would be the one where the man reportedly told you he felt it was okay to hit women and that this country would be better off if women stayed in their place. Supposedly he admitted to beating his wife."

"Ah." Molly nodded. "The Ashad case. That was the one where he called us for an officer standby so he could pick up some things from his house. In the first call he told me he came home to find his wife in bed with another man. Our unit got out there and it turned out they weren't married, and two days before that he'd smacked her around pretty good; so much so she ended up in the hospital over night. He said a few other things in that call that I believe the report confirmed weren't true."

"Yes, well, I'm not talking about that call. I'm talking about the one he made when he got out of jail. The one where he made the statements about killing his wife."

Molly considered that a few moments. "Julie, I don't remember him saying anything like that. He did make some statements about taking over his own investigation and he'd prove that our officers coerced her into saying those things. He rambled for a good fifteen to twenty minutes before he hung up. As soon as we disconnected I called the on duty sergeant and asked him to listen to the call."

"Well, he didn't need to. Kris took care of it and it doesn't jive with what you said."

"Excuse me?"

"I said, Kris handled it and apparently you reported to her that he made statements about killing his wife."

"Julie, I never talked to Kris about that call. I think someone must be confused with a call I heard she took, hmmm, two days before I took the call from him. From what I remember in the reports the victim made a call and it came in on a 911 line which meant it went to dispatch. I saw something in there that the vic called twice and was told that being afraid doesn't mean a crime is going to be committed. Unless and until an actual attack happened we wouldn't send an officer. Julie, you have to know Kris tells 911 callers that all the time. It looks like this time something serious happened."

"It certainly did. Fortunately no one was seriously hurt."

"How can you say that? The woman ended up in the

hospital."

"No thanks to you." Julie turned to her computer and began typing into an open document. A few minutes later, the print button keyed she looked at Molly. "It was bad enough that you didn't handle that call. Now I've had to add into the internal affairs report that you, once again, failed to take responsibility and tried to blame poor Kris for this incident."

"Poor Kris? Are you frickin nuts? Oh wait, don't tell me, she's slept with you too."

Sally put her hand on Molly's arm to stop her words.

Julie pursed her lips and studied the pages in front of her before continuing, "I should add that outburst into this report. However given the seriousness of the charges I will refrain for now. It's too bad this had to happen now because I heard from a friend at the county they were seriously considering offering you a dispatch position down there. You'll be lucky of you have a job at the end of this. Now, if you'll just sign at the bottom . . ."

"I'd like to read this first."

"Your rep is here. You can sign."

"We'd like to read it over, Julie." Sally cut her off and urged Molly to stand. Together they left the room.

"What the hell was that about?" Molly demanded

"Shhhh, come on, let's step outside. Maria, can you grab the phones a little longer, we have to talk."

"I've been here all day. It's time for someone else to do some of the work." Maria whined.

"Shannon should be back from her code in a few. It would be great if you can wait till then."

"I have so much to do."

"We all do, Maria. Right now though I need to talk to Molly, unless you want to be down one specialist for the duration."

"Fine. Fine. I'll deal with it."

"We can talk here," Molly started to tell her friend.

"Nu uh. Not with all the recording equipment around here and if we're here Julie will expect us to be working. We need to talk. Come on."

Together they left the station and headed to Java, Java. Lattes in hand they found a table tucked away in an outside corner. Sally read through the document and shook her head. "This is one of the most convoluted ramblings I've seen from her to date. It does look like she's trying to cover up for Kris, again. Maybe you're right about Kris providing sexual favors to Julie as well as the officers. The way Julie protects her you can't help but think something is up."

"Let me see that." Molly read through the memorandum, shaking her head and offering a few explicative's along the way. When she finally looked up Sally didn't need to ask, clearly nothing in the document was true.

"Why don't you tell me what you remember from that incident?"

"Sure, like I told the Red Queen—when I came back on duty, hmm, three weeks ago, there was some talk that a woman called 911 three times asking for help. She said her ex-boyfriend threatened to kill her. The first two times Kris told her there was no crime so no officer. The third call was for medical assistance. Two days later the suspect called and he rambled on about how our officers favor women and that he was going to do his own investigation. I figured since the call came on a taped line there we had his chatter first hand so I sat and listened. As soon as he hung up I called in the sergeant. From what Julie just said apparently he turned it over to Kris and Kris realized the whole thing escalated because she didn't send and officer in the first place so now she's trying to turn it on me."

"That sounds about right. Typical Kris."

"So now what?"

"It's been ages since I worked on one of these. Fortunately they don't happen all that often. It's too late today to make any calls, but I think we need to call in the big boys from the union. I'll call first thing Monday morning."

"Wait a minute. Are you saying I could lose my job because of Kris' sloppy call taking?"

"They might try. Actually, that last comment Julie made may be the most telling. She's not happy that County is about to offer you a job. Once you're gone from here you can talk about all the stuff that goes on. She doesn't want that, so she has to find a way to keep you from leaving. This will pretty much sew things up for five years. It will also protect Kris."

"Great. That's just great. What do I do now?"

"Don't sign this till we talk with an attorney on Monday. Don't worry, I'll handle it with Julie. Right now we need to get in there and for the weekend make sure you document every little thing you can, at least while Maria isn't around. You so know that the gossip queen will turn around and spread whatever she thinks you might say or do or hopes you say or do to anyone who will listen."

"You got that right."

"Are you okay to work?"

"You mean am I too rattled and angry to function? Close. I'll be okay." At least she hoped so.

CHAPTER TWENTY-THREE

Fortunately Maria left when Molly and Sally returned to the station with Julie taking off shortly thereafter. Kris went in a suck-a-long and Shannon took the lead position dealing with the public till the station closed. After that, without knowing what went down, Shannon pretty much let Molly be. Rare for a Friday night there were few calls leaving Molly to at least appear to be busy with paperwork. Several times she paced to the Serial Killer display at the front of the station. Each time she wished she could plug Julie into one of the crime scenes depicted. If they could photo-shop Carrie into a photograph and have her end up back in time, why couldn't they do the same to send Julie to that hellish experience? Clearly she'd picked up Gareth's imagination.

At 3:00 a.m. at the end of her shift she tore out the door, deeply regretting the day she answered the dispatch ad for Miwok P.D.

Driving the long, winding and fortunately empty road back to Napa the tears she held at bay all day fell. In frustration she pounded the steering wheel. It was almost as if Julie knew she'd spent three incredibly wonderful days with Gareth and just had to destroy any happiness Molly felt. Luckily there wasn't a CHP patrol car the entire stretch because tonight rules of the road were the last thing on her mind. All she wanted to do was go home and pour her heart out to Carrie. That possibility no longer existed. Best she could do was write a note, stick it in the desk and maybe, just maybe it would reach her former roommate. "And she'll do what?" Molly asked herself as tears spilled down her cheeks.

She stumbled from the car to the house and barely noticed the blinking light on the answering machine. "Probably a telemarketer without one of those nifty devices that hangs up when it gets a machine." Beyond weary she washed her face and fell into bed. Wanted, needed sleep eluded her. This time Julie and her sidekick Kris had gone too far. Kris screwed up. Big time. The victim could have been killed and they were trying to pin it on her. Enough was enough. This time she'd figure out a way to get the both of them off her back. Ten years of this crap was enough. But how? How could she end the abuse from the Red Queen and her hench-bitch? When sleep finally came it brought with it dreams of Julie in a flowing red gown chasing her down a hall way yelling "off with her head."

A loud ringing woke her what felt like too soon. Not that she didn't welcome the respite from the horrible dreams that plagued her through the night. After the third time she hit the snooze on the alarm clock and it still continued to ring Molly realized it was the front door bell. "Who the hell keeps ringing the bell like it's a xylophone in the middle of the night? My night anyway. Probably a Girl Scout or some school kid with their pesky cookies and chocolate that I so don't need right now. No, that's not true. I could totally chow down on a case of chocolate, it's the waistline that doesn't need it." She glanced at her robe and decided whoever the miscreant was at the door they deserved to see her in her worn t-shirt and bare feet. That ought to scare them away from invading her sleep again.

Her "What?" died on her lips when Gareth stood at the portal. His smile warmed her girl parts in ways she didn't know they could be warmed. What endeared him to her at that moment wasn't his smile, but the shy and yet longing look in his eyes.

"Good morn, Molly."

"Gareth. What are you doing here?"

"I missed you and thought to surprise you with fare to break your fast."

"You, you brought me breakfast?"

"Indeed. Merlin advised a cake from the pan is a favorite of your time. Vivienne showed me how to make these cakes of the pan."

"Cake from the pan? Cake from . . . Ack! Pancakes. You made me pancakes?" She peered into the grocery bag he carried.

"Yes, pancakes."

"Oh, Gareth, that's the sweetest thing anyone has ever done for me."

"That pleases me. Do you know what would please me more?"

"No. What?"

A smile played on his lips, showing her a bit of straight white teeth. "If I could enter and prepare the meal for you."

"Oh, oh, oh! What a duffis! Come in. My morning manners aren't exactly the best." Now she regretted the ratty old t-shirt and dearly wished she had one of those spiffy Victoria's Secret nighties that taunted with all too brief glimpses of body until the guy removed it.

In the kitchen, humming softly to himself, Gareth busied himself emptying the contents of the bag.

"Ah, Gareth?"

"Mmm?"

"If you excuse me just a moment, I'm going to throw on a robe or something."

He looked her up and down, he smiled, a smile that went all the way to his eyes, now hooded with desire. "Shall I help you?"

"Help me?"

"Put something else on?"

"Put something else on?" She shook her head. Why was she repeating his words. "Uh, um."

He reached her in one step, powerful arms pulled her into an embrace, "Molly, tis not the putting on I wish to do."

"No?"

"No. Tis the taking off I wish to help you with."

"Oh. I see."

"Shall I help?"

She smiled, "Uh huh. I'd like that."

In one movement he picked her up and carried her to the bedroom. In a flash he had her t-shirt off, pulled his sweater over his head and tugged off his jeans. The man was living eye candy. Molly felt her girlie muscles tighten and release their liquid warmth as merely watching the way the man's chest muscles bunched and stretch with each movement. The guys on the men's muscle magazines had nothing, absolutely nothing on Gareth whateverhisnamewas. Her last thought before he slid over her, warming her with his body was that at some point learning his last name might be a good thing.

Gareth slid a muscular thigh over Molly's legs, tickling her with the crisp hairs of his leg when he rubbed against her. With his finger he drew a strand of hair away from her face and studied her a moment before asking, "Did I come at a right time?"

"In more ways than one."

"Will you tell me why red rims your eyes?"

"Red? Oh, nothing."

"The only time I have seen such weary eyes is when a lady has been crying. Are these tears for your lost friend?"

"No. I'm happy for Carrie. Really. No, work upset me yesterday. Big time."

"The Red Queen."

"Yeah. The Red Queen."

"Tell me."

She shook her head.

"I am here for you in both good and bad times. If you only tell me the good things, then I am only there for half of you."

"Oh, Gareth. I don't want to burden you."

"No burden. Tell me."

She nodded. "I will. Not in here though. I want my bedroom to be an escape, a respite from problems. Okay?"

"Okay. Let us shower and then you will tell me over breakfast."

"Crap! I forgot about breakfast. Did I ruin the pancakes?"

"No. Vivienne showed me how to make the batter, but they were not cooked. We will do that together."

Gareth waited until they sat at the table to ask Molly what had upset her.

"I was kind of hoping you forgot."

"No. I did not. Now, tell me, was it your Red Queen?"

"Big time. Kris, the badge bunny? She has this habit of deciding whether or not a call merits an officer or not. With a domestic situation, you always send an officer, even if it's only for advice. A woman called twice and both times Kris said she didn't need help. The third time the woman needed to go to the hospital. I took a call from the suspect and when he said some weird things I reported it to my sergeant. They're trying to say I jeopardized the woman when it was Kris that did everything wrong. You know, I'm a pretty easy going person. I may not be the most exciting person anyone will ever meet, but I try to be honest and keep a level head. I try not to judge people and take things as they come. After all, we're all only human and if we do the best we can that's all we can ask, you know? Those two though. Man, I wish . . . I wish . . . You know what I wish?"

"Tell me, Molly."

"I wish there was a way to put them inside a photograph but instead of a happy ending like Carrie and Black Eagle I'd like to see them end up in the most horrible situation. Something utterly painful. Not only physically painful, but mentally tortured for eternity. We have this display at work on serial killers through the ages and I wish I could put her in place of the victims in one of the pictures. There. I said it. Does that make me a bad person?"

Gareth sat quietly and listened patiently. When she finished he sat contemplating her words.

"I shocked you, didn't I? You think I'm the most horrible person in the world. You think I deserve all the bad things that happen to me and then some. You think—"

"I think you deserve every moment of your anger. Have you asked Merlin for his help in this?"

"Huh? Why would I ask Mr. Merle?"

"Because the wizard could help you. Surely you know this."

Her fork clattered to the table. "Don't do this. Please. Things were going so well. Please don't go into storybook land and pull that 'I'm a knight of the round table' shit on me. I can't take it. I really can't."

"Molly? Molly, let me ask you this. Why can you believe that Carrie's Black Eagle traveled through time to come here? Why can you believe that he and Carrie went back to his time but you cannot believe I am one of Arthur's Knights? Why can you not believe that the legend that Arthur and his knights will rise in the time of the world's greatest need has happened? That I am proof that the legend is real?"

She stood, walked over to the sink and gazed out the window. "Because, because I'm not that special. I'm just an average person. Even if the knights of the round table were real, why would one of them wake up just to help me?"

"You are special to me."

"Oh come on." She snapped

He rose and started toward her.

She put her hand out to stop him. "Gareth, don't."

He stood an arm's length away. "Is this not your time of greatest need?"

"My life is pretty messed up. But a knight in shining armor to fix it up? One that's been asleep how many hundreds of years? Nu-uh. The legend is about the world, not one pitiful woman with a screwed up life. Besides, why would only one of you wake up?"

"That is the question that has puzzled me."

"Please. Even your language is changing. You started out with that old fashioned English and not knowing half the stuff around here and suddenly you can talk like an every day guy and know how to run a blender to make pancakes. It doesn't jive."

"That is Merlin's magical workings. Tis no difficult spell to change a man's way of speaking or teach him of a new world."

"Give it up Gareth. I'm done. It was nice knowing you while it lasted, but I can't deal with your games right now. I think you should go. Now. I'll clean up your stuff and leave it off at Treasures tomorrow or Monday. Right now though you need to go so I can go to work."

"Molly—"

"Please, I can't take it right now."

He shrugged and turned to head out the door. "You know where to find me when you wish my help, Molly. Even if it only my shoulder to cry on, you know where I will be."

CHAPTER TWENTY-FOUR

M olly only vaguely heard the front door shut. He was gone. The man she thought could be the one bright spot in her life was gone. "And I'm better off without him."

She looked at the clock and ran for the bedroom. Today was no day to be late for work. All eyes would be on her with the internal affairs investigation pending.

Cruising down 121, heading for Miwok she played her conversation with Gareth back in her mind. The man was certifiable. That was all there was to it. "King Arthur and the Knights of the Round Table my flaming ass. Who does he think he is? Oh wait. Wait! I know. He thinks he's one of Morguase's kids. Oh yeah and that makes him King Arthur's nephew."

Molly shook her head and pounded the steering wheel of her Jeep. "And I'm about as crazy as he is! What the heck kind of bimbo crawls in bed with a guy cause he has a hot body? Well Mr. Gareth whateverhislastnameis from Orkney has another thing coming. That jerk shows up on my doorstep again I am so calling the police. What a nut ball. And I thought Vincent was bad news with his sci fi conventions and dressing up like Mr. Spock. At least Spock was from this century, or the last one or . . . or . . . well at least he didn't talk like a bad imitation of Errol Flynn in Robin Hood. One of the companions my derriere."

The second she hit Highway 121 Molly floored the gas. Usually she just about broke the speed limit because she was running late for work. Today it was to get away from the crazy man. "He's probably got a million and one STDs to boot. Note to self—self, call for a full sex related test panel on Monday. He's probably a walking pharmacopeia of who knows what. Sleeping for hundreds of years waiting for Arthur to wake him up. Pulleez. I wonder if he knows how wacked he sounded."

Rounding the corner to Highway 29, Molly looked both ways and got ready to fly on the straightaway. Even in the height of tourist season, between the hours she worked and the fact she traveled out of the Napa Valley towards Marin meant she wouldn't have to deal with much traffic. From driving the route the past ten years she knew all the spots where the highway patrol hid waiting to pull over unsuspecting sightseers who imbibed a bit too much of the free wine dispensed at the various wineries. And, they knew her. The police community was pretty close knit, even if she weren't an officer or dispatcher. Not that they were beyond citing her if she really broke the law. Still, it felt good to punch the gas and revel in the freedom of getting away from crazy Gareth of Orkney.

She punched the button for a favorite Melissa Etheridge CD, cranked up the volume as *Testify* started to play and let the wind from the open top of the mustang. Moments later two highway patrol cars flew by going code three in the opposite direction, the flashing lights and whining sirens gave her a major adrenaline rush. "Musta been a crash back there." She shook her head, crashes out on 29 Highway were always pretty bad. The thought no sooner cleared her mind when she saw a helicopter streaking across the sky, flying low to the ground. "Hmmm."

Melissa got turned off in favor of the local news and traffic station, " . . . that's right, Alisa," a male reporter whose voice seemed to bounce ever so slightly leading Molly to think he must be in the news helicopter that'd just passed her, "there's a man, well we're guessing it's a man because, well what woman would don a suit of armor on a Saturday afternoon?" he snickered.

"So what you're telling us Neil, is there is a man in a full suit of armor on a, did you say white horse? Charging down Highway 29?"

"Exactly, Alisa. The horse, even from the air looks huge and appears to be in full medieval armor itself, right down to a plumb on its head. What's that?" The sound of mumbling carried over the air a moment before Neil came back on the air, "Gus, my pilot, says that the horse looks mighty mean. And there are now six patrol cars coming up from behind the horse, between them and the two CHP cars we passed coming up this way I think it's safe to say they're in hot pursuit on this knight in shining armor, racing his war horse across Napa Valley."

"Well, Neil," this Alisa woman chuckled, "Do you think he's pursuing a damsel in distress?"

"Could be. I'm telling you, that lance he's holding to the side looks like the real deal."

"Oh *shit*! Mr. Merle, I'm going to kill you," Molly screamed to the open air as she slowed just enough to turn the car around, kicking up a cloud of dust as she peeled out back towards Napa. "Please, please, please tell me he didn't put on that ridiculous armor of his and isn't riding a war horse that appeared out of nowhere. Please. I believe, I believe. Just don't let it be true."

Overhead the CHP helicopter flew toward Napa, pretty much confirming Molly's worst fears. It had to be Gareth. Who else would climb up on a horse, a white one to boot, and come charging in full knightly garb down the freeway? Hopefully he would surrender and keep his mouth shut about his being one of the knights of the round table. They'd lock him up and throw away the key and as delightful as that sounded right now, she wasn't about to try to explain it to anyone. Not that anyone would ask her, but she'd need to do the right thing and come forward and at least try to help Mr. Merle with his whack-job nephew. "This is so not good."

"Alisa, you aren't going to believe this," Neil's excited voice carried over the air.

"What's happening, Neil? We've got listeners calling in about this knight on the big white horse. Who is he? Is this an advertisement for a new King Arthur movie?"

"I don't know about a movie, Alisa, but another rider just arrived."

"You mean he rode up along the first?"

"No. I mean he just appeared from out of the blue. One second there was just this one guy charging down 29, jumping his horse over cop cars and, wait, right, Gus says there was a puff of smoke and suddenly the second guy was there and he's got the same kind of mean lance pointing out and oh my god! This is unreal. There are two more knights. I'm telling you, Alisa, this is unbelievable. One second there is nothing and suddenly there are three of them charging up behind the first guy."

"Neil, if it weren't for all the calls we're getting that these men on these big horses were just about dropping from the sky I'd think you were crazy. Apparently everyone is seeing this. Wait, wait, Neil, do you see a red Jeep CJ7? Apparently there's a woman with long brown hair driving it and she just blew through the police line that was set up to block those guys in."

"I do Alisa. I see her. She's heading towards the first rider and even from up here I can see she doesn't look too happy. Damn."

"What? Neil, what's going on?" Alisa breathlessly pushed for answers.

"The guy on the horse, the first one, he just jammed that

lance into the ground, jumped off the horse and threw back his helmet. One of the police officers tried to stop the woman and she pushed him out of the way and is stalking up to the guy."

"One of our callers said she's yelling at him."

"I can see her gesturing at him and the other three who have pulled up behind the first guy. Gees, those horses are *huge*. Okay, okay, one of the cops is trying to pull her back and she just rounded off a good punch in his gut and is now back to yelling at the guy. He's pulled off his helmet and with that long blond hair of his I have to wonder if this isn't some Hollywood set up. Especially since the other three have taken off their helmets and they have beards and long hair. Alisa, this looks like something right out of King Arthur and his knights or Robin Hood. Now that's weird."

"What? Neil? I can't see, neither can our listeners, what do you see?"

"A big black limo just appeared."

"You mean it drove up?"

"No, like the guys on the horses, one second there was nothing and then suddenly there it was. There's a guy in a suit with long white hair and he's approaching the man and woman. He just nodded to the other three and the first guy is turning to him and gesturing to the woman from the red car. A woman has joined the man in the suit."

"Neil, can you land and see what you can hear?"

"Good idea, Alisa, let's see if we can get clearance."

"See if you can pick up anything they are saying. What are the cops doing?"

"This is kind of weird, Alisa. One minute they were approaching, guns drawn and now they're standing back, almost like their frozen in place. What do your callers on the ground have to say?"

"I gotta tell you, Neil, this is odd, there's nothing but

silence. Like you said, it's as if everyone on the ground is frozen in place. Neil? Can you hear me? Neil? Neil?"

CHAPTER TWENTY-FIVE

"Are you crazy? Are you absolutely frickin crazy?" Molly stormed toward the four men who now stood besides their chargers. She barely glanced at Mr. Merle and Vivienne as they approached from the limousine.

Gareth turned, a smile of pure pleasure lighting his face. "Molly! My brothers have arrived! You see? I *am* a knight of the realm."

"No. No I don't see. What I see is three more whackos standing around in clothing meant to look like knights. What the hell are you thinking? Riding down the highway on horses with weapons drawn?"

She spun toward Mr. Merle, hands on hips no one could miss that the woman was absolutely livid. "And you! You couldn't have one lunatic nephew? You had to have four of them? This isn't funny. This so isn't funny."

Her watched beeped. "Oh shit. Shit, shit, shit. Now I'm going to be late for work. Major late for work and with an IA hanging over my head."

She spun again toward Gareth and shoved against his chest. "I'm going to kill you. I swear you are so dead. What are you thinking? No, wait, wait. You weren't thinking. Oh no, wait, you were thinking. You thought how else can I humiliate that woman? Sucker her into a trip to the coast, screw her senseless and then on the worst day of her life make it even worse by showing up like you're going to the renaissance faire with a bunch of your fraternity buddies and make me late for work. Very funny Gareth of Orkney, you flaming asshole."

She pushed Gareth out of the way and glared at the other three men standing close by, the two light haired ones barely containing their mirth. The dark-haired one the only serious one in the lot merely stood staring at her.

"Well done, brother." The one that looked just about exactly like Gareth told him. "The wench has fire. Art thou done with her?"

"Nay, brother," The other blond-haired one chuckled, "Me thinks she is done with him."

"Cease." The dark-haired one directed the others. "It appears the wizard has conjured quite a mess this time. Who art these people? Look to the women—" he gestured to the gathering crowd and a group of twenty-something women all in short skirts and shorts ogling the men. "Light skirts all about. What place is this, Gareth?"

"Oh shut up." Molly found a spot on his arm where the armor parted just enough for him to punch him. The large brunette looked at her as if a fly had merely lit on his arm.

"I will tell you, big brother. This is the land of Napa and this is my Lady Molly." Gareth came up behind her and laid his hands on her shoulders. "Molly, may I present my brothers, Aggravain, Gehris and Gawain."

Her head spun. She glanced at the sky for sanity, tears spilled down her cheeks. "Why, Mr. Merle? Why are you allowing this to happen? What did I ever do to you?"

Mr. Merle stepped over to them. "I'm not sure why this is happening, Molly."

"And these people. What is wrong with them? Why are they just standing there as if they are frozen or statues? What have you done to them?"

"Don't worry about them. Vivienne and I have merely placed them in a suspended state. When they wake they will have no recollection this—incident happened. They will go about their business without a thought."

"Sure. Like that's possible. Mr. Merle, that helicopter has a reporter on it. They broadcast this all over the Bay Area and beyond. The world knows these lunatics showed up on horses and were charging down the highway. And don't think for a minute my job didn't hear about it. Napa borders Marin and Miwok is the first town inside the county line. Trust me, they've got units standing by waiting for someone or something to come through there. I don't need this. I so don't need this and now I'm late for work. Someone just shoot me. Please. Put me out of my misery and just shoot me."

"Molly." Mr. Merle put his arm around her the way a favorite uncle might hold his distraught niece. "I may regret saying this, but I can make things right. I can move people through time. I can place you outside your work moments before you are due to arrive. I can even procure a latte for you so you don't need to go pick one up."

"How, how do you know I stop at Java, Java for a coffee before work?"

"Carrie told me. She often spoke of you and what you go through at the police department there in Miwok. Now, would you like me to take care of that and then after your work we can talk?"

She sniffed, "Sure. Why not? But this, this is too much to take in."

"Do you want me to make your forget?"

"No-o-o-o," she warbled. "I want to understand what's going on. Can you make everyone else forget and I'll remember?"

"I think we can do that." She saw him raise his hand a moment later she stood beside her car in the Miwok police department parking lot with an extra large cup of hot something—she sure hoped it was coffee if not a quadruple latte—in her hand. She glanced around the parking lot and softly called, "Thanks, Mr. Merle, I think."

When she walked in the station's door Shannon greeted her with a huge smile. "You'll never guess?"

Still shaken from what happened an hour before, well not an hour ago because it was now before what happened, happened. Or something like that. Just thinking about it made her dizzy. And did that mean she was an hour older or an hour younger? Reality check—at least the clock said she was on time for her shift and minutes ago she was over an hour late. "What?"

"Guess, guess, guess!"

"I had a rough night, Shannon, tell me."

"Fine. You're no fun. Kris and Goodwin both called in sick. Word is she's in the ER with a raging STD and he's not too far behind."

"That's not exactly news. The ER part is but the STD, we all know she's got herpes and shares."

"It is when her girl parts are swollen the size of a large grapefruit."

Molly dropped her bag. "What? Are you serious?"

"Total truth. Becca took her to the ER when they got off this morning. Apparently Kris was fidgeting so much during the shift Becca asked her what was going on. Right there in dispatch Kris pulled down her jeans, spread her legs and *showed* Becca. "

"Eeeuuuu, TMI."

"Like you wouldn't want the total 411."

"That's true. So Goodwin?"

"From what I hear that boy won't be needing any Viagra for the coming days."

"No way."

"Way."

"So what's wrong with them?"

" Apparently her herpes major flared up and she also got some kind of fungal infection on top of it. From what Becca said the combination makes you totally swell up and it smells horrific. Kris is out of commission for some time, maybe even longer than tonight."

"I wouldn't mind a week or two without her being around."

"Only a week or two?"

Together they laughed and Molly wondered if Mr. Merle had anything to do with their temporary good fortune. Her next thought was whether or not the same could be done to the Red Queen.

Chapter Twenty-six

"All of you, into the car. Now." Mr. Merle frantically gestured toward the limousine.

"You! I should have known," dark-haired Aggravain looked the elderly gent up and down with disdain.

"Aggravain, please, into the car. We will discuss this later."

"Where doth he order us?" Gawain asked.

"I believe tis that odd looking steed." Gehris responded.

Aggravain strode over and peered into the vehicle. "I like not this car."

"Like it or not, you either enter on your own or I'll whisk you in there. The good folk of this time are waking and Vivienne and I cannot hold them much longer."

"Speak for yourself, Merlin," Vivienne chuckled. With a flick of her wrist she caused the previously frozen in place helicopter to turn 180 degrees yet it still remained suspended in the air.

"What place is this?" Gawain asked.

"Tis called, Napa, little brother." Gareth informed him.

"Nap-on? I should enjoy such with the disappeared wench. What didst thou do with her, Merlin?" A grinning Gehris looked around the field that held now waking news people, tourists and police officers.

"That wench, as you call her, is my lady." Gareth, fists bunched, took a step toward his twin.

"Truly?" Gehris smiled back.

"Truly."

"It seems this Nap hath much to recommend it," Gawain

212

continued to look about him.

"Napa." Gareth absently reminded him while keeping his gaze on Gehris.

"Gentlemen, please, we can sort out wenches and ladies at my shop. Right now we need to get you out of this field and away from those who might see you."

"I've naught to hide from," Aggravain groused.

"You will if these folk see you. You would not like where people dressed in knightly garb in broad daylight for no reason are placed."

"I was dressed in the fighting raiment I wore on the last battle when I first arrived in this time and *you* told Molly twas for a play."

"Neil? Neil can you hear me?" The disembodied voice of the newswoman squawked through the air.

With a sigh Mr. Merle spun his hands in opposing circles and one by one the horses popped out of the field. Before the three recently arrived brothers completed gasping, they found themselves in the long black limousine with a smugly smiling Gareth leading the way.

"I like this not," Aggravain grit out while squirming from side to side.

Gehris chuckled, "You squirm as if ants crept within your trews, Brother."

"I will place more than ants within your hose, lout."

"Boys, boys," Vivienne reached out and patted the air. "Enough."

Gawain calmly looked about the vehicle. "Methinks this tis a convenient and comfy cart."

"You have that aright, brother. Wait till you behold the other treasures of this time." Gareth assured him.

"I like it not," Aggravain groused yet again.

"You like little, elder brother," Gehris smirked although one could easily see he had paled upon Mr. Merle began moving past the assembled gawkers who were beginning to arose from the spell he'd cast.

"I would know where our horses are, wizard." Aggravain demanded.

Gareth sniggered, "Beneath the hood."

"*You* do not amuse me little brother."

"I didn't mean to."

"Has the wench bewitched your tongue, brother?" Gehris asked while trying to look calm within the moving conveyance.

"There is much to recommend this time."

"Again you speak of this time. What do you mean, Gareth? What are these buildings and these devices that speed past us?"

"All in good time, boys. All in good time," Vivienne smiled at them. "Relax and when we get to Merlin's shop we will explain all."

"Not all," Gareth reminded her. "You have not yet been able to explain my presence although, I truly believe I am here to rescue my lady."

"The lady who disappeared as soon as Merlin arrived?" Gawain asked clearly interested in the news Gareth had to relate.

"The very same. I suspect Merlin has sent her to her labors."

"Ah, so I was right! The wench wouldst enjoy a tryst with me."

"Not likely. If you value your life, Brother you will stay well away from her." Gareth leaned back and folded his arms across his chest.

A moment later Mr. Merle stopped the car behind Treasures and with a flutter of her fingers Vivienne caused the doors to open. When all had stepped outside the long black conveyance, with a whoosh of his arms it disappeared.

Having witnessed Merlin's magic before his actions caused no surprise among the brothers.

"This way, boys." Merlin led them into the shop and up the back stairs to his apartment. "Gareth, could you start some tea for us?"

"I would have ale," Gehris clomped over to the window but before he could look out Vivienne caused the drapes to close. "What do you hide from me, Vivienne?"

"It is nothing I wish to hide from you. Rather to hide you from the people of this time. At least until we can get you into some modern clothing and get you settled in."

"Wha — ?" Gehris spun on her.

"Relax, Gehris," Gareth interceded. "I experienced much the same when I woke. Merlin and Vivienne have taught me much of this time."

"Gareth is right, but he, and now you all, have much to learn and not much time to do so. I now fear you are only the first of the companions to wake. I will need your assistance as the others wake and make their way here."

"So the legend is true?" Gawain looked from one to the other, hope lighting his gray orbs.

"It would appear so," a resigned Mr. Merle told him. "Now, I have much to tell you in a short time. Most important right now, I believe I need to check on Molly to make certain she has her life under control."

"I will go to her," Gareth started for the door.

"Perhaps later, Gareth. Right now we need to settle in your brothers. Molly is fully capable of taking care of herself. If nothing else she is organized and practical. She will handle her experience just fine."

The tea kettle whistled and Gareth turned to prepare the tea.

"I'm sorry, boys, perhaps later I will conjure you some ale. Right now though I need you to have your wits about you."

215

Merlin tried to placate them.

"We will listen," Aggravain spoke for the brothers. "Tell us, where is this battle we have woken to fight?"

"Good. As Gareth said, it appears the lore is true, at least part of it."

The kettle whistled and while Gareth prepared the tea the brothers sat quietly although if one looked close enough they would see a sliver of nervousness in their eyes.

When all had their cups Merlin stood before them. He cleared his throat and then cleared it again. He took a sip of his tea and swallowed then swallowed again.

"Tis rare to see you without words spilling from your lips," Aggravain goaded him.

"Yes, well I am searching for just the right words to explain to you what is going on or has happened."

"What happened?" Gehris chuckled. "It appears we mounted our steeds and rode from the field of battle to this land of Nap."

"Napa." Gareth once again reminded him.

"If you will all be still I will explain." Merlin looked to each of the brothers.

"Pray do, Merlin," Aggravain gestured to him to begin.

The elderly gent cleared his throat yet again. "Well if you recall, on the eve of the last battle a priestess of Avalon came to Camelot and told us that should ill fall upon Arthur you would all fall into a deep sleep and would awaken in the time of the world's greatest need. The last centuries have had such tremendous events — time and again I thought that would be the time. Wars of the Roses, discovering America, the Revolutionary War, the Civil War, World Wars I and II, the great depression—"

"It seems, Merlin, you think we are only needed for war." Gawain observed.

"I didn't mean it to sound that way, Gawain. I apologize

that it did. There were other great events such as going to the Moon and beyond. I only meant that there have been events of such magnitude that if we ever needed Arthur's leadership and your support they were it. While I am pleased to see you, I do not see why you have woken."

"I do." Gareth leaned toward the white haired gent.

"You do?" Mr. Merle asked, clearly surprised.

"Yes. As I have said again and again, my Lady Molly needs my help." He looked to his brothers, "She labors for the hellish Red Queen of Miwok, a veritable dragon and I believe I have been woken to vanquish the beastly woman."

"Ahem," Mr. Merle cleared his throat. "We do not slay evil doers these days."

"Truly?" Gehris looked from one to the other. "What do you do with them then?"

"Well, hopefully justice finds them. Some people of this time have a thing they call karma. The theory is that some greater being or energy will smite you if you behave badly. A form of justice."

"Have you seen this karma?" Gawain asked.

"It is not a tangible thing or person. It is an idea that does seem to have merit. That said, Gareth, I beg you, do not attempt to cause any harm to Julie Prince, Molly's Red Queen. The law of this time would treat you rather harshly for doing so and lest you think to tell them you are a knight of the realm, you would be locked away in what they call an institute. And while this is all very interesting to talk about, I do feel I need to explain some things to you all." Merlin looked from one to the other to ensure he had their attention. From the serious Aggravain to the impish Gehris to the lighthearted Gawain, he noted he was their sole focus.

"The first thing you must know is that in this time I am known as Mr. Merle. You call me Merlin or Wizard people will think you mentally weak at best."

"Merle?" Aggravain raised a brow.

"Aye, and he uses the first name Arthur. As if that would hide his true self," Gareth muttered.

"In each era I have chosen a name that should Arthur wake and hear it, he would know it was me. Although until Gareth arrived I thought I would know beforehand he was returning."

"So you are not all-knowing," Aggravain's tone indicated he'd long held that belief.

"Ah, Aggravain, a part of you will forever be your mother's son. At least in how you think on me. Perhaps that is for the best as you do keep me on my toes and remind me there is a part of me that is and forever will be human. Anyway, the earlier centuries it was easy for me to move around and do what needed to be done. It is truly only in the last couple where devices called cameras were invented and other implements that can track a person came into being that it became necessary for me to move about more frequently and change my name every few decades. Fortunately, as elderly as I look, few people pay me much mind. As to how you came to wake now, I am not certain."

"I suspect your magic helping Carrie Taylor may have moved things along," Vivienne quietly interjected.

"So you've said, Vivienne." Merlin nodded. "But how?"

"Before Black Eagle, had you ever used any of these modern devices to conjure?"

Merlin considered the question a moment before answering no.

"Then when you moved Black Eagle through time I suspect you interfered with the natural process of things. You and I and even Gareth have noted the sword glows a bit brighter day by day."

"The sword?" Gawain sat up straighter. "You hold Excalibur?"

Somberly Merlin nodded, "It has been with me all these centuries."

"How can that be?" Gehris rubbed his jaw. "We all know you oversaw Galahad throwing it into Avalon's lake."

"Ah, but the Lady of the Lake sits here with you. Vivienne and I spoke after that dark day and she returned Excalibur to me to hold for Arthur and his return. And yes, it does grow a bit brighter day by day."

"Then Arthur is awake?" Gehris rose and looked about the room as if he would find his king roaming about the halls.

"No. For some reason Gareth woke first and now, almost a month after his arrival you have woken."

"I suspect I know why my brothers have woken."

"Why is that?" Vivienne gently asked.

"Because of Molly."

"Molly?" Shaggy white brows rose to Merlin's hairline.

"Yes. She and I had something of a disagreement this morning. She does not wish to believe I am one of Arthur's knights. She says such is not possible. I asked her how can she believe in her friend Carrie traveling through time to be with the man she loves yet not believe I am one of Arthur's Companions. I woke to help her with her difficulties, of that I have no doubt. She did not take it well and ordered me to leave. I beseeched the gods for a way to show her I speak the truth and it occurred to me if I rode to her in knightly garb perhaps she would believe me. I was scarce out of Napa and I saw Gehris rode beside me followed by Aggravain and Gawain. If the arrival of my brothers could not convince her, then what?"

"Yes, what indeed. Which reminds me, as I said, I should check on her. I don't imagine finding herself deposited at her work with no explanation is setting well with her. If there is one thing about Molly, she likes order and clear reasons why things happen in her world. Before I go though, I need to ask you all not to leave this apartment, not until we have acclimated you to this time."

"The spell?" Gareth puzzled.

"Perhaps. Although there have been a few times you slipped into olden time speaking. What Gareth is saying so much of how we live has changed in the last few hundred years that the only way Vivienne and I could think as a way to ease him into this time was to cast a spell that gave him as much history as any recent college graduate. And never mind what I mean by that, if the spell works it will be clear to you. You need to fit in this time and at the moment I cannot think of an easier way to acclimate you."

"Will it hurt?" Gawain leaned back in his chair as if that would keep Merlin at bay.

"I felt nothing, not even a tingle, when they did such for me. All I noticed was that I had much more knowledge, almost akin to memories immediately after. Now I feel as if I have always known these things. My words are different. I speak in the modern tongue, as you may have noticed. Other than that I am no different than in our day."

Aggravain nodded toward Gareth, "Wouldst thou dress us as such?"

"You mean the jeans?" Merlin asked.

"Yes."

"If you like them, certainly."

"I would have them now, Wizard."

"Now remember . . ."

"Yes. I do."

"I would have them too. I could not help but notice how the damsels of this time looked upon my ugly twin and his legs in them." Gehris grinned.

"That is not my purpose for desiring them," Aggravin shot a wicked look at his younger brother. "After unknown years in my trews I require clean clothing."

"Of course," Gawain smirked.

"It is of no consequence," Merlin stood, uttered a few words and with a flash of his hands the three new arrivals wore t-shirts, jeans and modern boots. Gone were their medieval garb and accessories.

"Now," Merlin continued, "Vivienne, shall we cast the Make Modern spell so I may be off to check on Molly?"

"Agreed." Vivienne rose and stood beside Merlin and together the uttered the words to make modern men of the medieval warriors. One by one they yawned and then turned to each other and nodded.

"How do you feel?" Vivienne asked, looking in to each of their eyes.

"Hungry," Gehris grinned.

CHAPTER TWENTY-SEVEN

"I don't think it a good idea, Gareth."

"I do. I wish to see Molly."

Merlin shook his head. "I understand why you feel the need to speak with her. I'm concerned though that at the moment she may still be somewhat, well irked, at you. She's had a lot of information to process in a short time and we don't want to overwhelm her now, do we?"

"Then I should be the one to go to her."

"And do what, my boy? Gareth, before she met you, she was struggling with Carrie traveling back in time. Actually, she had a hard time thinking out of the box before then when Black Eagle first arrived."

"None of it my doing and she met me before Carrie left."

"True, true. Consider this though. When she first returned today, to stop you from continuing to ride after her, she seemed mighty peeved. And what was it you said about her not believing when you are from? Why not let me see if I can smooth things over a bit?"

"*You* smooth things over? The world's most renowned meddler assist *me* with my problems? What know you of courtly love?"

"More than you, my boy, more than you. Visit with your brothers, I'll be back directly. I promise."

With a flick of his wrist Merlin disappeared only to materialize a moment later in front of the Miwok police department. He paused to gather himself and take in the lay of the land a moment before entering. Knowing Molly, at least from what he knew from what Carrie had told him, when he transported her to the station, arriving in time for her shift, she would just go on in and act like nothing happened. This could be one of those times her strict level-headed-stay-in-the-box way of thinking would definitely be to her benefit. The Molly he knew had probably just plowed ahead, walked into the station and sat down to work without a thought about what happened moments before. Among the many things Molly Nichols did well, denial was high on the list.

He glanced through the glass doors and saw Molly standing at the counter engaged in conversation with a woman. Taking a step back he studied her — calm, cool and collected. Completely immersed in what she was doing and if nothing odd had occurred a short time ago. They spoke a few minutes more before the woman turned and headed out the door. Merlin gave her a quick salute on his way in and called out to Molly.

Molly looked quickly to her left and right before opening the waist high door and started to step out, froze and spun on her heel and walked back inside.

Merlin sighed. This wasn't going to go smoothly at all. If she wouldn't speak with him she'd probably blanked the whole episode from her mind. Or had he done it? Merlin thought back to his actions and words when he sent her an hour back in time and to the front of the station to arrive in time for work. Nope, he hadn't said anything. He doubted Vivienne would have done so. Then again —

He heard her call "thanks" just before she exited the service area, walked up to him, grabbed his arm and pulled him toward the door.

"I can't believe you *popped* in here."

"Molly, I merely wanted to see if you were all right."

"Not in here. There are cameras and audio all over the place."

"So?"

She glanced around the lobby area, "I'm not about to talk about what happened this afternoon here."

Well that answered one pressing question. She remembered what happened. Or at least that something happened. She stood impatiently at the door now propped open to the cooling evening air.

"Are you coming?"

"Of course. Uh, where?"

"Where? Mr.-I-can-send-you-through-time doesn't know *where*? Or did you want to blink us there?"

"Blink?"

"Like on that old TV show with the witch. You know, blink."

"Oh I see. Actually it wasn't *Bewitched* where the actress blinked. On *Bewitched* a fine actress named Elizabeth Montgomery wriggled her nose. You're thinking of *I Dream of Jeannie* where . . ."

"Mr. Merle! Do you really think I care about a television program at this point in time? You've turned my life into the craziest, most insane, most unbelievable circus that even Carrie with her wild imagination couldn't conjure. Television my ass."

Okay, the normally calm and staid brunette was in high dander. Peeved didn't even begin to cover it. "I see. Well why don't we walk where you'd like to chat as I don't believe with your surveillance equipment you really want us . . . blinking about."

"Got that right." She strode out the door, down the steps and took a military precise turn to the right and headed up the street. At the corner she stood tapping her foot, waiting for him to catch up. Women certainly hadn't changed in some respects over the centuries, that was certain.

With Merlin trailing behind she entered the coffee shop

and stopped so abruptly he crashed into her. "Gees, couldn't you see *that* coming either?"

"I am not a charlatan who pretends to see the future, Molly."

"Right." She walked up to the counter and ordered a four shot latte for herself and a peppermint mocha for Mr. Merle.

The addition of the peppermint mocha told Merlin her ire was cooling. At least he hoped so. She could still pour it over his head. Without a word she accepted the drinks and motioning with her chin headed over to a cache of chairs snuggled into a corner.

"I thank you for the mocha, Molly."

"Just because I bought you a drink doesn't mean I'm not majorly irritated with you."

"Of course not."

"Just so you know."

"Of course."

She sat, head bowed and stared at her drink. Merlin sat quietly by her side, waiting until he heard a sniffle. "Molly?" He softly asked.

Another sniffle and she looked up, "Mr. Merle, my world is falling apart. Bit by bit everything I thought I knew or believed or thought or counted on is just crumbling. I've lost my best friend, I'm on the verge of losing my job and it's pretty clear my sanity isn't too far behind."

"Believe me, you are as sane as I . . ."

She glared at him.

"You aren't crazy, Molly."

"I'm losing it, Mr. Merle. I'm really losing it. I'm just glad it happened today, on a Saturday, instead of on a Friday or Monday when the Red Queen's in the office. Then again, if I end up in the land of padded walls with old Dean, it wouldn't matter when it happened, now would it?"

"You aren't going to end up there, Molly. I won't let it."

"*You* won't let it. *You* cause all these problems in my life and expect me to believe that you'll keep me from going into the loony bin?"

Merlin cleared his throat. "I do need to explain some things to you. However, I'm not at all certain this is the time."

Molly waved her hand in front of her, "I've got as long as I need. Like I said, Julie isn't in, Captain Berger has already done his walk through today and Chris is in the ER or home sick. Shannon is covering for me so I've got all the time I need. You can start explaining any time."

"All right." He took a swallow of his mocha, not so much from thirst but to arrange his thoughts. "I came tonight mainly to be certain you were doing okay. I thought we could talk next week sometime."

"Mr. Merle, I'm losing it. Slowly, but surely, I'm losing it, so if you can give me some sense of normalcy, now, I'd appreciate it."

"I understand. So let me start . . ."

"Are you really King Arthur's Merlin?"

She certainly knew how to cut to the chase.

Before he could answer she continued, "I mean, well, that sounds crazy, but how could you be? It's just a story, right? It's just a great story that came down through the ages, right?"

"Would it help you to believe that, Molly?"

"No. I want the truth. I know you had something to do with Carrie and Black Eagle. If you *are* Merlin then it makes sense. But if you're just a nice old guy who likes to weave stories, then I just don't know. What happened today—I don't know if I'll ever wrap my mind around it. Do you have any idea what it's been like for me since I got to work today? How hard it's been not to totally wig out. We had the news on and there was nothing, absolutely nothing about what happened. Am I the only one who remembers any of it?"

"The boys remember and, of course, Vivienne and I do. The

others, no. When I sent you here to be on time for work we shifted time back to before the . . . event . . . happened. I couldn't send Gareth's brothers back. But I could shift the others to the earlier time."

"Why did you leave me with the memory?"

"Would you rather I hadn't?"

She slid the straw she used to drink her latte part way out and played with it in the cup.

"Well?"

"I don't know. I want to say yes, but then I say no. I'm just so confused. None of this makes sense. In my world King Arthur was a story, the Knights of the Round Table were part of that story, as was Merlin. For those living on Planet Molly you can count on the sun rising when it's supposed to and setting about the same way. Strange things like people showing up in your roommate's bed don't happen and that same roommate doesn't just disappear without a trace and leave you notes in old desks. In Molly-ville you don't meet gorgeous guys who make your heart go pit-a-pat who tell you they are from a group of medieval warriors who've been sleeping a thousand or so years and he's just now woken up to save your day. Molly-land is predicable, concrete and reliable. None of what has happened in my life the past two months or so is remotely predicable, concrete or reliable ergo I am losing it."

"No, Molly, you aren't losing it."

"Then I've already lost it."

"No. you haven't. These things have happened and while they have altered your world somewhat—"

"Altered my world *somewhat*? Try shattered."

"Yes, I can see how you might feel that way and I do apologize. I will admit I helped things with Carrie and Black Eagle along—"

"Helped along? What? What, he on his way here through time and you ran into him on the old time travel train and offered to give him a lift and just plopped him in Carrie's bed?"

"Well, no. I did have something to do with their situation, but Molly dear, I had nothing to do with Gareth's arrival in your life. No one was more surprised than I the day he popped into my shop."

"So there was a puff of smoke and poof, there he was?"

"Something like that. Are you sure you wish to continue talking now?"

"Yes. Confronting your fears is like that pick up the piece of paper and deal with it thing."

"Pick up the piece of paper . . ."

"You know, the time management — oh god, I can't believe I'm talking to you about time management. You who manipulate time. Anyway it's that thing where you pick up a piece of paper and deal with it once and send it on its way. You don't keep picking it up and shuffling it here and there. I do it with paper and I try to do it odd episodes my life. So please. Go on."

"Very well. I am indeed King Arthur's counselor, Merlin. Vivienne and I come from a long line of magicians, for lack of a better word, and have lived through the centuries guarding the tools Arthur will need when he wakes."

"Did, does, was, well Avalon. Was it real?"

"Oh my dear girl, it *is* real. It exists yet today, but no mere mortal can venture there. Vivienne and I know the way through the mists that guard the island. It is not a place anyone alive today would venture to, primarily because to go you must first believe. On the Dark Day I did transport Arthur there and to prepare for his return, in compliance with the legend, I sent the companions into a deep sleep."

"Weren't they supposed to wake in the time of the world's greatest need?"

"That was the belief. However, as you well know our

world has seen innumerable wars, plagues and other plights yet not a one stirred until a few weeks ago. Gareth believes he woke only to help you with your problem."

"So you didn't have anything to do with it?"

"Vivienne believes, well—"

"Go on. You know if you don't tell me, I'll ask her."

"Yes, well. She believes when I assisted Black Eagle to the present I did something to shift the ley lines."

"Ley lines?"

"They are what some belief systems consider lines of power or earth. Only a theory, the lines, but Vivienne blames me."

"It *is* your fault! All of this is your fault."

"I may have had something to do with it. Truly, Molly I only wanted for Carrie to be happy. I saw how Dean's treatment of her made her so sad and I felt I had to do something to help her. She deserved a good man. And then I remembered Black Eagle and how all he ever wanted was to meet a good woman."

"Wasn't there anyone living in the today world you could have introduced Carrie to? Wouldn't that have solved the problem without gumming up the entire universe?"

"I thought about that, but I could see they were meant to be together. So I brought him here. Some how either I misjudged my magic or universal forces chose that moment to collide and Gareth woke. Something happened about the time Black Eagle arrived that caused a disturbance great enough to wake, at least, the Orkney boys."

"Okay, I'll bite. How did Gareth find you?"

"That is not as hard as you might think. I hold Arthur's sword and a few other pieces of magic from Avalon including a time mirror. Within it's reflection it holds other times and places. For the most part you choose one and step into it."

She leaned forward, eyes flashing with eagerness, "So I

could walk through and go visit Carrie?"

"Would that travel for others would be so easy. I've often thought how if it were so people could, well make peace with themselves."

"What do you mean, Mr. Merle?"

"You know how, well —" He certainly didn't want to open any doors that shouldn't be opened, but he didn't want Molly to feel like he was holding something important back from her.

She leaned toward him.

"Have you ever heard someone say that they wished they had one more chance to tell someone something?"

"You mean like when your mom or dad dies and you wish you could have told them just one more time you loved them?"

"Exactly. I've often thought it would be such a gift to use the mirror to give people that final moment of peace."

She grabbed his forearm like it was a lifeline. "Then why haven't you?"

"Because it can be unpredictable. Because there would be the temptation to say something or try to undo something. Because one little act could change history."

"But you changed history when you brought Black Eagle here and again when Carrie went back with him."

"No. Not really. You see, history righted itself when Black Eagle went back to his own time."

"But you still changed it when Carrie went back. You changed my life and the lives of people she knows now."

"I don't think so. You see, I did visit Black Eagle a few years after I took his photograph and he was married to a woman who looked very much like Carrie. The first time she walked into my shop I knew she was the woman I saw him with so you see, history recorded her being there."

"Right and left me to pick up the pieces of her life. To make

230

excuses and figure out what to do so people don't think I'm a crazy lady or that I did something horrible to her."

"But you have had a message from her and perhaps she will write more." He made a mental note to himself to travel back to Black Eagle's village and ask Carrie to do that very thing. That was one of the problems with this world today. With instant messages and immediate communication, it was hard to cover up the fact that someone hadn't just moved but moved to another time. Even twenty years ago someone could move through time and all you had to do was say that they had moved to a remote area. Even remote areas today could have some sort of communication thanks to satellites. The way technology was advancing there was the growing chance his true identity would be discovered.

Either that or, as Molly feared for herself, he would be locked up in an asylum. Perhaps that was why the knights were waking — they could do so and blend in now more easily than if they did it say in a year when technology advanced even further. Yes, he would have to address Carrie's disappearance in some fashion.

"I suppose. I've been so bogged down I haven't tried to write her back. Well, I sent her one note, just a short one that I was glad she was happy. But I haven't checked to see if it's still in the desk I guess in part I don't want to know, you know? That as long as it's out there somewhere I don't have to find out for sure one way or the other."

"It's not like you to hide from things."

"No. No it's not. This though, this is out of my realm of understanding, that's for sure. But why is Gareth really one of King Arthur's knights?"

"Yes, dear, he is, as are his three brothers who arrived today."

"Then why is he here? Why are they here? Are more coming?"

That indeed was the question unless, as he'd just considered, they needed to wake now, before modern knowledge would discover them. Merlin cleared his throat, "As he has said, and I am beginning to believe, he is here to help you. That the sole reason for his waking is to help you. As to his brothers, or others waking, that we do not know."

"That's a nice idea, but Mr. Merle, how could he possibly help me? What does he think? That he can come riding in on his big white horse and rescue me? That's something out of one of Carrie's fantasy romance novels, not my very real world. And so help me, if he climbs back on that big white horse and rides after me again I will request a 5150 assessment on him and have him locked away once and for all. Anyone hears his rambling about being Morgause's son, they'll wrap him up tight for the rest of his life. My problems aren't insurmountable. They're just things I have to go through, you know? And really, what do I have to deal with? Taking care of Carrie's business and getting through this upcoming IA with the Red Queen. Piece of cake, right?"

"Perhaps. Have you considered that maybe simply having Gareth there to listen to you and not pass any kind of judgment could be a form of rescue?"

She considered that. "You mean a sounding board?"

"Exactly. You and Carrie always had each other to share your fears, worries and concerns along with your good times. Now that she is gone, perhaps Gareth is here to share those same things with you and before you say you can handle it on your own, consider things from his standpoint."

"You mean the whole chivalry thing?" She shook her head. "That'll send him packing faster than anything. It drove Vincent away."

"Vincent wasn't the man for you. As to the chivalry aspect. Yes, in part. Can you imagine falling asleep one day and waking up fifteen hundred years in the future? We still ride horses, but not the way he did. We still cook food, but it's much easier than in his day. Weapons, clothing, everything is different. Add in all the history that has come and gone it can be overwhelming. Having someone steady and as even keeled as you are is a gift to him. Perhaps you are meant to help each other."

"I can buy the being friends part, but you don't up and fall in love with a sixteen or seventeen hundred year old or however old man!"

"Molly! He's twenty-four."

"What?"

"Gareth is twenty-four. He didn't age while he slept. That is the magic of Avalon. He was in a form of, oh what do they call it in the science fiction movies—stasis! That's it. He was in a state of stasis!"

"And today? Are there going to be more episodes like today?"

"I certainly hope not," he muttered.

"What?"

"Oh, I said most definitely not. He understands better about your job."

"It's not him that has me worried. Although, that business riding after me on a horse in medieval armor was over the top. No, it's his brothers, especially the big, dark-haired one."

"Aggravain? Truly, his bark is worse than his bite. They understand about not charging after someone like that. Their arrival, well they didn't plan it. You see when they fell asleep at the end of the final battle they did so, they were on their horses. So that is how they woke. They were riding after Arthur and went to their rest. Their bond with each other, as brothers as well as comrades in arms, is quite strong so they were drawn to Gareth."

"I see." She paused and stared at the rough wooden table a moment. "Holy shit! Mr. Merle!"

"Yes, dear?"

"The others. How many knights were there altogether? Like fifty? Are they *all* going to wake up and come riding into Napa."

"Good lord I hope not," he muttered.

"What? You sure are mumbling a lot, Mr. Merle."

"Am I? Yes, well. No I don't expect they will."

"Mr. Merle, are they all waking up? Now?"

"No. I don't think so. After all, how many women need a knight in shining armor to ride to their rescue?"

CHAPTER TWENTY-EIGHT

"Need a knight in shining armor my ass." Molly told the front door of the station as she locked up for the night. They still had paperwork to do, but the station was closed to the public at eleven. "I can't think of any woman that needs some guy on a big horse to ride to her rescue."

"What are you rambling on about, Molly," Shannon asked her when she walked back into the records area.

"Oh my friend that came by today."

"The old man."

"Yeah, Mr. Merle. Thanks for covering for me by the way. He was the last person I expected to show up, but I did need to talk to him."

"So what were you rambling about with him?"

"Oh, nothing really. He asked me if I thought modern women needed knights in shining armor to ride to our rescue."

"And you said?"

"Heck no. There may have been a time like a thousand years ago when women needed a guy to protect and care for them. Today though? No way. Can you think of anything that you need a man to do for you?"

"Well yeah."

"What?"

"I don't know about you, but there are certain advantages in a relationship . . . and a knight. How romantic is that?"

"Right. I got that. I mean work things. We can pretty much accomplish anything we want including taking care of

235

ourselves in a rotten situation. It's not like the olden days when you needed a guy to fight your battles for you and stuff like that."

"True. Still, having a guy come in oozing testosterone and carrying me off to bed has its allure."

"You sound like Carrie. That ever happen to you?"

Shannon giggled. "Nope. Not likely to either. That's the stuff of romance novels, not real life. Although I have to say, it would be nice."

"So what would you do if some guy you were dating suddenly came riding up to you or after you on a big old horse? Would you think he was nuts or romantic?"

"Depends on what he was riding after me for. If he was just charging around for no reason on a horse I'd probably think he was nuts. If we had a fight or he wanted to do something totally dreamy and he came galloping after me so he wouldn't lose me I'd think it was pretty romantic."

"So if I told you I was seeing this guy and we had a bit of a tiff and I was on my way to work and he snagged a horse and rode after me . . ."

"Oh my god, you're in love and you haven't told me! Some guy did that, didn't he? Molly Nichols. Where did you meet him? What's his name? Does he have a friend? That would be soooooo romantic!"

Despite the pressure that was holding firm in her chest Molly laughed. "I'm not exactly in love, more like in like with a touch of lust. Mr. Merle, the guy who came by today? I met one of his nephews and we've seen each other a few times. He's a nice guy, kind of old fashioned in a lot of ways."

"What's his name?"

"Mr. Merle."

"You goober, the nephew, Mr. Oh-sigh."

"Oh. Gareth."

"Gareth," Shannon signed. "What a dreamy name. What

does he do? Did Mr. Merle do like a formal introduction? Is he hot? Does he have a friend?"

"At the moment he doesn't do anything. Well that's not true. Mr. Merle is the guy who owns Treasures, the antique store in Napa. Gareth helps out at the store. He only arrived here a few weeks ago and is still figuring out things. I met him when I was in the store one day and he and I sort of connected."

"You are holding out on me! You are avoiding the two main questions."

"Which are?"

"Molly! I'm so going to get you. Is he hot and does he have a friend?"

An odd tug settled in her chest. A tightness that wasn't painful rather it was anticipatory. Her girl parts clenched in expectation as if her body knew she'd get up close and personal with him before her mind could register the thought. Was Gareth hot? The man scalded her to her toes and then some.

"Well?"

"What? Oh, sorry, I was thinking. Yeah, he's hot. I haven't met any of his friends, but he does have three brothers who, ah, arrived today."

Shannon moved to sit on the edge of the desk beside Molly, "How long are they here for? Are they single? Which brother do you think I'd like?"

"Shan, they just arrived! I only saw them for a few minutes and there were three of them. I had to come into work so I didn't get much of a chance to talk to them. I don't know how long they're here for, or if they're single or if you'd like any of them."

Molly so didn't want to have this conversation. What she wanted to do was come to terms with the fact that the kindly old gent with the white hair and crystal clear blue eyes was

Merlin. Not just named Merlin, but apparently was the real deal.

And that meant King Arthur wasn't just a great story and that the Knights of the Roundtable were real.

And that meant Gareth was really one of those knights and he had in fact woken up in this time. *Well shit.*

"Well dang, find out!" Shannon told her, shaking Molly out of her spiraling thoughts about the weird situation that had unfolded today.

"You don't even know what they look like."

"From the look in you eye and the fact you said Gary?"

"Gareth."

"Gareth—was hot what harm can an intro do? Please? I haven't been on a date in forever."

"Whoa! I don't know word one on any of these guys so let's not rush into setting up my friends just yet, okay?"

"You'll check it out though, right?"

"What if they're assholes?"

"More than some of the cops we work with?"

"I'll check things out when I'm on days off this week, okay?"

"Promise?"

"Definitely. And Shannon, if things with the IA go the way I think they are going to go on Monday, I'll get word to you."

Shannon sat quietly for a few moments and finally drew in a ragged breath. "I know you can't talk about it. Or that they directed you not to. And I know you respect the chain of command not to, but if you do need to talk, like just emotions, I'm here."

"Thanks, Shan. I didn't do anything wrong and maybe this thing needs to run the course, like all the way to a court hearing, to expose what's going on around here. I'll be okay. After all, I've got my knight, right?"

CHAPTER TWENTY-NINE

"I like it not." Aggravain practically growled at his younger brother.

"You like nothing," Gawain chuckled. "Vivienne, hath you more of these pepper moke drinks?"

"Peppermint mochas," Gareth told him, making little effort to keep the smugness from his voice. After all, this was one thing he knew before his brothers.

"I like them as well," Gehris slurped his up with a straw.

With a flick of her wrist Vivienne refilled all but Aggravain's cups. "Are you boys hungry?"

"Aye," Gawain answered her with a smile. "I would enjoy dish of roast boar."

"Sorry, Gawain. No roast boar, however, Merlin does have what they call cold cuts."

"Cold . . ." Gehris stopped with his cup mid-lift.

"Cuts." Gareth nodded. "In this time meat comes in a wrapping, a clear wrapping, already cut and cooked for you."

"I like it not," Aggravain glared at his brothers.

"Why not?" A puzzled Gareth asked.

"How do you know tis truly meat and not some trick?"

Gareth shrugged. "I have eaten much of it. The different meats they have and cheeses will astound you."

The roar of a motorcycle drew the dark-haired brother's attention. Aggravain stood and walked from Mr. Merle's kitchenette toward the front of the shop. "I like not these cars."

Gareth followed him into the main floor of the shop, "They do take a bit to adjust to. Once you do though, you will see their advantages."

"And what of that? Tis is a metal horse?"

"They call it a motorcycle."

"I would have one."

"Mayhap in time Merlin will procure one for you."

"You hath ridden one?"

Gareth shook his head. "Mostly I have stayed here. Until last week I remained in this place Merlin calls Treasures."

"He held you here?"

"No. I had no where to go. There are things in this world that a man alone cannot face. Now that you are here, things will be better."

"And last week?"

"Molly and I journeyed to their ocean. Twas like home to me. Not that it hath been so long since I saw our home. Time passed, yes, but . . ." he sighed. "How do I explain it?"

"The great sleep?" Aggravain softly asked him.

"Yes. It felt to me as if I feel asleep but yesterday and woke this morn. Do you know we slept almost two thousand years?"

"So you, and Vivienne, say. And Arthur?"

Gehris and Gawain stepped into the shop. "What of Arthur?" Gawain asked.

"All Merlin and I know," Vivienne spoke from behind them, "is that Gareth woke but a few weeks ago and now you have joined him."

"I like it not."

"Aggravain, you tire me with your constant harping on what you do not like. Mayhap we can agree you like nothing and until such time as you do, you say nothing."

"You, Gawain . . ."

"Ah, there you are." Merlin joined them in the shop.

"Is Molly well?" Gareth turned and stepped toward the older man.

"Yes, yes, she's fine. Molly is practical and level-headed. Her work is a big concern to her right now, making other things seem less important. Not that you aren't important my boy. She is a modern woman with modern concerns."

"Yes, the Red Queen." Gareth nodded.

"Red Queen?" Gehris turned, wide eyed to his twin.

"Yes. My lady Molly labors for the Red Queen who commands those who displease her to lose their heads. Her friend, the Queen of Mean, was almost as evil."

"What happened to this Queen of Mean?" Gawain leaned back against a counter and crossed his arms over his chest."

"Molly said she died."

"So who rules the land of Mean now? This Red Queen?" Gehris asked.

"I know not where Mean is, but the Red Queen reigns in the Miwok police department." Gareth informed his brothers.

"If Molly is her subject, then why . . ." Gehris puzzled.

"Nay, Molly is not her subject," Gareth cut him off. "She labors there, yes, but in this time queens and kings do not rule as they did in our time."

"No?" Intrigued, Gawain asked.

"No. They have this situation, they call it democracy. The people choose who will rule them every few years or so." Gareth informed them.

"Truly?" Gehris asked.

"I like it not."

"Of course you don't, Aggravain," Gawain chuckled.

"Why not?" Gareth's brow furrowed in puzzlement.

"How can you know who leads you? How do you know the world will be consistent? Does your enemy become your friend? And your leader your enemy when they do this choosing? It makes no sense," Aggravain told them.

"Yes, well, all of this will make sense to you all before long. Right now, let us retire to my apartment and we can talk. I will try to answer your questions and try to help you to ease into your lives here."

"So you believe we are here to stay?" Gehris asked.

"I believe so."

"And the others?" This from Gawain.

"Ah, that is the question. Vivienne and I were surprised to find Gareth waking. Today was, well today was quite a shock."

"You did not know we would wake?" Gehris puzzled.

"No, well we weren't sure. As I said, we didn't expect Gareth. But it was just he that woke. It stood to reason that you might wake. It never occurred to us that it would be all three at once. As to the others, I, we do not know. Perhaps it is only you, Orkney boys. Or, perhaps the others will stir."

"To what end, Merlin?" Gawain asked.

"What do you mean, Gawain?"

"Why would we wake now? Is there a battle to be fought? Since another vanquished the Queen of Mean? Are we to defeat the Red Queen?"

"I believe I know why I woke," Gareth told them. In response to their raised brows he continued, "The legend says we will wake in the time of the world's greatest need. Merlin tells me there have been wars and struggles. Yet we did not wake. I know I woke to rescue Molly from the Red Queen."

"And of us?" Gehris put an arm around his twin.

"You are here to help me. She did not believe me that I am one of Arthur's companions. What better way to prove it to her than to have my brothers by my side?"

"Twould make sense."

Gawain laughed, "Something you like, Aggravain?"

CHAPTER THIRTY

After Shannon left for the night Molly paced around the darkened records area looking for something to do. Saturday nights in Miwok were either jumping with calls about loud parties or music, cars racing down the street and on a rare occasion, something like the bank break in a few weeks before.

Or, they were nights like tonight with virtually no calls, which meant no reports, and nothing to do. Unfortunately, while Julie had no problem with the dispatchers sitting in the comfy climate controlled little room playing on the computers, answering email, engaging in online gambling, reading books and doing crafts and crossword puzzles the records clerks were expected to be working every second. You couldn't even take a moment to take a breath after taking a call, even a difficult one like a suicidal caller. No, Julie expected the clerks to hang up the phone and in less than a second move on to pushing the next piece of paper or answering the phone or helping out a citizen. Nights like tonight when all the paperwork was completed, the filing done and not a single phone call in the past three hours it was an utter relief Julie didn't work or stop by on Saturday nights.

And, of course, tonight of all nights, she wished she had something to do. Anything. She would have even filed the never ending evidence reports. Unfortunately Deanna hadn't pulled any evidence for destruction or returns to a citizen in at least four months which meant when she did there's be tons of filing the onion skin forms that no one but Miwok used anymore in a few weeks. While Molly believed it made sense to review releasable evidence every two weeks, Deanna was one of Julie's favorites and therefore she could do what she wanted when she wanted. She made a mental note to keep an eye out for the next cleaning session and ask for vacation before the paperwork hit. Not that that would do any good. For the past five years it seemed Maria had some sort of work restriction in place when filing built up so that she couldn't help out. All the woman did was sit there stirring up trouble.

She paced around the work space one more time and stopped at the TRAK machine to see if maybe no wanted persons had come through or BOLOs for stolen or missing cars reported. Seeing not one piece of paper sat in the out tray she checked the paper supply — full up.

She wandered back to dispatch to see if they had any paperwork that needed to be handled. Nothing had materialized in the six hours since she'd last cleaned it out. Fortunately, an online gambling site held Becca's attention and Janette sat reading a book so neither dispatcher had any inclination to speak to her. Normally she'd welcome even a short chat with Becca. Tonight, however, she had no doubt if they said anything at all it would be about the pending IA. Despite admonishments not to say anything the dispatchers always had something to say about it, especially if it was something Kris might be involved with. Just before she shut the door Becca roused herself from her game to inform Molly, "Kris is going to be out the next week. Apparently whatever she has with the herpes infection is going to have her laid up for awhile."

"Thanks." Not that she cared. Still, there might be something hopeful in that situation, "Any of the guys laid up with her latest fiasco?"

"Just Goodwin. I guess he's got a temporarily permanent hard on and not cause he's panting for her. Can't wait to hear what his wife says *this* time."

Goodwin's wife was a former dispatcher herself. She, however, quit once she and Goodwin were married, preferring to be a stay-at-home mom. That didn't stop her from gossiping with Becca now and again.

Without another word, Molly headed back out to the records area. Most nights when it was this quiet she enjoyed it. Tonight, however, it drove her batty. The amount of mind chatter running around in her head just wouldn't stop let alone slow down. The sound of Gareth's voice when he asked her, "how can you believe your friend traveled back in time but you won't believe I'm one of King Arthur's knights who woke?" twisted around with the sound of Julie informing her an internal affairs investigation had been launched over the conversation Kris insisted Molly had a few weeks before.

"Note to self, ask Gareth what can a knight do for a lady accused of something she didn't do?" It wasn't like he could challenge Julie for Molly's honor. Now wouldn't that be something—Gareth against Julie with pistols at dawn! She shook her head, "wrong century." Still the thought of Julie being decimated on a field of battle had a certain appeal.

She wandered into the front of the station where what she began to think of as the Jack the Ripper display, had been set up. While there were more serial killers on the posters than Jack, his was the center piece. More specifically, the city council and the chief were using it to draw attention to citizens buying into playing a role in crime prevention. With budget cuts first paring back city services everyone had tightened their belt. This year heralded the first time a police officer had been laid off. In past years positions were eliminated through attribution. With a tremendous budget deficit an officer and two community services personnel had been cut. There'd been talk of sending dispatch to the county, which would have saved almost a million dollars a year. But Chief Krane was determined to keep them. Of course, why not keep the promiscuous badge bunnies who serviced him as well?

So they'd begun a huge public relations pitch to the community starting with the "See a Crime, Report a Crime" project. The posters depicted a series of unsolved crimes, with serial killers as the center piece. From what Molly could see, Jack the Ripper was the only one in the collection who hadn't been caught. Then again, in Jack's day, they didn't have cell phones and the internet. What wouldn't those prostitutes done if they'd had a cell phone to call for help?

Mesmerized she stepped to the large poster and in a bizarre combination of revulsion and fascination rested her hand on her abdomen. Against a dark background a faceless man leaned over a woman, one hand in her hair, the other holding a knife plunged into her stomach. The woman's face was only a tad clearer than the man's except you could see her mouth opened in a silent scream. Unbidden the thought came that one day she'd love to see Julie caught in a situation so hideous that her screams of agony would die in her throat.

Julie hadn't just ruined careers. She mentally tortured those under her. Two records clerks had committed suicide because of the woman's mind games. In both their notes they clearly stated that Julie left them no choice. She'd undermined their self-confidence so badly they had no desire to fight let alone live. The hell Julie had been putting Molly through for years, the sleepless nights, the migraines, the upset stomachs had been horrific. For many years Molly hoped she could lay just low enough to either get promoted to dispatch or get another job. Each time she lost an opportunity Julie would smile and spew platitudes about how she might have a better chance next time.

"Well, if wishes were horses." Molly sighed. "One can only hope. Imagine and hope."

She stretched out a hand, traced the woman's face, and

wondered if she could get a copy of the poster and photo-shop Julie into it. Would it work the way it had for Carrie? Would Julie spend eternity in the poster living on the edge of death? *Wouldn't that be retribution and then some?*

Molly shook her head at herself. *When did I get so cold hearted?*

Shocked at her thoughts she headed back into records and puttered around until it was time to leave. She logged off her computer, ran through the rest of her closing chores and headed out to her car. All she had to do now was get through tomorrow and deal with the IA hearing on Monday. Then she would focus on Mr. Merle's revelations. "Piece of cake. Right. I'm dating one of King Arthur's knights."

CHAPTER THIRTY-ONE

Sunday passed mercifully quickly with minimal interruptions. Apparently Kris needed to spend a few days in the hospital so no one had to hear her imitation of a screech owl over the air the rest of the week. Julie never came in on Sundays. Becca was too busy updating Viola on Kris and going on her own suck along. What bothered Molly, however, was that she was in fact bothered that she hadn't heard from Gareth. The guy clearly belonged in a safe place with nice soft padded walls because if he was the real deal it meant she was part of the most bizarre twist of fate. How could *she*, of all people be the person, a person, who met the real life Merlin? She was average. Just a regular person. Important people met characters like Merlin and Vivienne and Gareth. Not regular old Molly Nichols.

So either he was real or they both needed some other avenue to live out his fantasy life as a knight. It had to be a fantasy, his fantasy because if it wasn't, then she really did see four men on war horses riding along 121 yesterday. If he was the sane one, it meant Molly was the crazy one. No how, no way did she see the four knights riding in tandem, she didn't see the helicopter suspended in the air, or the highway patrolmen frozen in place or Mr. Merle arrive in a limousine from out of no where in a puff of smoke. It was a delusion, brought on by the stress of her job.

Mr. Merle, he was Carrie's so-called friend. Not hers and she heartily wished he'd return from whatever rock he crawled out of — after her life was put back in order.

She looked in the desk drawer when she got home last night, and again this morning, hoping for a message from Carrie, but nothing appeared. The first note could have been a fluke or Carrie didn't have access to the desk in her time or maybe Molly was the one who needed her head examined and everyone else was sane.

"Of course! That's it! I'm the crazy one. So why isn't someone kind soul locking me up?"

Every time thoughts of Gareth and the whole knight thing entered her mind she pushed it away. She'd take her three days off to deal with that. Get a few nights of solid sleep and she'd be just fine. It had to be the stress of IA. Once that was over everything would be normal and she'd find out Gareth was just a kook who liked to dress in tights and Mr. Merle was just that — Mr. Merle.

At least there were enough calls and reports to keep her occupied at work. Her hearing was set for three at the start of her shift the next day. "I suppose Julie thinks she's oh so kind not making come in early. Shit if I can't use the overtime though."

Amazingly she slept like a rock Sunday night and felt incredibly calm going into work Monday afternoon. She didn't even feel a ripple of trepidation when she drove by the area where Gareth's brothers apparently arrived. The sad part in Mr. Merle's explanation was that it made complete sense. Who wouldn't believe a bunch of Arthur's knights woke up and narrowed in like radar to where their brother happened to be charging down the roadway after her?

"Anyone with half a brain, that's who." She told her reflection in the rear-view mirror.

Latte in hand she entered the station. Julie had to have been hovering around the door because the instant Molly walked in Julie called to her. The way the sunlight filtered into the lobby a wavery light seemed to encompass her boss, making her seem to ebb in and out. *Wouldn't it be oh so nice if she did waver on out of my life forever?* Even more odd than the flowing-like light, the poster behind Julie, the very one Molly visualized Julie being stuck in the night before, seemed to pulse, glowing brighter and dimmer for a few seconds.

"What are you looking at?" Julie demanded.

"Just the crime prevention posters out here."

Eyes narrowed Julie primly told her, "It's beneath you to try to distract me."

"Trust me, Julie. The last thing I'd want to do is distract you."

Trailing Julie into the admin wing of the station Molly glanced again at the poster, wishing again she could stick Julie in one of them, even for a week. Certain that she had in fact well and truly lost her mind Molly nodded to herself. In her increasingly delusional state, a mere police department poster about a serial killer turned into a fantasy of Julie being trapped for eternity under Jack the Ripper's knife. Amazing how delusions could be of such a comfort.

Sally, already waiting in the interview room, gave Molly a weak smile when they walked in. Sally may have held the title of union rep, however she was a company girl all the way. She'd do whatever she felt gave her the most power. Not that she had any. Julie would never allow that.

"Well, let's get started," Julie said as she sat. "You know Lt. Lamertoni who will be conducting this investigation.

"Of course." Molly nodded. Lamertoni was another of the Kris fans. She'd caught the two of them in a rather passionate embrace in the hallway one night not too long ago. He'd never do anything about the blonde bimbo, confirming her earlier thoughts to let this interview go the distance and then appeal it. In front of an administrative hearing officer, with an attorney, would be her only chance at an honest hearing.

"I have a few preliminary statements to make and then

we'll get to the serious questions. I'm turning on the audio tape now. My name is Lt. John Lemertoni and I am the officer assigned to investigate the alleged mishandling of a domestic violence call taken approximately three weeks ago. Present are the alleged suspect, Molly Nichols, her union rep Sally Hawks and Records Manager Julie Prince. Molly, this investigation regards a serious dereliction of duty and could lead to your dismissal from the department. At all times I expect you to tell the truth, regardless of the outcome as lying could lead to further charges. Do you understand?"

"I do."

"Good. Let's begin."

Under her lashes Molly glanced at Julie. Four odd stripes seemed to frame her cheeks, almost as if straps had been fastened in place around her head and the woman rubbed her upper abdomen. She glanced at Sally and then at Lemertoni, but neither seemed to notice. She settled into what she now felt certain was her delusion. The fact that no one else reacted gave her a clear indication she had most definitely lost it.

"I know Julie went over some of this with you, but for the record I need to ask you a few questions again. Do you remember taking a call now three weeks ago from a domestic violence suspect where a man reportedly told you he felt it was okay to hit women and that this country would be better off if women stayed in their place."

"Yes, the Ashad case."

"What do you remember about it?"

Molly repeated the information she'd given Julie earlier, sticking to the facts as she knew them, finishing with reiterating that Kris said she handled the call rather than turning it over to an officer. She made an effort to remind Julie that the victim called 911 three times asking for help and that Kris told her there was no crime so no officer. Several times during the interview she glanced at Julie. The woman occasionally rubbed her stomach area, however she began to pull more and more on her shirt collar as if it were restricting her air flow. Lemertoni droned on and on about something with the case. There was nothing Molly could say that would change the outcome so she sat quietly waiting for the interview to end. An attorney would plug holes in their supposed tight procedures. Not that anything would happen to the blonde badge bunny.

" . . . have our decision by the end of the week. As usual, you are not to discuss this interview with anyone. Do you understand?" Lemertoni asked.

"I do."

"Wonderful!" Julie gushed, the first truly animated statement she'd made all afternoon. "There's a lot of work to be done and poor Maria needs to leave. Let's get to work, chop, chop!"

Molly may have lost her marbles, but Julie was, as usual, totally disconnected from the world around her.

Just inside the records area Sally told her to hold on a minute. The other woman walked up to Maria and exchanged a few words. It was clear Maria didn't particularly like what Sally had to say, but whatever it was, Sally had clearly gotten what she wanted because she smiled at Molly and motioned her to follow.

"What?" Molly asked, puzzled.

"I told her that experience was incredibly grueling and we both needed some fresh air. Let's go grab a coffee."

That surprised Molly beyond words. Sally never reached out like that.

Outside the station, out of audio range Sally leaned over, "You know they're going to pin the whole thing on you?"

"Yup. I knew that from the git go. And you know what? This time I don't care. Let it go the distance because they really don't want everything I know coming out in front of an administrative law judge and trust me, it will."

"That may not be in the department's best interest."

"The *department's* best interest? Do you think I care? I'm sick of them covering up every little thing that could out about Kris and Julie and the whole badge bunny brigade. I'm tired of always towing the company line. I've lost track of the hits I've taken for the team the past ten years. Enough is enough. This time I'm fighting back and let the chips fall where they may. Maybe if I had fought back ten years ago I'd be in dispatch now and Kris would be a bad memory."

"She keeps the guys happy."

"Oh come on, Sally! You don't believe that any more than I do. She's a quick, easy lay and the only reason every new guy through here sleeps with her is because he doesn't want to be the only one that hasn't. And if I lose my job for telling the truth, fine. I'll find something else do to. I'm done."

"Wow. This is a side of you I've never seen before."

"Well get used to it. At least for as long as I'm here."

"What's gotten in to you?"

"Sense. That's what. Sense. I used to think my roommate Carrie was missing out on life, real life, by reading so many romance novels and buying into a happily ever after. She was the one who always planned our vacations and adventures and along the way she met the man of her dreams. He's everything she ever wanted and more. I'm not saying I'm going to go out and fall in love like she did. But I'm going to start living my life, really *living* it. No more doing things to make someone else's life happy or good if it's not going to help mine. I'm not saying I'm going to hurt anyone or let anyone else get hurt. I'm just saying I'm not going to be the department's fall girl any more."

"Wow. Well I'm going to look forward to how this all plays out." Sally smiled, perhaps the first genuine smile Molly had ever seen form on the other woman's lips.

"I guess we should get back in. You know Maria is going to have a hissy and a half that we stepped out instead of just the hissy she had."

"What happened to putting Molly first?"

"I didn't say I wouldn't be courteous."

Sally answered with a solid laugh.

CHAPTER THIRTY-TWO

"Aren't you off duty?" Kyle Carpenter asked Molly, startling her out of another reverie of Julie being a serial killer's victim. The whole Jack the Ripper scenario had taken root with Julie being killed over and over again making Molly wonder if Gareth's arrival in her life had somehow sent her to the dark side.

"Wha — oh my god, what time is it?" She quickly glanced around the records area as if she'd never seen it before.

Kyle laughed, "Only 3:35. I only asked cause you're usually out the door at 3:30 and two seconds."

"For the most part. If I'm on a good call I don't."

"I don't recall hearing one tonight." He rested a hip on the edge of the desk. Kyle had always been a good guy, one of the few straight ones who hadn't succumbed to Kris' questionable charms.

"No heavy duty calls. I just got absorbed in this report and since it's my weekend tomorrow, I didn't see the need to go rushing out of here. At least not before Berger shows up. Thanks for uh, waking me."

"You got it. You need me to walk you to your car?"

Molly looked up at Kyle and felt like she saw him for the first time. He stood about six foot, broad shoulders, close cropped light brown hair and pretty green eyes although he wouldn't appreciate hearing the "pretty" part. A nice smile and pretty buff topped off a pretty impressive package. She didn't mix her bread with her honey, but maybe along with the other changes she planned to make in her life that should

255

be on the agenda as well. Yup, that's exactly what her life needed, a stable guy with a good job. Not someone who dropped in out of the blue claiming he just woke up. "That would be nice. Thanks."

Together they walked out through the front lobby and out of the building. Kyle bid her goodnight and turned to walk back into the station.

She arrived home with moonlight spilling over the walkway. Giving into an other worldly feeling she stopped in Carrie's room and rummaged around in what she now deemed the message drawer. Folded inside she found a brief message from Carrie,

All is well. I think you should consider a relationship with Mr. Merle's nephew.

Love Carrie.

Short, sweet and to the point. But how could Carrie know?

CHAPTER THIRTY-THREE

Despite thoughts spinning through her mind like a tornado on steroids, Molly slept like the dead. Well not quite. Images of Julie calling out for help from the Jack the Ripper poster were interspersed with Gareth standing beside it smiling. In each one he would step toward her, reach out and pull her into his arms and hold her as if his life depended on being up close and personal with her. She woke, refreshed. Refreshed and with a pleasant pressure between her legs. Well, pleasant, but with an itch she realized wanted only Gareth to scratch — and it wasn't the kind Kris spread around.

"Something is seriously wrong with me. How can I be thinking thoughts like that about a guy I barely know? Especially since if he's not the crazy one, I am? Maybe if I keep telling myself that I won't have to deal with the fact that Carrie's friend Mr. Merle is really Merlin."

She padded into the bathroom, took a quick shower and headed to the kitchen to make some coffee. Before she made it half way down the hall a creak from Carrie's room drew her attention. She stopped in her tracks and listened with determined concentration for a count of ten. When no further sounds came, curiosity won and she headed toward the room. Not that the old house didn't have its creaks and groans.

Inside the door she heard the sound again. Sadly, it was only the old tree scratching against the window. Not that she wanted someone to materialize there in her house. With a glance at the desk, she shrugged. "Might as well check and see if Carrie wrote back." A tug on the drawer revealed no further missives.

Padding back toward her original goal of the kitchen and coffee Molly shook her head. It wasn't realistic to think she and Carrie could pass messages back and forth for the rest of their lives. Eventually someone would catch on and if it weren't the right kind of person one of them could end up in the loony bin. That and the fact that at some point they'd both have to move on with their lives, each in their own time.

She filled the pot with water, scooped in the coffee and turned the maker on. The soft bubbling of the pot offered a sense of normalcy in her upside down world. The realization that it wasn't a matter of them both moving on, that Carrie had moved on, seeped into her thoughts. And it was time Molly moved on as well. Or at least considered it.

With the coffee made, she sat down to think. To try to make some sense of all that had happened the past few weeks. Gareth's words, shoved to the back of her mind in all the drama and upheaval the day before came back to her. Why could she believe Black Eagle and Carrie had traveled back in time but she couldn't believe he was one of Arthur's knights? Were the situations really all that different? Aside from Black Eagle stepping out of a photograph and Gareth waking up, both inside Treasures, they had more in common than different.

They were both men from the past. Both had old fashioned values. Both had a sense of right and justice. Both felt they ended up in 2021 to help their woman. Well, who would be their woman? Black Eagle determined he and Carrie would marry in no short order. And Gareth? Gareth decided he wanted to marry her after a night of some incredible sex. Well not that he wanted to marry her. That he felt he had to. Old fashioned values.

Gareth listened to her, to her concerns, her dreams, her ideas. He didn't get that glazed look in his eyes that Vincent did when she told him about the situation with Julie. Instead, he wanted to help. If nothing else, talking helped. And what if she lost her job? She had money put aside, rent was minimal, she could make do. Somehow she knew he wouldn't think less of her if that came to pass. Oddly, even though she hadn't known him that long, she missed him. She really missed him. Maybe there was something to Carrie's ideas of soulmates.

Taking a deep breath she rose, grabbed the phone and punched in Carrie's speed dial for Treasures.

"Treasures, where today the past becomes your future," a woman answered the phone.

"Uh, Vivienne?"

"Yes, who's this?"

"Oh, Vivienne, it's Molly, Molly Nichols."

"Hello, Molly. How are you?"

"Okay. Um, is Gareth there?"

"Yes, just a moment."

She heard Vivienne call out for Gareth who promptly came to the phone.

"Molly? How fare you my lady?"

"I'm all right. Um, are you free today?"

"To go to your city?"

"Oh, no. I'm sorry, I forgot. I've had so much on my mind and, well yesterday was a bit strange, you know? We'll go. If you want to that is, but I don't know if I can manage to get it together today."

"That's okay. I am enjoying talking and catching up with my brothers. There is so much for me to tell and show them."

"Yeah, I'm sure there is. Well, if you're too busy . . . but, Gareth, I need to see you. That is if you want to see me."

"Molly, do you wish to see me?"

"Well . . ."

"We do not have to go anywhere. I am happy to be with

you any time and any place you wish."

"Thanks. So, um, how about I pick you up in an hour or so and we'll have coffee or something?"

"Yes. I'll be here."

"Gareth, thank you. I need this."

A short while later Molly walked into Treasures and Gareth greeted her with a big smile.

"Hey." She gave him a little smile.

"Hey." He looked her up and down, the warmth of his gaze making her feel not quite so alone in the world.

"You sure you still want to get together?"

"I wouldst very much enjoy being together with you." Gareth took a step toward her, reach out and she walked into his arms. "I like the feel of you in my arms."

She smiled up at him and parted her lips as he lowered his for a kiss. His past kisses had begun with a tentative brushing. Today he crushed her to him, parted her lips with his tongue and tasted her as if she were a choice meal and he'd not eaten in days. No, more than days, weeks, maybe months. With one hand on the back of her head and the other traveling down her back she felt his desire through their jeans. He smelled of pine and wood smoke and tasted of peppermint mocha.

Pine and wood smoke?

She pulled away and peered up at him. His eyes darkened with desire and his smile left her feeling purely sinful.

His eyes. Gareth's eyes were a sapphire blue, dark sapphire blue, not turquoise blue. And he smelled of salt air, not pine and wood smoke.

At least she thought he did.

"Gareth?"

"My lady?" The sinful smile grew.

She forced herself to look away from those amazing eyes

of his and that sexy grin to look at his chest. Gareth's words about his twin came back to her. He said Gehris had a bit more hair on his chest. While the dark blue t-shirt he wore showed his pecs to perfection, she couldn't tell if he had grown some extra chest hair.

"My lady?" He purred.

"I thought we agreed to dispense with the lady business."

"My pleasure." He reached for her again and pulled her tighter in his embrace. "My brothers are upstairs. Shall we to Merlin's metal horse?"

"Merl . . . metal . . ."

The sound of metal rasping against metal seemed to have no effect on Gareth except for a slight tensing of his shoulders.

"Molly, step away from that heap of goat dung." A male voice growled from behind them.

"Huh?" She peered up at the blond man holding her. "I thought you smelled different."

"My smell?" He raised one arm and sniffed in the pit. "I bathed last eve."

"Dung for brains, step away from my lady." The mirror image of the man holding her strode into the room. That one had sapphire blue eyes.

Molly pulled away. "I thought there was something odd about the way you kissed me. My toes didn't even twitch."

"Toes? Brother, you have a way with women's toes?" The one holding her asked.

"More than my toes, buster. I don't find this funny at all." Molly shoved ineffectually at the man holding her.

"Neither do I, Molly. Clearly I am the one born with brains and this buffoon received naught."

"Naught? My dick outdistances yours by . . ."

"La, la, la, TMI," Molly sang with her fingers in her ears.

"TMI?" Gareth's twin asked.

"A modern term you best heed. It means you provide more

news that she cares to hear." Gareth told his mirror image.

Molly pulled away from the twin and looked up at Gareth. "Kiss me."

He smiled, that sweet and vulnerable smile that was Gareth's own. "With pleasure, my lady."

He reached for her and slowly lowered his head, never taking his gaze from hers. With his lips a hair's breath away he murmured her name and then gave her a light peck just before drawing a breath and giving her a kiss that curled her toes and then some. This man certainly made her girl parts sit up and take notice. This was Gareth, her Gareth. No doubt about it. She wasn't quite ready for the throat clearing behind them.

Gareth raised his head, but his growl was cut short by Mr. Merle pointing out they were standing in front of the shop window and did they really want to draw attention to themselves. Not that Molly minded all that much, which certainly surprised her given how normally private she was.

"Molly? Gareth, Gehris, shall we to the kitchen?" Mr. Merle asked with a grand gesture toward the cozy little room.

"Sure, Mr. Merle, ahhhh, Merlin." She glared at who she now knew was Gehris as she passed him and whispered to Gareth, "If that's your brother I'm sorry to say, but he's an ass."

"He is indeed, Molly. He is indeed."

They were greeted by another blond and a tall, dark-haired man as well as Vivienne.

"Molly, may I present my brothers, Aggravain and Gawain. You have, apparently, met Gehris."

"You mean the fake Gareth?"

"A poor imitation, is he not?"

"Very poor." She looked from one brother to the other. Of the four, Aggravain seemed the least likely to be related. With his dark hair and brooding scowl he looked decidedly out of place. Thing was, she could totally relate to feeling like the odd man out, if that was in fact his problem. The other three bore a strong resemblance with their blond hair and various shades of blue eyes.

"I did not fool you?" Gehris asked, hurt in his tone.

"Only for a second when I first walked in. But that was because it was so bright outside and dark in here."

"Then why did you kiss him?"

"Ah, well . . . it sort of . . . well he ah . . ."

"Twas a test brother. She did not return my ardor. Not for a moment. She is all you said and more last eve."

Gawain smiled.

Aggravain frowned.

Vivienne poured tea.

Mr. Merle patted her hand.

Molly realized they all looked to her for some sort of direction."

"Yes. Well. I called Gareth. When I called him I didn't think about you guys still being here. Gareth, you should have told me."

"Why? I would see you anyway, Molly. I was relieved to have heard from you."

"You were?"

"Of course. You were quite displeased with me when we parted yesterday."

"I guess I was. Gareth, Mr. Merle, I mean Merlin," she rose. "Look, I'm sorry. I shouldn't have come. I need to get my head on straight."

Gawain studied her and leaned backwards to see the back of her head. "Naught about your head seems amiss."

"It's a phrase. It just means my thinking was clouded. Really though, I shouldn't of come. Gareth, I'm sorry, can I call you tomorrow or later in the week?"

Merlin stood and walked over to her, "Nonsense, Molly.

Please, think of us as family. Sit and tell us what is wrong."

The old gent looked at her as ever, with kindness and compassion. Five pairs of eyes turned to her as she sat beside him, all with gentle caring in their gazes. Even Aggravain seemed to care. She couldn't help herself and started to shake as tears began to track down her cheeks. "I'm so sorry, I'm so, so sorry. Oh my god, I can't believe I'm falling apart like this."

Gareth pushed back his chair, rose and pulled her into his arms. "Come, we will talk."

Chapter Thirty-Four

Upstairs Gareth guided her to a comfy, over stuffed couch. He took a moment to settle her and before leaving only to return a barely a minute later with a glass of water. Tears flowed unchecked and the warmth of his embrace went to her heart. She cried for what felt like an eternity, pouring out her heart in deep wracking sobs. Unmindful of how her tears soaked his shirt Gareth held her close, murmuring gently how he would protect and care for her. A long while later she dozed in his arms, feeling safe and secure for the first time in a long, long time.

It had been so long since she'd cried. It wasn't something she did. Her world was black and white. No grays. Things fit into neat compartments and they never spilled for one to the other. Tears had no place in the practical place she'd built for herself. A world where she might get irritated, but no one hurt her. She never cared about anyone deep enough to hurt. No one except Carrie and now, suddenly, here was Gareth.

The little scars on his hands and arms stood out in stark relief in the waning afternoon light. Tiny lines around his eyes were gentled by the look in his eyes. He was sturdy and strong and his strongly hewed muscles didn't come from going to the gym four or five times a week. They came from riding, hard riding, on one of those huge war horses she'd seen yesterday and from wearing heavy armor. No light-weight Halloween costumes. They were the real thing and he was the real deal. She knew for certain he was the knight he proclaimed himself to be.

"Gareth?" Her voice sounded raw even to her own ear.

"What, Love?"

"I'm sorry."

"For what, Sweetheart?"

"For coming over here and falling apart. For soaking your shirt. For letting your brother kiss me. For, for, for not believing you. You really are one of King Arthur's knights, aren't you?"

His expression serious, he nodded. "Yes. I am. Proudly so."

"I'm so sorry I didn't believe you."

"I understand. Were you to have appeared in my time I would have thought you a strange, perhaps mad, creature. What, why do you now believe?"

She snuggled closer to him, wrapping her arms around his neck and loping a leg across his lap as if she could get close enough he'd never leave her. "Does it matter?"

He shook his head. "No."

"I, I guess. Gareth, my world has been so up-ended. Nothing in it makes sense. Nothing but what my heart says."

"And what does it tell you?"

"That you are good and honest and true and that you really are who and what you say you are."

"The heart never lies, Molly."

She toyed with a button on his shirt. "Carrie always talked about soulmates and how we look and look until we find our one and only forever guy . . . or girl. She always said she would know when the right one came along. I think I knew that about you the first time I met you. Remember? When we came into the store and you were in your armor?"

He nodded.

"I think I knew then you were someone special to me. That I would fall for you and it scared me."

"Why?"

"Falling in lo — falling for someone puts your heart on the

line. If he doesn't feel the same, it can be a lot of hurt. A hurt you never quite get over."

"Can I tell you something?"

"Anything."

"I too knew the moment I met you that you were my other half. I knew in that instant why I had woken. Not to right some great ill in the world, but to love the only woman for me. I love you, Molly Nichols."

"Really? For real?"

"I will never lie to you, Molly. I love you. I feel as if I woke loving you and tis no spell of Merlin's. It is me, the man, who loves you and will love you for all time. I will do whatever needs be done to prove this to you and to win your love."

"Now can I tell you something?"

"Anything." He told her, quoting her own words back to her.

She drew in a deep breath. She'd never said the words before and they lodged somewhere in her throat. But it was time they were said and to the only man she could and would say those words to. "I love you, Gareth. It scares me, but I do love you."

"I am glad, Molly, because I mean to spend my life with you. I hope to make you the happiest woman alive."

She cupped his jaw. "You really are out of one of Carrie's romance novels."

"No, not out of a novel. I am a real, flesh and blood man."

The smile forming on her lips felt good. "I'm glad. While imagining sex with a fantasy man can be fun, it doesn't feel quite as good as the real deal."

He grinned, "So you like my deal, huh?"

"You do have a nice package."

He gave her a quick kiss. "Do you feel ready to come to know my brothers now?"

"Yeah. And apologize for making a scene before."

"They will not mind. I'm sure Merlin has told them a bit about you."

"He really is Merlin, isn't he?"

Gareth nodded

"And his ancestor, the one who took Black Eagle's picture, that wasn't an ancestor at all, was it?"

"I do not know the tale, but I suspect it is one and the same."

"So that's the story," Molly told the assembled group a short while later. "Julie always defends her dispatchers and particularly Kris. She'll twist facts so that it's never their point. And don't dare tell her that you weren't there when something happened because she'll tell you that you can't take criticism. And then if you show her who really did it she writes you up for not being a team player."

The four Orkney boys looked at her with varying expressions of commiseration mingled with the desire to understand.

Gawain finally spoke up and asked, "What is this writing up, Lady Molly?"

"Molly, just Molly. It's putting on paper what someone did wrong. Or what you think or want them to have done wrong."

"I see, Molly jus . . ."

"Tis simply Molly. There is no just before my lady's name." Gareth quietly told them.

"Molly." Gehris tasted her name. "Tis a fine name. I like it. Do you ever tire of my misbegotten brother I would gladly court you."

Molly laughed and it felt good, "No chance of that, Gehris. It's Gareth or no one."

"I like this Julie, not." Aggravain growled.

"For once, Brother, we agree that something is not to be liked," Gawain chuckled.

"How can we help you, Molly?" Vivienne quietly asked.

Molly signed and leaned back, closing her yes for a moment. She opened her eyes as she took in a breath. "In an ideal world I'd have you do a reverse Black Eagle on her. I'd have you stick her in one of those serial killer posters we have up at the station and have her linger between life and death for eternity. That sounds pretty mean spirited, doesn't it?"

"Not to us," Gehris told her. I know not what this serial killer or poster is but the people of my time have inflicted some most painful tortures. If it is a just ending to this Red Queen, so be it."

"Well, a poster is a picture. Like a painting except there are lots of the same picture. And a serial killer, well I'm sure you had them. It's someone who kills again and again without a reason except he, or she, enjoys it. The act becomes a ritual where they do it again and again exactly the same way." She shuddered, "I know I might say I want to put Julie in one of those posters, but even if it were possible, I'm not sure I would do it. I just want her to leave me alone. Well, leave me alone and give me the job I want in dispatch. It's not like I'm asking for a lot. Being in dispatch would make me happy. It's all I ever wanted to do."

The brothers looked at each other in such a manner, eyes meeting and gazes holding, as if they shared a silent communication.

Merlin cleared his throat, "So. A fantasy. A dream. An imagining. Yes, Molly?"

"Right."

"And imaginings are simply that. Things that our mind plays with to help us feel better, right?"

"Right. Besides, it's not like you or Vivienne would do something nasty to someone. And you guys don't know magic, right?" Molly looked at each of the brothers in turn.

"There is much you feel is right," Gehris smiled at her a beat before turning to meet each of his brothers' eyes.

Molly smiled back, "I guess so. But you don't seriously, magic isn't common, it's not what you guys do, is it?"

Gawain rose and filled his cup with cool water at the sink, staring at the flowing water as if it fascinated him. Finally he spoke, "We are warriors, Molly. We uphold the law. We protect the weak."

"I'm not weak." She felt her jaw clench as she looked at him.

"No, love, you are not," Gareth pulled a strand her hair behind her ear and held her closer on his lap.

"Not weak," Gehris told her. "Weak need not be physical only. It can be someone in a position where they cannot protect or defend themselves. The Red Queen dominates you. She is your ruler and she is an unjust one."

Now she chuckled, "You're not going to run her through with a sword now, are you?"

The four brothers laughed and in unison told her, "Nay."

"Good. And you know what? Just talking to you guys I feel better. I told Sally I was ready to let the chips fall where they may and I meant it. With you guys here, even if you have to leave, I feel like I've got someone at my back, at least for a time."

"I will not leave you, Molly," Gareth held her tighter as if that alone would hold him firmly in this time.

"I don't think he will, either," Merlin told her. I truly believe these boys have woken and will live out their lives in this time. And well, err, Molly?"

"Yes?"

"Now that you know who Gareth and his brothers and, well, Vivienne and I are, you won't reveal our true selves, right?"

"No problem there, Mr. Merle, ah, I mean Merlin. Seriously, if I said anything people would think I was crazy. Your secrets are safe with me."

"Thank you, Molly."

"And no magic, right?" Once again she looked the brothers over.

They looked to each other and nodded in silent agreement.

This time it was Aggravain who spoke. "None have the power of Merlin or Vivienne. Not even our mother despite her best attempts."

Molly nodded, "Well good. And honest, guys, just being able to talk about what happened is the best medicine. Thank you all, thank you for listening."

"If you are Gareth's lady," Gawain took her hand, "then you are our sister. We will always defend you and your honor and listen to your woes."

"Thanks, Gawain. That means a lot." She glanced at the kitchen clock. "I didn't realize how late it was. I better get going so you guys can have your dinner or whatever. And Mr. Mer . . . Merlin, I hope you didn't loose a ton of business because I was sitting in her all afternoon."

"Not at all, Molly. The bell did not ring once so I suspect no one in Napa sought treasures today."

"I guess I should get going." She stood and Gareth rose with her.

"Nay, do not go. Stay and share a meal with us and then I will take you home."

The sexy smile on his lips told her she'd be getting more than a good meal.

271

CHAPTER THIRTY-FIVE

"Thanks for dinner, Merlin. Gees, I still can't get used to the idea that you're Merlin, the real live, living, breathing Merlin from King Arthur's court."

To her surprise, all four brothers stood as Molly rose from the table. "You guys are major into the gentleman thing, huh?"

"I am the only gentle man you need, Molly." Gareth smile as he reached for her hand and led her to the door. "I will see you all on the morrow."

He tried to usher her out the door but only got as far as the threshold before Gehris arm shot out and grabbed him. "Where do you go brother?"

"To escort my lady home."

"And she liveth so far that you needs not return till morn?"

"I do not return till the morn because I will stay with my lady."

Gawain strode to the door, "Then we will accompany you!"

"That's okay guys," Molly looked up at Gareth for his assurance that he'd support her on this. "We'll be just fine by ourselves, won't we?"

"My lady speaks aright. I will see you all in the morn."

With that he ushered Molly out the door and hurried her toward the Jeep. Things were going quite well with their escape until Gareth tried to guide her to the passenger side.

"I don't think so."

"Twill impress my brothers."

"Yeah, and cost my insurance big time. No way."

Grumbling he escorted her to the driver's side, then climbed in the passenger side.

Glancing in the rear view mirror Molly caught sight of the three brothers standing outside Treasures watching she and Gareth drive away. "Gareth, are you sure you don't want to visit with your brothers? You haven't seen them in a, in a, in um, a few years."

"Tis as if I saw them but yesterday. No, Molly, my place is with you. It is my intention to never be far from your side." He reached behind her to toy with the hair at the nap of her neck the rest of the way to her house.

Inside the door Molly turned to the big blond and looked up at him. "Gareth, thank you for being so patient with me. For understanding that I, well that I didn't quite believe you about, you know."

"There is no need for thanks, Molly. I understand why you would doubt me. If I did not live the story myself I would doubt what I have seen since my wakening."

"And you're sure you don't want to be with your brothers? Or that they might need you?"

"Merlin and Vivienne are with them. They cared for me when I arrived; they will do no less for my brothers. And, they are grown men. They will find their own way in Napa and this world of yours. My place, as I told them, is with you."

"And if Aggravain likes it not?" She smiled up at him.

Gareth pulled her into his arms, "Surely you heard Aggravain likes naught."

"Was he like that in your time?"

Gareth shrugged, "He is the eldest. Much responsibility falls to him. But tis late and I have no wish to speak further of my brothers this night."

"No?"

"No. In fact, I do not wish to speak further tonight at all

except to tell you I love you and to share sweet words between us."

She couldn't help but smile. They kicked off their shoes and hand in hand headed toward Molly's bedroom. When offered something to drink he declined while reaching for her blouse and began to undo her buttons.

With a smile into his kiss she released the button in his jeans and none too slowly peeled the zipper down. Together they tugged down each other's jeans and Gareth backed Molly to her bed. Lying back she reached for him and slid her hands down his arms. "Mmm."

"Mmm?"

"I love how your arms feel."

"Why?"

"Ah, oh," she smiled at the feel of his knee nudging her legs apart, happy to open herself to him. "They're warm and satiny smooth and I can feel your strength. And I love to feel your muscles in my hands when I kneed your shoulders. The tiny scares on your back remind me that you're a man's man. Gareth, you need to know, just touching you turns me on."

"That is good to know, Molly my love."

He dipped his head to kiss her.

She wrapped her arms and legs around him, and savored the long, slow, and oh so passionate kiss. He tasted of the cider they'd had for dinner coupled with the slight flavor of the hot fudge from the sundaes they'd introduced his brothers to. Holding him felt so good. Just so good. For a long while he lay atop her and in her, kissing her slowly as if to memorize ever bit of her mouth. His fullness felt so right in her pleasure spot. So thorough was the kiss all she needed to do was squeeze his member buried inside her, knowing his would begin to move her to ecstasy only when he was ready to claim her.

But she couldn't wait. Not much longer.

Sensing her need for him, Gareth began to thrust inside her. She raised her legs to take him deeper, eliciting a groan of sheer pleasure from her man.

Her man?

Yes, yes, her man. There was no doubt Gareth was hers. He'd woken for her. To protect her. In her heart she knew he'd be there for her, at all times, for all times. He didn't just feel good. He felt right. Being here, in her bed, him buried to the hilt inside her was everything right in the world.

The intensity of her climax took her by surprise and she shuddered from head to toe. Gareth's voice shook when he called out her name a moment before he rested his forehead against hers, waiting for his breathing to slow. Before he fully caught his breath he gave her a quick kiss and murmured, "I love you, Molly."

"Gareth?"

"What my, dearest?"

"I love you too. I really do."

"You make my life happy. I have waited long for the woman of my dreams."

"I'm glad you woke for me."

"You believe me now, don't you? That I woke to be with you?"

"I do, Gareth. I think I did before and what I didn't believe, what I really didn't believe, was that someone as good as you, as right as you, could be in my life. I didn't believe I deserved someone as wonderful as you."

"It is you who is wonderful, Molly. And if you will have me, I will spend the rest of my days showing you."

"Have you? Oh, Gareth, more than anything. Yes. Yes! Wait. Did you just propose to me?"

"Do you doubt it? Do you wish me to leave your bed, to remove myself from your body, and go do one knee to ask you in a more formal way?"

"Nu-uh, this way works just fine."

"And your answer?"

"Yes. Oh, Gareth, I love you. I really love you and yes, I can't think of anything better in the world than to be your wife."

In the dim light cast by the moon through the windows, she saw his smile, the brilliant white flash of teeth and self-satisfied male. "When?"

"When?"

"How soon can we wed? When can we post the bans?"

"Post the . . . oh we don't like do all that these days. Well I suppose in some places they do something like that, but not for me."

"I am pleased to hear that. I saw on one of your entertainments in the little box, what Merlin calls the vision, a mere clerk can do this."

"Justice of the peace. Yeah, we could do that." She didn't know why that was an unhappy thought. Not that she ever really expected a big huge wedding with her in a white dress with a mile long train and a fluffy white veil. But she did want some sort of ceremony with her friends watching the happiest day of her life.

Then again, just being with Gareth, becoming his wife, *that* was what mattered. As long as they were together, what did all those trappings matter?

"But . . ."

She realized he was still speaking.

" . . . I wouldst prefer something more formal with my brothers and your family in attendance."

"I, Gareth, I don't have any family, just some really good friends."

"Then they will be as your family. Whilst I would wish to make you my wife in an instant, I would rather we make of it a great celebration. Unless you wish otherwise."

"Well, to be honest, I would like to have a party than just you and me, but whatever you want. After all, it's about us and our future, right?"

"And I think your friends and my brothers would wish to be there to wish us well."

I think so too. So we can plan it for a few weeks?"

"Whenever you wish, Molly, however you wish."

She wriggled under him, enjoying the feel of him hardening while still inside her. "And this?"

"Whenever you wish as well."

CHAPTER THIRTY-SIX

"Are you sure you don't mind if I leave you off and go take care of business this morning?" Molly asked Gareth while they walked to her car the next day.

"Of course I will miss you, love. But I do understand. We will tell our news to my brothers and then you will do as you must. We will be together tonight, yes?"

"If you want."

He smiled that sexy grin of his that made her tingle to her toes. "I want."

"I want too."

"Then mayhap we should . . ."

"Uh-uh, much as I prefer to be naked with you, I do need to take care of a few things today. You're sure you want me there when you tell your brothers?"

"Most definitely."

A few minutes later they pulled up to Treasures and hand-in-hand walked in. The assembled group couldn't miss the bright grins either wore.

Aggravain stood and looked his brother up and down, "You appear most pleased, brother."

"I am. Merlin, while tis early, have you any ale?"

"At this hour?" Molly looked slightly askance at him.

"You prefer wine?"

"Um, coffee would be good."

"Then coffee you shall have," Vivienne winked at her and in a flash produced a steamy cup of coffee that tickled Molly's taste buds.

"Well," Merlin rubbed his hands together. "Did you two pass a nice evening?"

"An exception evening, Merlin. We have news." Gareth smiled down at his lady and she nodded. "I asked Molly to do me the honor of becoming my wife. She has agreed."

Gawain rose, a broad smile creasing his lips, "You will be my sister?"

"Appears so. Is that okay?"

"It is most welcome news. Merlin! Ale!"

"Boys! This is Napa, home of the best wines in the world. Molly, would champagne be amiss?"

"Oh, Mr. Merle, if you have some that would be awesome. I don't think a little will be a bad thing, do you?"

The elderly gent thrust his arms before him, spun them in circles three times and with a pop a bottle of Domain Chandon Brut and seven delicate crystal glasses appeared on the table. With a grin he pointed a finger at the bottle and popped the cork. To Molly's delight he then had the bottle rise into the air above the glasses and watched as and equal amount of the amber liquid poured into each. Vivienne came to stand beside the white haired wizard and together they caused the glasses to float off the table and into each of their hands.

Standing in a circle, each with their glass raised, it was Aggravain who spoke, "Congratulations to my brother and his wife to be."

Gehris grinned at his elder brother, "It seems we have found something you like."

"I do. I like Molly very much and, Molly, should my younger brother forget himself, I would gladly take you to wife."

"Thank you, Aggravain. But, I don't think Gareth could ever disappoint me."

"So," Merlin toasted the couple, when is the big day?"

"Soon," Gareth told him. "Soon."

When all had drunk their champagne Molly turned to Gareth and after a quick kiss told him she'd see him later. Walking out of Treasures she felt not only happier than she'd felt in a long time. She couldn't think of a time she was happier.

A short while later, breakfast dishes and glassware cleared from the table, Vivienne popped out and Merlin went about the business of his work day as Mr. Merle, proprietor of Treasures Antiques. The brothers assembled upstairs, their smiles at Gareth's news fading as they took in his grim expression.

"What ails you, brother?" Gawain asked.

"His Lady Molly," Gehris answered

"Not Molly, but what she must face on the morrow when she returns to her work. The Red Queen seeks to make her life miserable. Molly may lose her job because of Queen Julie."

"Can you send a challenge to the Queen's champion?" Gawain asked.

"The people of this time do not have champions. No, the Red Queen must be stopped in another way. If there ever existed a time I wish I knew more of our mother's doings, it is now."

"What would you do, brother?" Gehris asked.

"Molly lived with a friend who fell in love with a man who stepped from what they call a photograph. The friend, Carrie, now lives in the man's time, in the past. At Molly's work they have a display of what they call posters that show evil men. What they call serial killers. No matter what their title, they are malevolent beings. Molly confided to me that it would please her to place the Red Queen in one of those posters, as a victim of one of these killers."

"Then we will do so," Aggravain growled.

CHAPTER THIRTY-SEVEN

"Are you certain you knowst how to maneuver this metal horse?" Gehris asked his twin.

"Of course. I watched Molly many, many times. Tis simple and, buffoon, it is called a car."

"Car, horse, what only matters is that you can bring us safely to our destination," Gawain peered out the window of Merlin's big, black limousine.

"There is naught to worry, brother. And I have seen that the knights that patrol the streets of this time give great leeway to cars such as Merlin's."

"I like it not." Aggravain grumbled from the front passenger seat.

Gareth signed, "All you have said since you arrived is that you like naught, Aggravain. May I suggest you cease to speak till you have news for us? Perhaps something you *do* like?"

"I hath said more! Was it not I who suggested the way to make things right for your lady? And, without me, you couldst not complete the task we have set for ourselves. Now, if you can make this conveyance move, do so before Merlin and Vivienne discover our plans."

With that Gareth repeated the steps he had seen Molly take and got the vehicle moving. Taking special care to use the turn signals, despite several rather jarring lurches, he made good time driving up to 29 and making his way to 121. Passing the field where his brothers appeared beside him he slowed, looking to see if any of the other knights had appeared. With a twins' knowledge Gehris peered out the back seat and told

Gareth, "No others have woken. It would seem only our family has found its way here to the Land of Nap."

"Napa," Gawain mumbled beside him.

Aggravain turned from looking out the windows as well and shook his head. "Mayhap this is merely our family's chance to make right what was done wrong so long ago."

To himself Gareth marveled at how relaxed his brothers were with his driving. Even with Molly's skill maneuvering the metal horse he felt quite nervous when he first rode with her. With a smile he wondered what his brothers would think should they meet Bessie and her friends out at Pt. Reyes.

At the turn for Miwok Gareth slowed and told his brothers they were nearing Molly's work. He glanced over at Aggravain and into the rear-view mirror to make certain each was dressed in modern garb. It hadn't been easy to convince them to leave their swords behind.

With careful precision he pulled in to a parking spot outside the police station, grateful he did not have to engage in what Molly called parallel something or other. As one the four brothers left the limousine and walked into the station. If there was one thing years of fighting and sharing their lives did, they knew how to guard each other's backs without a word.

The brothers entered the lobby, stopping briefly to look at the serial killer posters.

"What strange likenesses," Gawain muttered.

"Tis what they call posters in this time. Not all that different than our paintings except they can produce many in a short span."

"And this is where Molly would wish the Red Queen to reside?" Aggravain stroked his lightly stubbled jaw.

"It is." Gareth nodded.

Turning and flanked by his three tow-headed brothers, Aggravain approached the front counter of the station and waited for the woman to approach, not at all surprised when her gaze traveled up and down each of them. Women always found them to be of interest to say the least.

"Can I help you?" She spoke through a device in the glass.

"We wish to speak with the Red . . ." Aggravain began.

"Julie Prince," Gareth cut him off. "We have business with your Julie Prince."

"Okay. Can I tell her who you are and what this is about?"

Gehris, a warm smile on his face, approached the window and speaking low told Shannon, "Tis a secret dear lady, but one I wouldst share with you if you would but step aside where I may tell you."

Gareth smiled to himself. Of all of them, his twin knew best how to charm a lady. His grin broadened as he watched the woman with the name "Shannon" written on her blouse, moved toward the gated doorway to the glass wall and opened it to speak with Gehris. Before she knew what was happening Gawain, Gareth and Aggravain slipped in past her and quickly made for Julie Prince's office. As they passed one of the internal cameras Gareth had told his brothers about Aggravain slid his hand across the lens. If their dark-haired brother spoke true, he knew how to prevent their images from being seen.

As one the three eldest brothers stepped into Julie's office and shut the door.

"Wh-wha-what are you . . . who are you? Stop right there or I'll have you arrested." The older woman sputtered.

"I think not," Aggravain glared down at her. "We come to speak with you and will then leave you in peace."

Julie rose, hands planted firmly on her desk. "Get. Out. Of. My. Office."

A blond brother on either side of him, Aggravain placed his hands on the desk and leaned toward Molly's nemesis. "Sit, lady, else we will seat you ourselves."

Sputtering she sat and reached for the phone. Gehris placed his hand firmly on top. "Best you listen to my elder brother, Red Queen."

"Red . . . what are you lunatics . . . hel—"

Seeing her furtive movement toward the phone Gareth swiftly moved to her side and clamped his hand over her mouth. "You will listen old woman."

Her frustration showing with her narrowed eyes and rapid breathing, Julie sat.

"Good." Aggravain nodded. "Now listen and listen well, Red Queen. You have abused the Lady Molly one time too many. May you spend eternity knowing the fear and pain she felt each time she was within your presence."

He held his hands before her, fists clenched. Slowly he turned his palms upward and unfolded his fingers. Quickly turning them once again palm down he flicked his fingers at her.

With an abrupt turn he spun from her and marched to the door, pulled it open and with his brothers behind him, strode from the station.

Several women had come into the records area to see what the fuss was about and as the brothers departed they heard an array of comments from, "nice buns" to "love the hair," to, "anymore at home like them?" to, "he can dive into my pants anytime."

As they marched past Gehris, Gareth overheard him tell the women who greeted them upon their entry that he would call her soon and that yes, they would double something with Molly. Unsure of Aggravain's magic and intent on departing the building post haste, Gareth made a mental note to take his twin to task later about his intent toward Molly.

A slip of paper in his hand, Gehris slipped in beside his brothers. With a determined yet unhurried pace the brothers entered Merlin's car and headed back to Napa. In the rear-view mirror Gareth saw a dark cloud descend over what he was certain was the police station.

CHAPTER THIRTY-EIGHT

After a restless night Molly rose early Friday and prepared to go to work. After the excitement of Gareth's proposal she was disappointed when he didn't come over the night before, but totally understood. He told her he'd missed his brothers and after last night he'd be with her every night for the rest of their lives. She completely understood and it was just as well since she wanted a little time to prepare for whatever happened at work today. There was had no doubt in her mind that when she arrived there would be a decision rendered in the IA and that she may well be turning around and heading back home minutes after her arrival. The sick feeling in her stomach could only be a premonition of hearing she'd lost her job. Well, be that as it may, at least she'd turned in her resume at a local employment agency and they said they'd get right on finding her a new job. Even if they didn't have something for her off the bat, the job counselor assured her they had some decent temp assignments.

With a pain-filled sigh, she headed to work. She had to fight the urge to double over from the pain in her stomach. Losing a job was one thing. Losing her shot at her dream job for the rest of her life was excruciating. Just the fact that the IA had been filed would keep her from transferring to any other police job. Even if validation came at the administrative appeal level, someone would always know she'd been involved in one, that she'd been suspected of malfeasance. And during a background, despite the investigator telling you that if someone says something negative they ask you your side, no one had ever heard of that happening. Even if they did, management sides with management and investigators side with management because they like their cushy jobs.

No, her police career ended the day Julie filed the IA against her. And all to protect her precious badge bunny cunt-Kris. If she managed to keep her job she was forever doomed to work in records and under Julie's special care.

"Why couldn't Carrie drag me back in time with her?"

"Why?" she answered herself.

"Yes, why?"

"Because then you wouldn't have met and fallen in love with the most amazing guy ever. A guy who loves you for yourself. That's why."

"Lovely, and now I'm having conversations with myself. Well, at least I'm not answering in a different voice, right?"

Arriving at the station she skimmed the parking lot looking for the telltale bobbing blonde head. It appeared Kris decided to forego servicing any of the officers in the parking lot today.

An eerie stillness encompassed the lobby area when she walked into the building. The silence reminded Molly a bit of the way a room sounded when an air conditioner suddenly cut off. Utter silence while at the same time other noises sounded incredibly loud. The air even had that moldy-like dampness you felt when a dehumidifier had been used.

Half the lights were either out or turned off. Given budget cuts that either meant they were trying to save money by not having them on or Chief Krane decided to close the station earlier than usual. The latter made more sense if she was being terminated. After all, if there was no one to work the night shift, why have the station open and the lights on?

One bright light caught her attention just before she reached the Dutch door into the glass encased reception area. A sterile silvery light shined over the Jack-the-Ripper poster. As if drawn by an invisible force Molly started toward the poster. Each step seemed to be more and more difficult to complete. She was sure her feet were encased in cement. So sure she even looked down to be sure. A dark spot marred the otherwise spanking clean tile floor. Bending down Molly dipped her finger at the edge. Not that she had a lot of experience, but the substance sure felt like blood. A smear in the same shade lay on the Ripper's cheek.

She took a closer look and the woman victim looked a whole lot different. Instead of the dark-haired victim with a blur instead of a face was a honey brown haired one, sheer heart stopping terror forming a hideous mask on her face. If Molly was the fanciful type she'd swear it looked like Julie. She peered again at the Ripper character and his face looked a bit different from what she'd seen earlier. In fact, he looked a bit more feminine, almost like the victim originally looked.

Clearly the stress of the IA affected her thinking ability.

"Molly?"

Startled out of her reverie, Molly turned to the sound of Shannon's voice calling her from the Dutch door.

"Shan? What's going on?"

"We're . . . we're not sure."

"The woman in the picture. It's Julie. How did anyone get her to give up a picture for that? Who got her to do it? Does she know? Of course she doesn't. She'd never allow something that hideous to be put on display."

Shannon ignored her babbling. "Molly, something bad happened."

Inside the reception booth Molly took a long look at her co-worker. The pupils of Shannon's eyes were dilated so far she could barely see the blue irises. The stark whiteness of her face was almost frightening. Only the quiver of Shannon's lower lip indicated she was alive.

Molly laid a hand on Shannon's arm. The little bit of oatmeal she'd eaten for breakfast sat like a lead lump in her stomach and threatened to make its way up her throat any second now. Not since Kurt Ames tried to kill himself by jumping off the Golden Gate bridge had anything felt this bad. "Shannon?"

"Nichols, good, you're here," Sgt. Dickerson walked up to them. "We've had some strange news today. Come on into briefing.

Several officers, Sally and most of the dispatchers sat around the briefing table. Even Kris looked stricken by whatever had happened.

"Have a seat, Molly." Dickerson held a chair out for her.

Dang, they are making a bigger deal out of that IA than even I thought they would. Are they all here to arrest me?

Molly performed a mental role call, making note that both the swings and graveyard officers all sat around the table. Were they going to kill her and hide her body?

Before she could take further stock, Chief Krane entered briefing with Captains Berger and Cohen behind him. Lts. Lemertoni and Johnson followed. But what surprised Molly the most was the appearance of one of chaplains.

Krane cleared his throat, "Some of you know, some of you have heard rumors and a few of you haven't heard anything at all. Apparently Julie has disappeared."

"Disappeared?" One of the officers scoffed.

"Did she go on vacation and just forget to post it?" Officer Jagarski asked.

"Maybe disappeared is a bit strong," Berger told the group. "After almost thirty years her behavior or whatever happened seemed strange to us."

"Seems pretty dramatic if we've all been called in and the Sheriff's department is patrolling our streets and dispatching for us." One of the sergeants spoke up.

"I suppose it does," Krane scratched his chin. "However, considering how it happened, whatever it happened . . . it is a bit strange and we do want everyone to be on their guard."

"Well?" Jagarski probed.

"Yesterday afternoon several young men came into the station to speak with her. According to Maria there was a mix up over evidence or something. They met with Julie and left a few minutes later."

A sick feeling started working its way up from Molly's stomach to her throat. Young men? Evidence? But it couldn't be. Not unless Merlin transported the Orkney boys here. They couldn't drive. Okay, they could have mounted their horses, but that would have been on the news. Okay, so she just jumped to a conclusion. Right?

"So did these guys do something to Julie?" Becca tore her gaze away from Officer Westly, her current flavor of the month, long enough to ask.

"We don't think so. Right after they left Maria saw Julie stand in her doorway a few minutes before she headed down the hall, we think to the ladies room because her scarf was found in there. Sally said she saw Julie walk back into her office. Thing is, when Maria went into ask Julie a question maybe five minutes later, she wasn't in there. Her computer was on, her phone off the hook, her coat on the back of the door and tea still in her cup. In other words there was every indication she planned on coming back. That she hadn't left the building but no one saw her leave her office again.

"A bit later Maria went in again to see about whatever she was looking for. Nothing had changed and Julie still wasn't in there. When her shift ended Maria asked Sally to follow up on a report for her and the both of them went to look in the office. Still no Julie. Since a few of the documents looked private Sally got one of the sergeants to lock up. At that point he looked in the drawer and both her purse and cell phone were in there. No one has seen Julie since."

No one except me. Molly thought. And she wasn't about to tell the assembled group that she saw Julie sitting in the poster in place of the original victim. That would earn her an instant psych for sure.

"So do we think those guys did something to her?"

"No. No. Not at all. I mention that only as a lead in to what happened. At the moment we have no idea where Julie is. She had no vacation scheduled, no admin time off, she isn't anywhere in the station but her car and all her work belongings are here. No one saw her leave the station last night. We did have Hill Valley PD to go over to her house and see if she'd gone home and we contacted all the local hospitals."

"Are you thinking she was kidnapped?" Jagarski asked.

"It's possible. That's why we're here." A bald-headed man she hadn't noticed before stepped away from the wall he'd been learning on. "I'm Deputy Martinson with the Sheriff's department and this is my partner, Deputy Fernandez. With no sign of struggle and no ransom note, as yet, we don't have much to go on. We'll be meeting with each of you about the last time you saw Julie and try to make sense of her disappearance. Keep in mind even the littlest detail could mean something."

"Are we stuck here or can we, you know, grab a coffee or something?" Shannon spoke up.

"No one here is under suspicion, at this time. We're just hoping someone may have seen or heard something that may be of help figuring out what happened to her."

"Thanks. Although right now, I could use something stronger than a coffee." Shannon looked around the table.

Yeah, me too, Molly thought. *Something a lot stronger.* She so was not going down the road that Merlin did some of his mumbo jumbo and put Julie in the poster. Surely he knew she'd been joking, just complaining, when she made the suggestion. And since Vivienne told him no more putting people in pictures magic anymore, he'd listen, wouldn't he? She had to talk to him. And fast.

"You don't think she's dead, do you?" Jess, one of the other dispatchers asked.

Molly studied the dark-haired woman. Jess was one of the wannabe badge bunnies. When she started with the department, she'd been a size 7. In the seven years she'd been dispatching the woman ballooned easy to a size 20 if not a 22. Jess didn't make her brownie points by sleeping with the officers, although she'd made a solid attempt to try to. With her dark hair and growing girth, it wasn't going to happen. She did have one thing though and that was information. For some reason that information got her a promotion to lead dispatcher in the past year, over two other candidates with more years experience and ability. Jess was the only one who'd ever gotten up in the middle of a hot call and walked out of dispatch because it shook her up too badly. And still they kept her on.

"No, Jess, we don't." Krane calmly told her. "At the moment we just feel this is an odd situation that needs to be looked in to. So, if you'll all report to your duty stations, these gentlemen said they'd prefer to chat with the officers first so those of you were are due to go off duty can do so and the rest of you, if you are up to it, can hit the streets. Anyone has any doubts that they can do their job today, no worries. Just let me know and we'll give you admin for the day."

Molly filed out of briefing along with Maria, Sally and Shannon, followed by the dispatchers. Each one had their own ideas about what happened. The records staff held with Julie just wigging out and losing her mind because of all the nasty things she'd done. After all, why couldn't she have had a psychotic break down that ended up with her just walking away from it all?

The dispatchers, on the other hand, figured Julie'd given in to someone for some wild and crazy sex that was still going on.

Despite Merlin promising he wouldn't do any more magic, it sure sounded like he'd been up to his old tricks again. She needed a coffee . . . make that a quad latte and then to talk to Gareth.

With their calls routed to county dispatch there was no need for all four records clerks to be inside the station. If Julie'd been there she would have insisted they sit there and do something, even if there wasn't a thing to do. Maria and Sally gave Shannon and Molly their coffee orders as the junior clerks left.

On the way out Molly stopped in front of the poster.

"You sure are fascinated by Jack, aren't you?"

"Shan, look at the victim and tell me I'm not crazy."

Shannon studied the poster and slowly told her, "You aren't crazy."

Molly grabbed her friend's arm and pulled her out the door. "You saw it, didn't you?" "You saw Julie in the poster, didn't you?"

"Huh?"

They made their way down the steps before Molly spoke again. The last thing she wanted was for the outside microphones to hear what she had to say. "I know it sounds crazy, but when we get back, look at the poster and tell me the victim doesn't look like Julie."

"O-o-okay."

While they waited for their coffees Molly pulled out her phone and called Gareth. Merlin answered immediately, almost as if he expected her call.

"Mr. Merle, it's Molly. I'm at work."

"Is everything okay, Molly?"

"No. Not really. Mr. Merle, you didn't do anything like what you did with Carrie recently, did you?"

"What I did with . . . what I . . . you mean did I take a photograph?

She paced across the worn wooden floor of Java, Java oblivious to the smell of freshly ground coffee or the other patrons with their tempting pastries walking by.

"Yeah, you didn't like do something to like help me out or anything, did you?"

"Goodness, Molly. No. That isn't the sort of thing one does lightly. Did something happen?"

"Yeah. Something did, but I don't want to talk about it on the phone. Is Gareth around?"

He sounded out of breath when he came on the line and explained they had been training in Merlin's yard. "Molly, are you home?"

"No. Not yet. Gareth, listen, something happened at work—"

"Did the Red Queen dismiss you?"

"Nothing like that, yet. I need to see you though. I don't get off till three in the morning. Could we go for breakfast around seven or so?"

"I will meet you at your home after three."

"That's not necessary. You should sleep and I'll—"

"No, love. I will be there."

Back at the station Molly didn't want to draw too much attention to the poster until she had a chance to talk to Gareth. Merlin was the one with the magic, but Gareth might have some ideas. Maybe she wished too hard near a magical object or something like that. Knowing Merlin as long as he had, Gareth would be able to tell her.

Inside the records area Shannon admitted that one of the people in the poster sure did look a lot like Julie.

When the Sheriff's investigators called Molly in they only chatted briefly. After she told them she hadn't been on duty the day before, in fact not for the past three days, they sent her on her way.

CHAPTER THIRTY-NINE

"You did *what*?" Shaking from head to toe in a rare burst of anger Merlin looked from one brother to the other. "Tell me you didn't really do what you just told me!"

"We did not do what . . ."

"Silence, Gehris," Aggravain growled.

"What were you going to say, Gehris?" Merlin softly asked.

The stunned look in the younger man's eyes told the wizard Gehris was more than aware of his anger.

"Twas my idea," Aggravain sighed.

"Pray tell, *what* was your idea?" Merlin demanded.

The dark-haired brother drew in a deep breath and sat. "Best you sit as well, Merlin. The tale is not a short one."

Grumbling to himself Merlin sat.

"Tis this way." Aggravain began. "When we heard of the evil Molly's Red Queen caused to so many, we knew we must needs do something. When Molly said she wished to see the evil queen in the Ripper painting we saw the solution before us."

"*How* did you put Julie into the poster? That tis a magic that took me many years to perfect."

"Twas not so hard. I read your notes on the man you brought for Molly's friend and with the basic magic our mother taught, we bound the Red Queen into the poster."

"Aggravain, you cannot simply put someone into a poster!"

"We did not. We went to her and gave her an opportunity to make things right. She refused. We meted out justice. She will spend eternity at the mercy of the killer in the picture with her."

"My boy, do you understand, they will look for her. No stone will be left unturned until they find her. When they see her image in the poster they will think, that is . . ."

"What will they think, Merlin?" Vivienne's soft voice carried over to him.

"Well they will think. Hmmm."

"The people of this time do not believe in magic. They will merely think the artist created an image that also resembles this Julie."

"Be that as it may, we need to find a way to undo this situation."

"I am seeing Molly in the morn. She has already guessed what happened. Mayhap she can help set this aright although, I cannot imagine she is not pleased to be rid of that evil one."

"Tis true, Merlin. I liked her not in that short time we met with her," Gawain nodded as he spoke.

Molly saw Gareth sitting on the porch swing waiting for her when she pulled in shortly before four in the morning. She'd barely pulled into the garage and he was beside her, pulling Molly into his arms. "I missed you, My Lady."

His kiss melted her down to her toes and had her girl parts sitting up and taking notice. She'd never bought into those heroines Carrie used to read about that fell into bed in the midst of a crisis. Right now, with Gareth's kiss making her feel all warm and vitally alive, the idea of tumbling him then and there held a certain appeal. Yup, some super sex with her hot guy and then talk.

"Want to take this some place more comfortable?"

In the dim dawn light she couldn't miss his grin.

Hand in hand they made their way to her bedroom. While Gareth seemed to want to take things slow and sensuous, Molly wanted hot, body pounding sex. The need to be skin to skin with Gareth, to feel alive as only he could make her feel, over rode any desire for gentleness. The man certainly knew how to please.

They dozed for a bit in the afterglow. Gareth's arm around Molly, holding her close, reassuring.

A few hours later, their breakfast made, the couple sat down at the light pine kitchen table to eat. She didn't want to ruin the mood, but with work in a few hours, she had to talk to him about what had happened the day before.

"Gareth, something weird happened at work yesterday. Julie disappeared."

He swallowed and nodded his head but said nothing.

"Gareth, she's gone. Poof, like gone in a puff of smoke."

He nodded again.

"Doesn't that strike you as odd? That a woman who showed up for work pretty much every day for thirty years suddenly just vanished?"

"The Red Queen tortures you no more?"

She stood and walked over to the coffee pot, not so much because she wanted more coffee but to have something to do. Bringing the pot back to the table she confirmed Gareth's assertion. "I have to ask, Gareth, did Merlin do something to Julie?"

"Merlin?"

"Yes. Merlin. Older guy. White hair. Does magic. Did he do anything to Julie?"

"You asked him this yesterday, did you not?"

"I did."

"And he said?"

"That he had nothing to do with it. But Gareth, listen, this is way weird. Remember those serial killer posters in the lobby?"

"Yes."

"Well Julie disappeared. Some guys showed up on Thursday afternoon. Everyone saw her a few times after and then bam! She was gone. Disappeared. Vanished. Like she'd never been there. And there's no trace of the guys that came in on the videos. It's like they never existed."

"What has that to do with your posters?"

"Gareth, don't you see, she's *in* one of them! I know it happened. She's stuck in a poster for eternity."

He reached for her hand. "Then your troubles are over."

"No, no they aren't." She stood and paced across the room. "Don't you see? Somehow she got stuck in there and there's only one person I know of who can do that. Merlin had to put her in there."

"Love, if Merlin said he did not do this, then you can believe him. Perhaps the fates decided your Red Queen had done enough damage in the world and this was her just desserts."

"I don't think fate works like that."

"You didn't think a two thousand year old knight could wake in your time either, yet here I am. My brothers as well."

"You don't think that maybe I caused it, do you?"

"How could you?"

"Well, by wishing when I walked by some sort of magic object or something?"

"Nay. It takes more than an object to make magic. You need words and intent. You had nothing to do with this, Love."

She drummed her fingers on the table, thinking, trying to figure out what to do next.

"Tis what you wished, Molly."

"I know. What do I tell the Chief and the investigators?"

"Nothing, Molly. You tell them nothing."

"But, but . . ."

"Nothing, Molly. Consider this. The people of your time do not believe in magic. If you go to your people and tell them a woman in the poster looks like your Red Queen, what will they say?"

"That, that, well that . . . yeah. That she resembles Julie, but there is no way I could explain that if it is her how she got there. And maybe it isn't her or doesn't even really look like her. I've been under so much stress lately with Carrie leaving and the IA —"

"And my arrival in your time. I saw how difficult it was for you to accept my wakening. Truly, Love, I am sure tis only a resemblance."

"You're right. Gareth, you are so amazing. I feel so much better. It's like a light finally came on in my life. Have I told you how much I love you?"

"I wouldst hear it again and often."

"Would you?" She couldn't help but smile. "Why don't I show you?"

His smile warmed her to her toes. At the hall doorway he bent his head to kiss her and in a total lip lock they made their way to her bedroom. All thoughts of Carrie, work and the day's dramas faded in the wake of his sensual assault. They undressed each other in seconds and tumbled back into Molly's bed. As he entered her Gareth told her again that he loved her. It didn't matter from where or when he came from, only that he was in her life and planned to stay there.

They woke with Molly's alarm and while it was tempting to call in sick to work and spend the rest of the day in Gareth's arms, the aftermath of Julie's disappearance called to her. She had to find out if the other woman turned up and, if she didn't what they were going to do about it.

When she dropped Gareth off at Treasures, he promised her he'd see her when she returned in the morning.

With latte in hand she arrived a bit early for her shift, eager to hear if Julie turned up. She made a quick stop in front of the Ripper poster and the victim still resembled Julie, but there was something different about it. Something she couldn't quite put her finger on. Maybe it was just that the character looked a little more frightened. With a shrug she walked into the records area to learn Julie had not turned up and until she did, Leslie Thompson would be the acting manager Basically one of Julie's yes people, Leslie could sometimes be persuaded to do the right thing.

Midway through her shift a tall, well-dressed, dark-haired man entered the station. When she heard his British accent she almost asked if he were another of the knights woken up. She caught herself before hand, thinking if one had, they'd surely show up at Treasures.

Shannon stood by Molly's side chatting with the man who told them his name was John Ripley and he'd come to be livescanned in preparation for starting to work as one of their new officers. Even though the city had initiated cutbacks, this John was one of the officers Krane managed to convince the city they needed to hire.

"You get all the luck," Shannon whispered before Molly opened up the Dutch door to let John in.

"Why?"

"Because you get to live-scan Mr. Gorgeous. That's why?"

"Why don't you come downstairs with us and I'll start to teach you how to do it. Julie, Leslie and I are the only ones who know how and if Julie doesn't come back, we should have someone else who knows."

"Seriously? Molly, you are the best."

A short while later, the live-scan done and John left the two women finally had a few minutes to talk about what had happened with Julie.

Shannon sat on the outside of the curving front desk and leaning on her elbows ask Molly what she thought about the events of the past few days. Mirroring Shannon's movement, Molly leaned forward and shook her head.

"I don't know what to think. It's just all so weird. If she left the building the cameras never picked her up. Nor did they pick her up if she went downstairs to evidence. I could see Julie wigging out and leaving but not without her purse. Then again, maybe all her nasty machinations finally fried her brain and that's exactly what she did do."

"So what happens now?"

"We do our jobs, the same as usual. The public depends on us and we need to keep it together and do our jobs to the best of our ability the way we always do."

Shannon glanced around the records area, "I suppose dancing on the desk in celebration of her departure would be in bad taste."

Molly giggled, for the first time she could remember, she giggled out loud in the station. "Sadly, yes. That doesn't mean, however, we can't have a drink after work or on days off some time."

"We should. We should have our own special bon voyage party for Julie. You could bring your new guy and I'll . . . I'll dance on a table and see if someone likes what he sees. Unless . . . does Gary?"

"Gareth."

"Do you think maybe one of Gareth's brothers . . ."

"Hmm, One of his brothers is a pretty nice guy. I can see if he's dating or not."

"Could you? Would you?"

"Sure. Why not?" *Why not indeed? If the brothers are here to stay, they might as well meet some fun women.*

"You still think the woman in the poster looks like Julie?"

Molly shook her head. "No. That was all just stress from the changes in my life. Unless someone was playing a really bad joke and photo-shopped her in, there is no way Julie would pose for a picture like that."

A moment later someone came to the front counter and Shannon rose to help them. Molly looked around the station. Julie's disappearance was a breath of fresh air. Even if she did some back, her sudden departure would factor in to whether or not she was fit to run the department. And, if she'd been kidnapped? Well that took time to recover from and management would be watching her for signs of PTSD for years to come. Yes, life without Julie in it was good.

"So there were no problems at your work?"

Snuggled up against Gareth in the aftermath of his warm welcome home Molly smiled up at him. "Not a one."

"Do they still search for her?"

"They will. They need to be till they get some kind of answer. Kidnappings hit the news for a few days and then, unless someone does something to keep it in the forefront, fades away. I don't think anyone, even her bevy of sycophantic dispatchers miss her. We're all kind of glad she's gone."

Gareth leaned over and kissed the tip of her nose. "I am glad you are pleased. And do you still miss Carrie?"

"I'll always miss her. But I'm so very happy for her. By the way, speaking of being happy, my friend, Shannon, from work? She was wondering if we could get together some time and double date. She's not seeing someone and I thought that maybe, well, if you wouldn't mind . . ."

"Yes?"

"Do you think one of your brothers would like to meet her? Go out with her?"

Gareth nodded. "Gehris and Gawain have both asked if there may be a lady in need of their services."

"Gehris. Shannon is kind of adventurous and I think Gehris."

"Then we will do this double. He will be pleased."

Molly looked up at him, into his amazing sapphire blue eyes. The warmth and adoration she saw in them made her heart beat a little faster. Her gaze traveled down to his strong, lightly beard stubbled chin, to his broad chest and six-pack abs. Gareth of Orkney wasn't just a pretty face on top of a gorgeous body. It was his heart, his daring, his love for her that made him the only man she knew she could ever truly love. "Gareth, I love you, I love you so much."

"And I love you, my Lady Molly. I will forever be your knight in shining armor."

ABOUT THE AUTHOR

From earliest childhood Regan was an avid reader and upon discovering Alexander Dumas and Charles Dickens she was hooked on books that carried the reader away to a different time and place. Preferring the quiet of her room and a good book to spending time with people she traveled far beyond those four walls.

It was while working as a police dispatcher, first for the California Highway Patrol and then her local police department, she began to write fiction, primarily time travels and romantic suspense. In the spring of 2009 she returned to the day job she always liked best, working as a legal secretary. Although, curled up in her bunny slippers with her furfaced children, Missy, Lulu and Ollie, while writing is one of her most favorite things to do.